SHELTERED BY THE
SEA LORD

LORDS OF ATLANTIS

USA TODAY BESTSELLING AUTHOR

STARLA NIGHT

For inquiries:

Starla Night
starla@starlanight.com
https://starlanight.com

ONE

Starr opened her eyes.

Cold gray light from the port window reflected on the slatted ceiling. Her bunk rocked with every swell.

There was no sound of an engine. No captain. No crew. Only the splash of seawater against the hull and clanging from something unsecured sliding across the deck overhead.

Her stomach growled.

She rolled upright and rested her clean tennis shoes on the floor.

It would be so easy to lie down again...

Do this. Get up and eat food before you lose the will. Again.

The voice in her head sounded distant.

Her stomach growled again.

Now, Starr.

She donned her personal protective gear, first putting on the plastic pants and then snapping on the long-sleeved jacket. She slid protective glasses on her face, fit her mask straps over her ears, and pulled the hood tight.

Her warm breath felt moist.

Suffocating.

Now.

She opened her portable medical kit. Antihistamines, antacids, eyewash drops, nasal spray. She sucked in a breath through her mouth. Her nose was always stuffed. She counted the long tubes. EpiPens. One...two...down to two? Not enough. She grabbed both, stuffed them into her jacket pocket, and closed the medical kit.

How could she ration them?

How could she not?

Starr opened the door, crept out of the stateroom, and closed it behind her. The empty captain's cabin was to her right. The guest cabin to her left was filled with network and security equipment. Tool sets, cables, testers, switches. Neatly stacked. Utterly useless.

Past it was the small bathroom, called the head on a ship, and the door that led to the silent engines. She couldn't smell anything, but the air had an aftertaste of oil. Sour.

Stairs led to the kitchen, called the galley.

A large wave shoved the floor beneath her shoes.

She grabbed the railing and ascended the steps. Just before the top, she paused.

Seating cushions slid across the polished wood. Rough waves had tossed them off the benches and overturned abandoned coffee mugs. The contents of a cracked mug stained the floor.

Next to it rested one small brown sphere.

Her breath stopped.

A honey-roasted peanut.

More were scattered across the floor. And the counters. They rattled like caltrops across the galley.

Her heart thudded in her chest.

Peanuts couldn't make her sick just by looking at them, but the dust floating in the sunbeams streaming through the enclosed windows could.

Her throat tingled.

Oh, no.

Go, Starr.

She raced through the galley and burst out onto the deck.

The gray Atlantic stretched in every direction.

She ran to the side, gripped the rail, and tore off her mask, gasping. The wind whipped strands of hair across her face. Her lips tingled and turned numb.

No, no.

Her heart thudded out of control. One hand quested in her pocket. Her fingers closed around the EpiPen. Could she even use it properly? She could barely feel it in her cold, trembling fingers.

A film descended over her. The day seemed to recede. Her vision grew narrow, as though she were looking out through a periscope on the infinite ocean.

None of this matters. You're not here.

The film wrapped around her chest embracing her in tight plastic. Her breathing slowed, and the tingling of her lips went away.

Panic, not an allergic reaction, had caused the sensation.

She released the EpiPen and followed the railing to the back of the boat. Her movements were mechanical, almost mindless. Her stomach growled. She needed food. Here was the lifeboat. Wherever the captain and crew had gone, they hadn't taken the lifeboat.

Where had they gone? Why had they left here? Had

they washed overboard? Were they all dead? Had they left her to die?

Alone?

Her heartbeat accelerated.

The film thickened. *What does it matter? Alive or dead, it's all the same. None of it affects you. Nothing affects you.*

Her thoughts echoed. Nothing affected her.

She undid the clumsy bow ties, pulled back the tarp, and opened the tub of emergency supplies. Unlabeled silver granola bars filled the tub. Starr selected one and a bottle of water, resealed the tub, and retied the tarp. She carried the water bottle and unlabeled silver-wrapped bar to the edge of the ship and knelt.

A rogue wave slapped the hull. Droplets of seawater sprayed her.

She wiped the spray off her face with the back of her hand. Seawater was fine, but the slightest hint of fish, shell-fish, or seaweed spelled death. She squeezed the emergency meal bar.

She needed food. She needed to survive.

Please don't kill me.

This food wasn't contaminated. It might be safe.

Might.

Unlabeled wrappers ought to be illegal. Of course, even labels could be misleading.

She'd lived her whole life trying so hard to be safe. Trying so hard to isolate herself from dangers. And now, alone on a ship in the middle of the Atlantic, she enjoyed the ultimate isolation, but she was in more danger than ever.

Somewhere, her half sister was worried sick about her. Somewhere, her friends were searching the networks trying to figure out where they'd been betrayed.

Somewhere—in front of her or behind her or to the side—was a giant platform being constructed in the middle of the ocean. It floated over the recently rediscovered city of Atlantis, the city of mermen who had revealed their existence to the modern world, defying the laws of their ancient race, to seek their soul mates. One of those human soul mates had been Starr's half sister, Bella. And soon this platform would become a meeting place for the two races, human and mer.

But someone did not want the mer to arise.

They would do anything to destroy the platform.

And the mermen.

Bella had asked for Starr's help. What had started as a project to keep Bella safe had morphed into a quest to bring down the mysterious terrorists threatening the mer. The group, called the Sons of Hercules, was bent on destruction. Even in the middle of the Atlantic, the mermen weren't safe. A traitor had infiltrated their platform right before the mer held a grand opening.

Starr knew what it was like to fight a hidden adversary. She'd been doing it her whole life. Her traitor was calling from inside the house—inside her body.

But she had underestimated the Sons of Hercules.

She'd been coming to the platform in secret, and her secret must have fallen into the wrong hands. Now she was adrift. Helpless.

The film calmed her panic.

She tore open the plastic.

The bar was brown and mealy. No nuts that she could see, but peanut dust could be on anything, and it wasn't as if her stuffed nose could smell.

Her stomach growled.

Starvation was a real possibility. She'd always imagined

dying from something she ate, not from starving in the middle of the Atlantic.

Starr pressed the bar to her lips. Licked. *Food.* She was so, so hungry.

She took a big bite. Chewed.

The tingle started in the back of her nose. An itch that she couldn't scratch.

She choked.

Oh, she wanted to swallow. So bad.

Her throat tightened.

Nuts.

Literally.

She spat the contents over the side of the ship and washed her mouth out with bottled water and spit that over as well. Then she sat, EpiPen resting against the side of her thigh, and waited.

An invisible hand squeezed her throat.

Don't think. Don't panic. This is fine.

The invisible hand clenching her throat tightened.

The world faded.

She threw the bar over the side.

Heat suffused her face, and spots of red hives appeared on the backs of her hands.

Hives were not caused by dangerous thoughts in her mind.

She jammed the EpiPen through the side of her thigh, depressed the trigger, and waited.

A sharp pain, and then her body shook as if she'd gone on a race for her life. She gasped. Her throat loosened, opened, and sweat poured down her forehead. Her cold hands turned clammy. She felt sick.

Traitors ruled here, inside and out.

She removed the empty EpiPen and threw it into the

water. With trembling hands, she quested in her pocket and drew out her last pen.

She couldn't keep doing this.

One way or another, she was going to die out here.

The world narrowed and faded as her mind receded.

From a distant vantage point, she saw the allergic reaction fade, thank God. She returned the last pen to her pocket. Her body stood and shuffled to the captain's chair. Her eyes peered over the control panel. Her hands methodically tested the controls. Radio, satellite navigation, fuse box. If the satellite connection was working, then she could look up how to start or repair a boat. And she would do it in this state. As an automaton. Because this was how she survived.

Nothing turned on. Everything remained dead.

She was a little piece of driftwood, alone in the mid-Atlantic.

No one was looking for her.

Even though days ago, she'd been within hours of reaching the platform.

Starr shuffled downstairs again and back to her cabin. She removed her protective gear, rinsed it, and hung it to dry. She poured a thimbleful of Sea Opal elixir—the concentrated liquid steeped in the mer's healing Sea Opals—into a cap and swallowed an antihistamine.

Once, her half sister Bella had thought the elixir might cure Starr's allergies. It had cured her nephew's leukemia, even though the healing hadn't appeared at first. Starr had been taking it for much longer. Hope died hard.

Then she got back on the bunk and curled into a fetal position.

The gray light splayed on the ceiling. She stared at it the same way she used to stare at the ceiling in the hospital.

This is fine. It's not happening. You're not here.

Her therapist would be so sad for her. She'd spent years trying to tear down the film and become a real person. Three days in isolation, and she powered down like a computer.

But no one was coming.

And this was the only way her mind could survive.

TWO

Gailen wasn't supposed to be here.

He pinched withered, slimy leaves from ancient plants, seeking the dormant life inside. Around him, the ruins of old Atlantis spread out in all directions like the shattered rubble of his naïve dreams.

Once, it had been a sprawling city that could rise above the ocean and sink below with the pull of a lever. Human roads and statues and ornately carved buildings had dazzled with their craftsmanship.

The new Atlantis warriors had managed to raise the ruin three stages, into the middle of the ocean, but had been unable to extend up to the surface. As they'd excavated, searching for clues about the Great Catastrophe that had caused it to be destroyed in the first place, aggressive, creeping vines had climbed up through the mechanisms, crowding out the mer and choking off their ability to explore. And no matter how they battled the vine, it only grew back stronger.

By following it back to its source, in the center of the

chunks of barnacle-crusted marble, Gailen had discovered an abandoned garden.

Maybe the key to gouging out the strange vine's heart lay here. Or maybe the foreign tendrils would grow into a plant he recognized. Maybe one of the other dormant plants he'd uncovered would grow into something legendary, not found since the humans sank the ancient city and sent the mer into hiding. Something that made his labor in this little plot of silt, while everyone else escorted dignitaries and repulsed All-Council raiders, important.

He clawed at the soil. His index finger caught on an old root. He shifted his fins into human feet, rested them on either side of the root, and tried to clasp the dead wood. But his thumbs were permanently fused the wrong way and would not bend.

A curl of bitterness tainted his tongue.

After all this time, he really ought to be used to his disability. But somehow, it came as a surprise every time.

He yanked on the root, and his fingers slid off. He drifted a few feet away with the rest of the muck.

Ah well.

Gailen cracked his back and stretched.

Across the ocean floor gleamed beautiful new Atlantis. Its young Life Tree gleamed like a star casting pure, holy light over the ocean. The castles of the city bobbed around it, giant green spheres anchored to the seafloor, in two complete rings.

One castle was Gailen's.

He had lovingly carved its interior, smoothing the rough spots, and filled it with the most bountiful garden. It was all ready for a bride.

Between the ruin of ancient Atlantis and the glimmering hope of the new Atlantis, steel chains anchored the humans' floating platform to the seabed. The mermen had put in huge concrete blocks and stretched wires up to the surface. The humans had attached a communication bubble filled with machinery, and two warriors sat inside at all times, breathing the machine-made air and conveying messages to and from the surface.

Those warriors were doing important things.

He shifted to fins and kicked back to the ancient garden. This stump in the center was deader than his chances of finding a bride. He grabbed his neglected trident and jammed it into the soil beneath the root. He buried the blades deep into the thick, woody heart. This creeping vine was solid. He tried to lever the trident, but his palms slid off the staff. He jammed the trident base against his shoulder, planted his now-human feet, and forced it up and down.

The vine moved but did not break.

A roving patrol swam overhead. One of the warriors called down to him in a teasing tone, "Do not disrespect your trident by using it to rake plants, Gailen. Lieutenant Diras will take it away from you."

Gailen yanked his trident free, straightened, and strove to return the warrior's light tone. "It is my trident, Endi."

"He will say 'do not disrespect the warrior who crafted it.'" Endi made a show of impersonating the grave lieutenant. His partner laughed, and both looked at Gailen to share their amusement.

Normally, he could find amusement in anything. But lately, smiling had been harder. "*I* crafted it."

"Did you? He will not believe you. All the tines point in the correct direction!"

His partner feinted at the jokester, but they both laughed.

Gailen didn't. He used to joke about it himself. These warriors weren't the ones who had changed.

He smoothed one finger along the flat edge of his carved trident. "Where are you going?"

"A special assignment." Endi veered toward the far edge of the ruin where Lieutenant Diras waited. "To glory, honor, and finding our brides!"

They swam on, cheery and excited.

Once, he had had close friends.

One by one, they had found their soul mates and left him behind.

Once, he'd thought finding a bride would be easy. Atlantis sent warriors to the surface all the time. How could he fail to find his soul mate? He'd been so young, and he'd had so much hope.

Once...

He barely knew the new warriors who flocked to Atlantis. Rebels and exiles fleeing their traditional home cities for the hope of a new life. They were all fit and willing, and their souls glowed brightly in their chests displaying their loyal enthusiasm. King Kadir had welcomed every new defector to Atlantis just as warmly as he had once welcomed Gailen. They defended Atlantis for this historic reunion between the races.

One bright soul separated from Lieutenant Diras's special assignment group and kicked to him. A smaller form followed.

Uh-oh.

Do not pity my struggle.

He turned away and roughly raked the tines through the rubble.

Queen Elyssa hovered over the ruined garden. "You're working hard."

He could not help his bitter laugh. It vibrated in his chest with a choking sensation. "Hardly."

Her young fry, Prince Kael, shifted to human feet and tore into the rubble pile, spreading out what he'd raked.

"You're about to have to work twice as hard." Queen Elyssa shooed away her young fry. "Kael, baby, why don't you stack the rocks? Here, like Mommy."

Her busy prince tossed the rocks, immune to her distractions.

"I do not mind." Who could feel anger at a young fry? Prince Kael was the hope of Atlantis—and their race. "This task is all I can do. If it takes me twice as long, at least I will be occupied."

"You're always occupied." Queen Elyssa looked at him too sharply. "You do a lot, Gailen."

She was exceptionally kind. She always had been. "Yes... This garden will take a lot."

"Just think how wonderful it would be if it could bloom as it did in the past. All the warriors who still don't believe in us would change their minds. Even the All-Council would be amazed."

"If anyone bothered to visit this small plot during the reunion ceremony, yes."

Queen Elyssa tilted her head. Her soul glowed steadily with the power of a vibrant queen, but her smile faded. "Do you really think what you're doing is unimportant?"

Playing in a dead garden was certainly not as important as securing the city from the All-Council or any other enemies who threatened them.

Bitterness lanced him again.

He shrugged.

Queen Elyssa glanced at the edge of the ruin. "It's been days since the first search for Starr turned up empty. The second search party will have so much more ocean to cover, and you're from that region. I was surprised you didn't volunteer."

"I did volunteer." He buried his trident in the loosened soil by his human toes. "King Kadir cannot afford to search for a misplaced warrior on top of everything else."

"Misplaced warrior?'

He lifted his hands, thumbs jutting out. "If I was captured by raiders or attacked by a predator."

"Kadir didn't say that. Weren't you one of the warriors who freed him from the impenetrable All-Council prison?"

A lifetime ago, perhaps. "No one remembers."

"I remember. You saved the city a bunch of times, Gailen. And that was with no thumbs." She held out her hand. "Come on."

A flicker of danger zinged through him. Only a husband was allowed to touch his bride. If any other warrior tried, even to save her life, he could be exiled.

But that was the ancient rule. Modern queens were different, and Queen Elyssa waited patiently, knowing his struggle and smiling gently as he overcame it.

He tucked his trident to his side and gripped her fingers with his own, his thumb jutting away from her wrist.

"Let's go, Kael." She kicked with her fins, tugging Gailen with her.

Gailen pushed off the ground with his human feet and shifted to fins, modulating his expert strokes to match her pace. They approached the gathered warriors. Queen Elyssa shone with resonant power, and all naturally turned toward her, sensing her approach even if they had faced away.

Lieutenant Diras stopped giving his orders and touched his earlobe, which was a gesture of respect in his former city. "Queen Elyssa, you grace us with your presence."

"Thanks. How are things going?"

"I have divided the warriors into two units and am assigning the leaders now. We will find Starr. I promise you."

"I know you will." She lifted Gailen's hand. "Gailen will lead the third unit."

Rejection tightened Lieutenant Diras's face. "We do not have a third unit."

"Oh, that's okay. I'll make one." She turned as the lieutenant's brows lifted in shock and waved to a warrior patrolling the ruin. "Iyen, come over here."

The skilled warrior kicked to their gathering. Iyen's gaze roved over the open ocean while Queen Elyssa detailed the assignment. Even though he was listening intently, he never took his eyes away from danger.

"When Gailen finds the boat, you swim back and gather everyone else, okay?"

Iyen nodded once.

"Good." She smiled at the rest of the warriors with warm encouragement. It filled their small gathering with hope. Just like her young prince floating importantly by her side. "Be merciful, help others as you can, and take care of each other. This is the most exciting time in our history, and I can't wait for you to come back and celebrate."

All the warriors straightened. She made them feel like they didn't have to compete to be honored. Everyone who worked together would be celebrated together.

The other units departed, but the lieutenant stopped him and Iyen. "Two warriors cannot evade the dangers of the open ocean. Do not risk a good warrior's life on reckless fantasies."

"Oh, sorry." Queen Elyssa turned serious. "Gailen swam this route by himself when he came to Atlantis, and Iyen is so capable that he won't interfere with Gailen's method. Really, I assigned a second warrior because it'll be hard to stay with Starr and summon reinforcements."

The lieutenant blinked hard. His mouth opened and closed even though he vibrated his words in his chest.

Gailen's heart swelled. Queen Elyssa legitimately thought that he, a damaged warrior, could find Starr and swim the ocean alone despite all the dangers. She didn't think he'd been lucky before. She thought that he was skilled like Iyen. It had been a long time since anyone had thought that.

She opened her arms in what she called a virtual hug to him and Iyen. "I know you'll find Starr and bring her back safely. We're counting on you. Good luck."

Gailen tucked his trident into his side and kicked away.

As he was leaving, the lieutenant once more tried to influence Queen Elyssa. "Does the king know you are changing patrols and reassigning warriors?"

"How responsible of you to ask." Queen Elyssa gestured for him to join her and Prince Kael. "In Atlantis, we welcome every question, even if it challenges a person in authority. Let's go speak with my husband together."

The lieutenant's face blanched, and he looked like he was swimming toward his doom, but he followed Queen Elyssa toward new Atlantis.

Gailen's energy soared. For the first time in a long time, he was doing something important.

Iyen swam like a ghost by his side. The silent warrior had been part of Atlantis since the beginning, but they had never been close.

Despite Queen Elyssa's confidence, it *was* dangerous to swim in the open ocean with fewer than five warriors. The distant sirens of angry goblin sharks and the heavy drumbeat of giant squids pinged him as they flew through the vast undersea wilderness. On his signal, they ascended the water column into the mid-ocean, where swift currents interlocked. This was a dangerous region. Warriors from all different cities would pass by, hunting the migrating fish. And although some were friendly now, many still were not.

And there was always a risk of being captured by the All-Council...

Iyen disappeared without a sound.

Gailen turned to look for him.

The vibrations of foreign warriors hit him without warning. "A lone warrior? It must be a rebel or an exile. Catch him."

A trident flashed to his right.

Gailen pivoted into a trap. Five warriors surrounded him and blocked off his escape.

He floated in the middle of the scouting party with his trident before him in readiness. A small hunting dagger was strapped to his biceps. He was so unused to being in a defensive position that he hadn't fully armed himself.

"Well, what have we here?" A familiar All-Council representative strutted in front of Gailen. He rested one hand behind his back and frowned. "Wait, I recognize you. A weak, disobedient exile from Aiycaya." Representative Rikoy smirked. "So, even the Atlantis rebels do not want your broken form?"

"I am an honored warrior who tends the Life Tree," Gailen snapped, even though he'd been assigned the position because it was easier than patrolling.

"You are the last guardian of the city? The king is short-sighted for giving a cripple such an important position."

"Says the male kidnapped from within his army who has only one hand," Gailen snapped.

"What?" Representative Rikoy clutched the hand he had been hiding. It had partially regrown, the wrist extending into a small palm with five finger nubs. "How did you know? Were you there when Aiycaya fell to that modern bride and I..." He straightened abruptly and looked at the hardened warriors, then rested his injured hand behind his back again. "That does not matter. I lost my hand heroically fighting off Atlantis invaders. You are swimming alone, and so your king must have finally realized you were good for nothing but chum."

The All-Council warriors, bristling with weapons, stood poised to attack.

The representative's eyes narrowed. "Or perhaps we could hold you. You might be worth something to him. Yes. Your softhearted king will either be forced to capitulate to our demands, or he will watch you die."

Gailen's heart thudded. He did not want to prove Lieutenant Diras right.

Representative Rikoy glanced at the warrior to Gailen's left. "Yes, good. Use the net to contain him. We will drag him to the limits of the anathema city. One way or another, his death will cause suffering."

But that warrior was not wielding the net, and it swung over Representative Rikoy. He ducked. The net tangled on his trident. "What is this?"

Another net flew over the warrior on Gailen's right.

Iyen zoomed past.

"It must be an ambush," Representative Rikoy shouted.

"This damaged warrior was sent as a decoy. Retreat. Retreat!"

The warriors fumbled over each other.

Gailen jackknifed and kicked out of the chaos. Iyen paced him. Together, they kicked hard, leaving the confused All-Council warriors behind.

"Thank you," Gailen vibrated roughly. His heart still thumped with battle vibrations. "That was close."

Iyen nodded once.

"Perhaps we should rise. The All-Council is less likely to linger near the surface. They risk running into humans."

Wordlessly, Iyen ascended. When Gailen pointed out the rogue currents that pushed in unusual patterns, he accepted Gailen's new directions without comment.

His silence allowed Gailen to calm. But it also gave him far too much time for bitter thoughts.

Iyen had been with Atlantis just as long as Gailen had, but he had not been ambushed and captured.

Gailen couldn't escape on his own. He couldn't do anything.

Lieutenant Diras was right. Gailen had nearly been used against King Kadir during the critical ceremony. He should have told Queen Elyssa he was happy staying behind. There was nothing to be gained from swimming here. More capable warriors would find Starr's boat. Why did he think he had some kind of special sense that would lead him where others failed? He fooled no one but himself.

Iyen floated upright in the current. The surface glimmered overhead with the sun. "We have gone as far as the current could have pushed the boat. We should turn back."

He was right.

But...

"Sometimes, the wind will act in concert with the current and push surface debris a little farther."

Iyen blinked slowly but oriented again on the current. The siren of a territorial bull shark warned them to move quickly. They battled long tendrils of jellyfish and deviated around vicious swordfish spearing a frantic ball of cod.

Twice more, Iyen looked at him, silently asking to turn back, and twice more, Gailen vibrated aloud, "Just a little farther."

But why? Why did he keep going on? When they finally returned to Atlantis, other warriors would have already celebrated finding the missing Starr themselves. Gailen knew that, and yet...

They swam through another reversing current. Unless the boat had hit at just the right angle, the reversing current would have pushed it back—and they would have already seen it.

So, this was the end.

Iyen looked at him a final time.

A war fought in Gailen's chest. It was time to turn back. It was time.

And yet...

Gailen barely vibrated the words, "You stay here. I will look a little ahead and return."

Iyen grimaced, stopped kicking, and scanned the ocean.

Gailen swam forward on his own. If the boat had floated into the reversing current at just the right speed, it could have pushed through. The most likely new direction was off to his left.

But he veered off to his right. Because... Well, there was no reason. Just a deep sensation he wasn't supposed to stop here. He had already come this far knowing there was no point. Perhaps, he was just delaying the inevitable. Or perhaps...

Perhaps...

A shadow cut through the distant sunlight. Fish swam beneath the curved hull of a vessel.

His heart jumped.

He had found Starr's boat.

THREE

Thunk.

Thud. Thud.

Thunk.

Someone walked across the deck overhead.

Starr slowly came out of her comatose state.

Was that...?

"Starr?" A soft masculine voice called down the stairs. "It is Gailen. From Atlantis."

Her mouth stayed shut. Her fingers trembled but couldn't move.

She felt like she wasn't inside her own body. She couldn't respond. Extreme depersonalization. That's what her therapist called this.

"Starr?" Gailen's voice receded.

He was leaving.

She sat upright and rested her shoes on the floor. Slow, deliberate motion. *Inhale, exhale. Inhale.* "I'm in here."

Too quiet. He might not even have heard her. She closed her hands into fists and rested them on her knees.

Thud.

He had heard her.

Thud thud thud.

He was coming down the stairs. "Starr, Queen Elyssa sent me to—" His hand rattled the doorknob.

"Don't come in."

The rattle stopped. "Queen Elyssa sent me to find you. We have been looking for days. The other warriors turned back, but I... Are you okay?"

Prickling warmth seeped into her chest. They *had* been looking for her. Someone had. And this warrior with a firm, upbeat voice, Gailen, hadn't given up. The warmth melted away the plastic film, and she stood. "I'll survive, I think. But I'm allergic to the peanuts scattered all over the ship. I'll put on my protective gear and meet you on the deck."

"What is allergic?"

"Allergies. Peanuts make me sick."

"Peanuts? They are small and brown, right?"

"Yes." She pulled on her gown and gear. "That's why I can't come out. Someone dumped them all over."

Thunk thunk thunk. Creak. He had disappeared up the stairs again.

She dressed and pocketed her last EpiPen. Fear fought with exhilaration. She had been rescued. All she had to do was hold out until she reached the platform.

Calm descended over her. And the room receded a little. She was still too emotional. And that was dangerous.

The film kept her safe.

She checked her protection systematically. Mask, hood, eyewear, gloves. Fully covered, she cautiously opened the door and climbed the stairs.

A nude man with iridescent orange tattoos knelt and swept peanuts into a cupped palm. He was fit, the way all mermen were in pictures, and his knee rested at the right angle to block her view of his male member. He glanced up at her with an open smile and lifted his hands full of the honey-roasted peanuts. "This is the last I found."

Oh, thank goodness.

She really was rescued. Everything was going to be okay. "Thank you."

Gailen did a double-take. His jaw dropped, slack, and he blinked as though stunned.

Huh?

But he shook off his surprise. "Where did you want these?"

"As far away as possible."

He strode to the deck and dumped the peanuts over the side.

She followed.

He turned and held out his hand. "I am Gailen. Nice to—"

She backed off. "Wash your hands."

His smile faded.

Part of her felt bad, but the film wrapped her in protective coating and sharpened her tone. "If even the smallest bit of peanut dust touches me, I'll react."

"Peanut dust?"

She nodded.

He opened and closed his hands. The thumbs didn't move with the rest of his fingers. They jutted out and angled down toward his wrists.

Oh, had he thought she didn't want to shake his hand because he had a mild deformity?

But before she could ask, he hopped over the railing and plunged into the ocean.

That was one way to wash your hands.

She pulled off her mask and leaned against the railing.

He looked so free diving just beneath the water. There were no boats in any direction, and she hadn't heard any motors, but he had found her. How? She was a small needle in an oceanic haystack.

He surfaced. Seawater dotted his brow and sparkled on his skin in the afternoon sun.

It warmed her arms.

He kicked out of the water and grabbed the railing. His feet stretched out in fins, but as he pivoted over the hard metal, they shrank. By the time he landed on the deck once more, they were ordinary human feet.

Gailen was inhumanly beautiful.

In profile, he was a little taller than her, but every inch of his body flexed, hard with rippling muscle. The iridescent tattoos flashed like an Orange Crush soda can. The colors looped across his muscle in generous swirls. And in his eyes, warm brown was embedded with threads of that same iridescence that almost seemed to glow.

He once more smiled and held out his hand. "Nice to meet you."

She grasped his strong fingers through her glove. "You too."

His smile intensified.

It did strange things to her. Awareness prickled up her arms. He was all male, focused and powerful, and that generous smile promised he would carry her to safety through a hurricane if he had to. A sharknado. Her heart thumped hot and hard.

Huh?

Was that...? Some type of reaction...?

She let go and cleared her throat. "What do we do now?"

"Wait."

"Wait?"

"I am traveling with another warrior. When I do not return, he will find us and convey our location to the others. We will figure out together how to rescue you."

More waiting. She sighed. But at least she wasn't alone.

Gailen would keep her safe.

Sensual tingling seeped into her veins, ticklish and sweet. He was really very good-looking, and she wasn't used to a man—or anyone—looking at her like she was the most fascinating woman he'd ever seen. Especially since he seemed so shocked when he first saw her. Now he looked like he was tasting her lips with his heated gaze, sliding lower to her tightening nipples, nipping her feverish skin with his even, white teeth.

Her breath caught.

And then the film descended, cutting off her emotions and cooling her chest. The tingles faded, and Gailen was just another good-looking nude warrior.

In sync, his smile faded. "You are unwell."

"I'm starving."

"I will hunt." He pivoted to leap over the rail.

"No, wait. I couldn't get food out of the galley because it was covered in peanuts, but you can."

"The galley is clear now."

"I can't risk the dust." She braced herself for an argument.

"What do you need me to do?"

No argument? Rare. "Bring out cans and wash them. But don't wash off the labels. I need to make sure there's nothing inside that can make me sick."

He did as she asked, returning to plunge the cans into the ocean and stacking them on the deck. She sat cross-legged and sorted the ones she could probably eat from the ones she had to be careful about.

He watched the process with curiosity. "Why carry food that makes you sick?"

"I brought my own, but I didn't plan to be stuck at sea. And the electricity went out. My cold food spoiled."

"But you brought this food."

"I didn't bring it. It was the captain and crew. I'm used to not being able to eat anyone else's food, which is why I always bring my own."

"Why can you not eat anyone else's food?"

"It's my allergies. The illness I have."

He sat cross-legged as well with his arms covering his male member. "Drink Sea Opal elixir. Your bright soul will react to its healing resonance."

"Oh, I did. I have a bunch in my cabin. I've been drinking it every day." She tapped her stuffed nose. "It doesn't seem to be doing any good."

His forehead wrinkled in adorable confusion. "But you have a bright soul."

She shrugged one shoulder.

"You are very bright. I almost think..." He focused on her chest. "Elixir should affect you strongly."

She touched the place where his gaze drifted because that was where mermen claimed to "see souls." Scientists debated what that meant, and why people with so-called brighter souls got more healing benefits from their Sea Opals than people with dimmer souls. Starr was supposed to be one of the lucky beneficiaries.

"I have a theory about why it hasn't cured me."

"Is it because you are hiding?"

"Hiding?"

"When I boarded this boat, I could not sense you. But

after a short time, your presence grew. Just now, when you told me to wash off the peanut dust, a barrier hid your soul. And now the barrier is gone again."

She lowered her hand. "You see that?"

"Sense it. And sometimes see it, yes."

He could see the film.

She felt opened up, as if he could crack her chest and see what was inside. No one sensed when she retreated. No one ever knew when she disappeared. This warrior had just met her, and yet he already knew a secret.

Her hands trembled.

Oh, yeah. Low blood sugar.

She forced herself to focus. "Can you go into the drawers and pull out a can opener?"

He returned to the kitchen. She had to describe the can opener, and when he was sure that he'd found the right thing, he plunged into the ocean, then landed again in front of her. He leaned down.

There was almost no way to avoid looking at his...

Male. Cock. Long and thick and swirled with iridescent tattoos. A good size, relaxed and large enough to grasp in her fist. Was that extra-large? Or just from this angle? Maybe it was ordinary, but she hadn't seen many in real life to compare. But she had a sudden, pounding need to explore his in detail.

She swallowed drily. "Thanks."

Their fingers brushed, and she nearly dropped the can opener.

His eyes twinkled with a smile that stole her breath. "You are welcome, Starr."

A hint of peanuts infiltrated her thick, mucus-clogged nose.

Oh, no.

She jerked her hand back and covered her mouth. "Did you eat the peanuts?"

"One. To test its flavor. But I washed my hands." He tilted his head. "Is that a problem?"

Maybe not. Please not. "Sometimes."

His face dropped in shock. "If *I* eat it, *you* get sick?"

"It's on your breath."

He stepped back and covered his mouth.

She quested in her pocket for the EpiPen. Her fingers closed around it. Her heart thudded like a countdown timer.

Maybe it was fine. Maybe she'd imagined it.

They faced each other, her sitting and him standing, both holding their hands over their mouths and looking terrified. At least she assumed she looked terrified. He looked sick with guilt.

That was one of the many reasons why she hadn't dated much. The few times she'd risked opening up, her potential dates had decided she was too much work. Too picky or too fragile. Or, after one memorable incident, that dating her was too stressful.

Her throat tingled.

Panic-induced stress? Or a real problem?

Gailen turned and bolted into the galley, leaving her alone on the deck.

The film descended like a welcome friend, wrapping her securely. *Concentrate. Breathe in, breathe out.* Her hands steadied.

Gailen raced back with a bottle of Sea Opal elixir. "Drink this."

His gesture dislodged the EpiPen.

Her stress spiked, and the film tightened protectively.

She accepted the bottle and calmly swigged the elixir. The liquid lodged in her closed throat.

"Swallow," he urged.

She forced it down. The elixir sat in her stomach like a rock.

Breathe in, breathe out. The straw to her lungs narrowed, requiring more and more force to get each breath in. The familiar invisible hand squeezed her throat.

"It is not working." He stepped back. "Your soul is hiding. The elixir cannot resonate with your light."

Interesting.

Yes, red marks had popped up on her hands. Hives.

This was not her imagination.

She readied the EpiPen and depressed the trigger. An instant later, her heart raced and the invisible hands strangling her loosened. *Breathe in, breathe out.* The adrenaline in the EpiPen flooded her veins with a sudden fright, like nearly being crushed in a car accident. Her hands trembled, and sweat broke out all over her body. She couldn't stop shaking. But she was alive, again.

For now.

And he knew.

Gailen sat at a safe distance. Resting his elbows on his knees, he settled his chin on his palms. "You are *very* unwell."

She could not respond to him. The boat, the ocean, everything retreated, and she saw him as though looking through binoculars. Her body was not under her control. Her response—or silence—was not her own.

"I have never seen elixir fail." He set the can opener on her can and, using his toe and stretching out his full length, pushed it to her. "You were hungry."

Her distant self shook her head. It was too dangerous

now. She was out of epinephrine. Another incident would kill her. This one still might. She had no backup.

"Am I still dangerous to you?"

She didn't know, and she wasn't going to get close enough to find out.

He scrubbed his face. "I have never heard of this illness, allergies. The mer do not suffer from it. I did not understand. Forgive me."

She wanted to ease his self-recrimination. But her distant self did nothing. She was unreachable and would be for some time. *I know it was an accident. Just be careful, please.*

"Thank you. You do forgive me." His shoulders slumped. "I will do better."

Wait, did he somehow sense what she wanted to say?

"I can see a flicker inside." He responded to questions she didn't ask, somehow seeing through her resting dead-person face. "I know you want to talk to me."

He could see her? He could really see her?

"Your soul shines a little stronger now. But it is still faint behind the barrier." He studied her without judgment. "What can I do to help you?"

Oh. That was so sweet. She just wanted to tell him...

"Talk to me," her distant self said.

Ah. It worked. She was still not in control of her body, but her body's pilot had managed to convey her message. So, one of the things she'd practiced with her therapist had finally worked.

Talk to me.

And Gailen did talk to her. He talked to her like it was his mission.

He told her about the search parties sent out to look for her. He told her about a garden of dead plants in the ruin of ancient Atlantis, and how he usually tended to the Life Tree in the new city center, and how he had planted gardens inside the floating castles of all the warriors. He got to see secret spots, meet new queens, welcome the influx of rebels, and watch over the growing families. It sounded incredible, but at times, a dry bitterness tainted his tone.

He didn't seem to hear the magical words he was saying. Gardening was the only job he could do because of his thumbs.

"I do not mind," he cautioned as though he had to defend himself. "Plants are interesting. Sometimes, you must treat them gently or they will die. But sometimes, cutting them to the ground is the only way to make them blossom."

Wouldn't it be amazing to see the gardens he described? Being allergic to every known substance, including every type of pollen, meant the closest she got to stunning beauty was her screen saver.

He darkened and turned his hands over, flexing the thumbs. "Do you know how I was injured? Everyone knows. Others share if I do not." He glanced at her.

No, she didn't know. She'd studied their computer systems, not their dating profiles.

"My origin city, Aiycaya, lost its sacred islands to a hurricane. Our sacred brides sheltered on a modern island, Haiti, and the All-Council refused to let us contact them in case we accidentally revealed ourselves. Our city lost all hope of young fry."

Right. This was a familiar story. In the last hundred years, the all-male mer populations had dwindled. Many cities' secret, tribal islands had emptied due to modernization and natural disasters.

"But then King Kadir traveled the ocean—he was not a

king then—and insisted we must change to survive. We must surface and choose modern brides to save our race, even though it meant revealing ourselves. It was whispered that a few warriors had left their cities to follow him, even though he was always chased out at trident-point. No young fry had been born in Aiycaya for over a generation by that time. I decided to follow him."

Gailen frowned more deeply. "I told my plans to my closest friends, but they would not come with me, so I left on my own. My second lieutenant ambushed me at the edge of our territory. He shamed and dishonored me before the king. It was terrible, but nothing changed, so I tried to escape again. And again I was caught."

His chest rose and fell.

"Perhaps the first time, I shared my plans too loudly, but the second time, I was quiet. Careful to tell only the friends I most trusted. And yet I was caught."

His voice broke.

"First Lieutenant Tibe tortured me. It was endless. When he broke my thumbs, he said if he caught me trying to escape one more time, he would kill me."

He lifted his thumbs. They wiggled back and forth, toward the front and back of his wrist, but would never close.

"So, the third time, I left in secret. And he did not catch me again."

How awful.

"But this is funny." Gailen leaned back on his palms and gazed at the pale sky as the first twinkling stars appeared. "A short time after I left, Aiycaya rebelled. They revealed themselves to modern humans and reconnected with their sacred brides. Now, Aiycaya has more queens than Atlantis. If I had only stayed, loyal and quiet, I would have my thumbs and my honor. I would not know my friends were so eager to betray me. I would live in my father's castle, making my ancestors proud, and I might even be a second lieutenant myself by now. I might have my own bride, my own young fry..."

He let out a long sigh. And then he forced a bitter smile, as though he wasn't the kind of person who could be dark for too long, but he was still fighting his pain. "Of course, I would not have met you, so, I should forget my regret and be happy."

How unfair.

"Do you get told that a lot?" she asked, managing to slip a question past the cold pilot commanding her body.

"Told what?" he asked, not seeming to mind that this was her first response in at least an hour.

"To forget your feelings and be grateful you don't have it worse?"

"No." He tried to force his thumb between his index and middle finger. The knuckle twisted. "But many warriors died for their ideals. I only lost my thumbs. And the more cities that rebel against the All-Council, the better chance our race has of surviving. I should be happy my home city is flourishing, even if they did not rebel until after they had tortured me for the same crime."

It was internal, then. "You can still be annoyed."

"Annoyance is a waste. Like regret. Or anger."

"Don't," she said. "Don't feel bad that you feel annoyed because you 'should' feel something else. Just feel annoyed."

He grimaced. "I am a warrior, not a young fry."

"Yeah, well, I met a lot of kids in the hospital sicker than me, but I was still sick. And every time I went in, I lost things. Friends. Foods that I could eat or places I could go. I had all these dreams, all these plans, and they all disappeared. It sucks."

"Sucks?"

"It's bad. No fun. Sure, don't torture yourself about what might have been, but sometimes you have to. And if you're going to do it, just do it and get it over with. It's okay to look at the lost future and be sad."

"Lost future..." He straightened. "Do you ever fear the real future? That it is already too late, and you will end up alone forever in a shelter of your own making?"

"Every day." She rubbed her clammy, cold palms on her protective fabric-covered knees, approximately twenty feet from the tiny cabin she'd been stuck in for the entire journey. "Every single day."

His gaze fixed on her. The orange threads glimmered in the starlight.

He got her. Soul-deep, he understood.

And she was having a real conversation again, immediate and close-up. She'd come back to herself. He'd talked her through the hardest part and she'd come home.

Thank you, Gailen.

She uncapped the Sea Opal elixir and took a good swallow on her dry throat. Bella said that warriors could see elixir because the water looked shiny to them. They sensed its resonance just as they sensed souls.

And now she was back to waiting. "When will your friend come?"

"I am surprised we have not seen him. I do not think he would summon the other warriors without telling us." Gailen peered over the railing into the darkening water. "Time flows differently above the water."

"Do the other warriors know how to repair a ship?"

"No."

"Then how will they rescue me?"

"Queen Lucy knows how to drive boats," Gailen mused. "But she is escorting vulnerable dignitaries across dangerous areas of the ocean to Atlantis. We can pull you back to the platform on a smaller raft."

"How long will that take?"

"In surface days? Some. We move faster beneath the water."

A few days. She would starve. Rescue was so close and yet still so far. "Too bad we can't just slingshot across the ocean and land right on the platform, huh?"

"If you were a queen, you could use such powers to increase your speed."

Oh, yes. The magic of queens. Bella had told her all about it. Somehow, they channeled power from the Atlantis Life Tree into a protective shield, a telekinetic force-shove, or healing. But queen powers only worked under the water. And these powers were a recent discovery. Sacred brides never had the powers, but modern brides who hit the apex of Maslow's hierarchy of needs self-actualized themselves into wielding underwater magic.

Even though she knew about it from Bella, she'd never heard of a slingshot power. "Is flying a new queen power?"

"No, but queens are creative, and I have seen many unimaginable wonders in Atlantis. Wonders I could not have seen if I had stayed in Aiycaya." He lightened as if all he needed to feel better was to remember a small benefit from his monumental mistake.

Well, she was glad she could make him feel better.

She opened the can of peeled new potatoes, speared one with her fork, and rubbed it on the back of her hand. Her skin didn't react. She touched it with her tongue, licked it, and waited. No reaction, so the label was probably accurate. She chomped and chewed. Mmm. It tasted way more than okay. She scarfed it down, her stomach growing heavy for the first time in days, and she couldn't stop eating. Oh, yes. So good. She was going to hurt herself.

He watched companionably.

She chatted around her mouthfuls. "Why were you surprised when you first saw me? Did you think I was a guy?"

"No, I knew you were not a guy. Is that common?"

"It's common when I meet people I've only chatted with online."

"What is online?"

"Um, communication where you can't see each other."

"Ah. A cell phone. You only hear voices."

"If I did voice-over IP, then they'd figure out I'm not a guy pretty fast. I mean chatting on forums. Using letters. Writing. Do you know what I mean?"

"Yes, like archives. Only the All-Council can enter those."

"Yeah, a lot of the online world is closed like an archive, but some things are open. My skills are actually related to opening closed archives or keeping secret archives closed."

"That would be very useful for us."

He stretched. His muscles rippled down his back and across his chest. Even though she had to tug her jacket in close for warmth, he seemed perfectly comfortable in the chillier evening wind.

"We all wish we knew more about our past. The All-Council controls our knowledge. King Kadir once worked in the archives, and after he rebelled by using the knowledge he stole to locate the ancient ruin, it seems that many things we 'knew' about ourselves and humans are not true. And if we are going to live on the platform in harmony with humans again, then it would be good to know what caused the Great Catastrophe."

"Isn't the All-Council archives a bunch of tablets stored in a stone fortress deep beneath the Indian subcontinent?"

"It is well-guarded," he conceded. "They must regret having lost King Kadir."

So, invading an undersea fortress was a little different from the hacking she was used to. "Well, I'm going to do my best to secure the new platform. Whatever happened in the past, it's pretty clear that someone doesn't want me to investigate right now, and that someone is a human."

Which was her domain.

And now that she had food in her belly, food that hadn't tried to kill her, she was starting to feel cheerful again about this rescue.

Gailen acknowledged his mistakes and didn't double down when he was wrong. If she had to spend a week on this boat with only him, she might just survive.

Which was kind of funny. Usually, people found her cold or awkward in person. And usually, she had to fight their well-meaning mistakes to keep herself alive.

"I guess we just have to wait here until someone comes." She rested her spoon in the can and leaned back on her hands. "The only problem is that the longer it takes me to get to the platform, the less time I'll have to find the criminals before your grand ceremony. And you have how many people coming? Hundreds?"

"Many," he said. "Former sacred brides seek their lost sons and husbands. Some warriors from traditional cities wish to spy on Atlantis, but others come in good faith. Modern bride candidates will offer themselves to their soul mates. The All-Council will certainly fight the gathering. Raiders antagonize us now, but King Kadir expects armies."

Because they had to, probably. Bella had told her the underhanded means the All-Council had used to stop Atlantis in the past, but this event was the big one. It would cement Atlantis as the new center where humans and mer coexisted again. The traditionalist All-Council had to take a position, had to do *something* to maintain its power, or else their ancient rule would end.

But that was a merman problem. Starr had to stop any human interference.

"So I just hope your warriors arrive in time." She sighed.

"There is another...option."

Warning, like the changing pressure of an incoming storm, pinged in her belly.

Gailen's demeanor changed.

Even though he was still in the same position, he looked bolder. Darker. More dominant.

The curves of his biceps swelled with capable strength. The ripples of his quadriceps bulged with ocean-crossing power. And the promise in his firm jaw made her tremble.

She swallowed. "Oh? What's that?"

"We can escape now if you are my soul mate."

Little sizzles of fire streaked up her arms, leaving trails of goose bumps like ghostly nibbles on her flesh.

If he was the one nibbling her, she could like that. She could like it very much.

She wet her lips. "If? Is this the kind of thing you can test?"

"There is a test." Gailen rolled onto his knees.

His cock rested against his thigh. Swirled with tattoos, it lengthened in reaction to her. She was lost in a sensual pool of need. He drowned with her, silently promising to carry her deeper, save her, and savor her while he slid every lengthening inch into her swollen, wet pussy.

The images slicked her with throbbing need.

She sucked in a deep, shaking breath. The wind was suddenly still, the falling evening suddenly too hot. "Test?"

His irises glimmered with promise. "Accept my claim, and transform into my bride."

FOUR

"Bride?" Starr's voice squeaked. Her soft, rounded cheeks flushed a beautiful color. "Me?"

Dark amber tendrils escaped from her covering and flipped in the wind. She was wrapped in so many protective layers that he could only see the gentle shape of her body beneath. Feminine curves were hinted at. He wanted to peel back all the wrapping and taste her, starting with her trembling lips and going down the column of her neck to where it disappeared in the covering.

He crawled forward on his hands and knees, staying at her level. "You."

Her eyes widened. Her soul glowed bright as it had the first moment he had seen her. Now it made her even more beautiful. "How?"

He rested on his knees before her. "Accept my kiss."

She swooned forward. She was going to accept...

And then she closed her eyes and clenched her fists, resting them on her knees. A thick substance surrounded her, encasing her light. Strangely, the substance did not extinguish her light, the way humans normally fluctuated with their powerful, uncontrolled emotions. He could still sense her brilliant resonance deep inside. But it was no longer able to connect to her body. Her expression flattened, and her shoulders froze.

This was also like before. It made his stomach dip. "Starr, you are going away from me again."

She did not respond.

And this time, he could not sense even the flicker. The barrier was too impenetrable.

She hid herself. From him, now. She made herself immune to the mer, to the elixir. She cut off her soul mate bond. More than cut off. She repelled him. Right now, he would never think that he was her soul mate.

The rejection stung.

A smart warrior would respect her unspoken wishes.

But Gailen was not smart. "Do you wish for me to talk to you again?"

No response.

If anything, the substance grew thicker, repulsing him more actively.

His presence was not what she wanted. Distance. She needed him to go away.

And she was as locked in as she had been after her shaking sickness.

Was the peanut substance still on his breath? On his fingers? Was he dangerous to her?

He stood and walked around the ship. The waves rolled the deck and made it difficult to walk. It was tough on the surface. Could he wash off the dust, or was that dangerous too? He had so many questions about this illness. She'd seemed fine and then, moments later, she'd been dangerously ill. He'd caused a horrible rattling noise in her chest. She'd looked panicked, unable to draw in a breath.

He never wanted to be the cause of her panic again.

And she spoke defensively about it, the same way he spoke about the life he should have had if he hadn't been stupid.

It's okay to be annoyed.

That helped. Just a little, it eased his anger.

He returned to her on the deck. She was still locked in silent introspection.

His soul tried to reach her and failed. His chest felt cold.

He vaulted the railing and dove into the water.

No sign of Iyen.

Night fishes rose with the last light of day. Perhaps he could hunt. His first trident thrust went awry, and the fish sheltering beneath the boat scattered. How stupid. Even a young fry could spear a surface fish, but Gailen, because of his thumbs...no. Because he was angry and hurt and... panicked? Yes, this burning fear in his chest was panic. He could not reach the woman he thought, possibly wrongly, was his soul mate.

If he had never left Aiycaya, never gotten injured, never defied his king...

It's okay to be annoyed.

He was annoyed. Constantly.

His heart calmed.

He needed to not cry about his past mistakes. Focus on being present. Learn how to help Starr.

He rinsed his mouth as he had once rinsed the cans for her. They would have a week or more together. He would rinse many more cans, and he would hunt. Here was an edible seaweed trailing from the keel. It was not a fish, but it was something. He hopped onto the deck with a handful of seaweed to offer her.

She was standing, staring blankly over the side. Her light flared. "I thought you left."

The knowledge hit him straight in the chest. *She is my one.*

And then the barrier intruded, blanketing her light and flattening her expression to a vacant, absent look.

His heart ached. He opened his hands to show the seaweed. "I collected food for you."

She backed away. "I'm allergic."

He threw the seaweed over the side. "Forgive me. I am learning this new illness, and I have never been complimented for skilled thinking."

She blinked.

And then, like a cautious firefish, once more her soul light flickered bright enough to be seen.

"This pleases you?"

She covered her chest with both hands.

"I can see your soul light even if you cover your chest."

After a long moment, she spoke. "I know. This is for me."

"For you?"

"I have to be careful of how much I feel." A hint of a frown crossed her brow. "Knowing you can sense me anyway helps." Her brow smoothed and her eyes, formerly glassy and dull, brightened as she seemed to return to herself. Her shoulders slumped and she rubbed her forehead. Her soul brightened.

His chest warmed in response. Resonance. And even though he should be careful, he couldn't help but smile. "This too is allergies?"

"If you mean that I'm allergic to emotions, then yes. It's just one more allergy." She gestured at the seaweed. "I'm sorry I can't eat it. I'm allergic to seaweed. And fish. And shellfish."

He flexed his fingers. "Then it does not help that I ate seaweed to remove the peanuts from my breath."

"Yeah, it's been long enough you were probably okay on peanuts. Um, about what you were saying about soul mates..." She hugged herself. "Without going into too much detail, how do we know if the test works? If I kiss you, will I transform immediately? Or does it take time?"

Her soul fluctuated dangerously.

And his, already linked to her, did as well. Was she thinking the same as him? He fought his excitement, too used to being disappointed, but still hopeful. "You have already drunk the elixir. Our kiss increases our resonance, and when our souls resonate strongly enough, you will transform. But I cannot kiss you now."

"You can't?"

"Because of your illness. I do not want you to react to the seaweed I have eaten."

"Oh. You're right. But... Ah."

He reached out to take her hand.

She backed away.

He curled his seaweed-tainted fingers into a fist. "If I eat your food, then we can kiss."

"Can we? I mean..." She seemed caught between a smile and a frown. She reached up under the hood and scratched her scalp. "I don't even know if we *can* kiss. That would be so ironic if we were soul mates and we couldn't kiss. And we probably shouldn't test it." She rubbed her thigh where she had jammed the medicine tube. "Not without some plan to protect me if it goes wrong."

"In the ocean, I will protect you."

"But you can't protect me from myself."

"Starr." He captured her gaze and held it before she had the chance to disappear completely. "Tell me about this illness, allergies, and why it makes you hide away from me when you are sad."

"They're kind of two separate things." She nodded slowly and hugged herself. "That's a good topic. That'll calm me right down."

She sat on the deck again, and he joined her at a safe distance. She hugged her coverings closer and put her shoulder to the ever-present surface wind. "Allergies happen when our bodies try to protect ourselves too hard from something that doesn't really mean us harm. It's a massive overreaction. We have a saying about cutting off our nose to spite our face, and allergies are like cutting off our whole head to prevent a little scratch. In my case, I'm allergic to peanuts, soy, latex, pollen, dust, dairy... The list goes on. Food allergies are the worst because they trigger my asthma, so I can't breathe, but the other environmental ones just make my skin red and itchy. The dietary ones that don't kill me give me indigestion. I can't live a normal life because almost everything in normal life will cause my body to react."

"Can you tell your body it is not in danger?"

"I did allergy treatments for a lot of things, but we couldn't risk anaphylaxis. Shellfish is terrible. Fish and seaweed aren't as bad, but they can still give me contact rashes and indigestion. And that's why I can't risk exposing myself to you."

"I am not shellfish, fish, or seaweed."

"I know, but if something comes from the ocean, usually I can't touch it. And you come from the ocean."

"But now, I am a man."

Her gaze trailed down his body to the curve of his back,

his lower abdomen, and where his elbows once more rested on his bent knees. Delicate color splotched her pale cheeks. She swallowed hard. Her voice turned raspy. "Do you really want to kiss me?"

"Yes."

Her chest lifted and fell.

He reached into the woven bag tied at his waist, pulled out his mating gemstone, and started to hold it out for her— no. The seaweed.

A half-empty plastic bottle of water rested next to her. It was regular water, not the shiny color of the elixir, but it should still work. He rinsed his gemstone and his hands, then his mouth with the bottle of water, and just for good measure, poured the last over his head. The constant surface wind dried him quickly.

She watched him avidly, and her attention made him stand taller, as a warrior.

Her lips parted.

The barrier thickened, hiding away her light.

She quickly covered her chest. Trying to hide...no, not from him. Trying to hide, somehow, from herself.

This barrier was so powerful. She had learned to live with it, just as she had learned to live with her allergies. If her allergies were her body's overreaction to her physical world, this barrier was an overreaction to the glow of her soul.

He rolled to his knees again and rested before her. "Starr. This barrier is a powerful danger. It will repel me. And I think it has caused your elixir to not heal you."

Her soul flickered deep inside. "I think the elixir isn't healing me because allergies are natural. It's not a foreign illness. It's my own body."

"There are many kinds of illnesses, even the illnesses of your soul."

Her brows lifted, then her gaze turned inward.

He was losing her.

And she knew it too. She rubbed her chest, trying to fight the barrier, but she couldn't. "I can't risk it."

"You must. Once our bond is strong and the healing energy of the Life Tree flows in your veins, you will not suffer the allergies that have endangered you up to now."

"I will always suffer. Going into the water with you, with seaweed and fish everywhere, I might suffer more. And if I react..." She shuddered.

"That will be no problem."

Her gaze narrowed. "If I react, I can't breathe. You think that's no problem?"

"Yes." He took her hand. "Because under the water, united with me, you will never have to breathe again."

FIVE

Starr's world cracked open.

Gailen offered her the holy grail.

She would not have to breathe. Their souls would be united by their kiss.

Her heart thudded. Excitement pushed against the band tightening around her chest. She wanted to draw in a great breath and dance. Twirl. Sing. But the protective film squeezed like a corset, and unless something changed, it would cut her off again.

She withdrew her hand. She had to force herself not to feel anything.

The shadows beneath Gailen's eyes deepened. Pulling away hurt him.

She didn't want to hurt him.

Drawing away like this had never hurt anyone but herself, so trying to fight against it was like trying to fight against a DDOS attack. The attackers came from everywhere, and unlike in the movie *Hackers*, she couldn't shout out cute names and stop them. They descended like a swarm of bees.

Bees. Another thing that could potentially kill her.

The warrior in front of her rested on his knees, patient. But darkness and sadness showed in the hollows of his eyes. He looked haunted, hunted. He had been through a terrible experience, worse than her, but similar enough. And she knew what she was missing. It was why she'd gone to therapy in the first place.

"I'm sorry," she managed to say, distantly and emotionlessly, while pressing on her chest hard enough to leave a bruise. "Whether bad or good, it does a hard reset and forces me to stop feeling."

"When I said you were my soul mate, was your emotion bad or good?"

She knew the answer.

But even thinking it made her heart lift and the film tighten, so she said, "I don't know."

He looked devastated.

And that hurt.

It...

Nothing. She felt nothing, actually.

The film cut her off.

Which wasn't fair. If she was feeling happy and then she felt hurt, the two emotions should cancel out and return her to neutral. But it didn't work that way. Like if her protective system was already on overdrive from allergies, she should never get sick, but she was sick all the time.

Anyway, she shouldn't care so much. They had just met each other. They'd known each other for an afternoon.

Although the sun was down now.

He rested on his heels. "You are gone."

She was. Sitting in her isolation booth trapped in her mind. Again.

"Do you want me to leave you?"

Aw. She wanted to ache for him—for being so nice, for understanding her—but she felt nothing inside but deadness.

"Talk to me," her distant self ordered.

Hey, that was actually what she wanted.

He crossed his legs. "What do you wish to know?"

It was really good not to be alone.

The night passed, and his voice—his presence—kept her company. Pulling an all-nighter was pretty normal for her, and she was too rested from all the hours her body had shut her down during this voyage.

But every time she allowed herself to think about going with him, the film tightened and she lost herself again.

It wasn't just the prospect of kissing this warrior. An almost uncontrollable urge deep inside told her this was it. This would save her. Not just right now, but for the rest of her life.

What would it mean to descend beneath the water and open herself up to an entirely new world? An entirely new ecosystem, environment, allergens and risks, and things that she didn't know how to navigate? When she'd booked this boat at the last minute, she'd still calculated exactly what she'd need. Things had gone wrong, but her calculations had been right. If she left the boat now and entered the water, everything would change. She had no backups. She might be committing suicide.

And her allergies were unresponsive to Sea Opal elixir. Yes, she didn't need to breathe. But what would happen underwater instead?

The worry sharpened his features. The night must be lightening. The dawn had come.

She didn't want to spend another night on this broken-down ship.

A squiggle of nerves zipped through her empty stomach.

She was hungry again.

"You are coming back to me." Gailen's voice was rough from talking. He had so much endurance.

He handed her a large Sea Opal. His fingertips brushed her hand. He closed her cold fingers around its smooth shape. "This is yours."

His gemstone.

The large, heavy pearl filled her palm like one of those relaxation eggs. Holding it soothed her deeply. It was slightly iridescent, with a warmth and fire deep within.

Each Sea Opal was worth so much money because it could be transformed into so many healing drugs and things. And it was beautiful as a gem. They now knew it was the resin of Life Trees and not a naturally forming rock.

"It's beautiful," she said distantly.

He tilted his head. "But it does not increase your soul's resonance. Or, perhaps it does, but the barrier remains strong. Let me in, Starr."

She wanted to.

Her chest remained tight.

His kind eyes looked sad.

He was so gorgeous that a question in her mind demanded why her? Was this a joke? She knew what she was like. She didn't go outside, she didn't exercise, and the only reason she wasn't a fat slob was that any comfort food she wanted to enjoy would only kill her. She was doomy, she was gloomy, she was a submarine of her own sea.

But he was a merman. He swam in the sea.

He would find her in any sea.

And she was not alone there anymore. While her mind

and her heart fought about everything else, they agreed on that one thing.

"It feels like you're trying to reach out, but an algae coats you and you cannot escape it." He lifted his hand to her cheek and stopped a millimeter away, so close that she could feel the heat of his skin. "Can I touch you?"

Oh. Yes.

She tightened her grip around the Sea Opal, trying to focus on its shape and not on what he was about to do.

She nodded.

He touched her cheek.

She flinched.

He stopped.

She took a deep breath in through her mouth and released it shakily.

His fingertips touched her cheek and brushed back to her hairline until his palm cupped her jaw. His thumb jutted out, unable to touch her. And that was okay. Part of her was unable to ever touch him.

The iridescent threads in his eyes glimmered. Warmth, strength, steadiness transmitted to her.

Everything would be okay.

She leaned into his warmth.

He eased closer, ever so slowly, and curled his arm around her back. His thigh brushed hers and his gaze dropped to her lips. This was every heart-aching fantasy she'd ever had of an anime hero and heroine finally together. Her lips tingled.

The heat of him burned through her protective clothing. Her senses went crazy. She tensed. But it was too late now. She'd already used her last EpiPen.

But the tingling didn't remain in her lips. It zipped through her veins to her cold fingertips and back up to her chest. And then it swarmed and descended lower, pinching her nipples and aching between her thighs.

She sucked in another desperate breath. *Don't think about it.* She rarely felt this way. Well, she did, but not with real people. "This feels so sudden. How can everything be completely wrong and this be completely right?"

"I do not know. But it is."

She never jumped into anything. She had to know all the exits, know who would listen and who was dangerous. She had to know the ingredients of every object, every person, she allowed into her life. And this male was a complete unknown. His label was off, and she couldn't read any of his ingredients.

And yet, she also craved him. He was the food her soul craved.

He nuzzled her cheek, and his warm nose drew a line toward her lips.

She trembled.

He pulled back a millimeter. The fire in his eyes burned. He wanted her as much as she wanted him, but he was allowed to show it. "Yes?"

Only one last little protest gasped deep within her. "What if I'm allergic to mermen?"

"You cannot be allergic to your soul mate."

She wanted to believe that.

So she did.

Starr leaned forward and kissed him.

His lips felt hot and also very male. Harder and firmer than she'd imagined, and they moved with their own will that was totally unlike her fantasies, but oh so wonderful. He nibbled her, teasing her mouth open. Wet heat seared her as their liquids combined. His tongue delved in, filling her with sensual commands. *Open, embrace, yield.* Each demand made her feel like she was falling, and with every languid stroke, he promised to catch her. Her soul met his and entwined.

He pulled back. His thumb stroked her cheek as he studied her intently. "Your throat is open?"

She nodded. For the first time in a long time, she could breathe.

Laughter bubbled inside her. He'd sounded so confident when he said that she couldn't be allergic to him. Did he doubt that now?

He smiled and leaned in again for another kiss.

His kisses stoked her inner fire, feeding it as he pretended to quench it with gasoline. Her body throbbed, aching for this warrior. He pulled her into his lap. His hard male member pressed against her cleft with promise. He would command her, own her, and join with her body. He was the only one who would ever breach her defenses so completely. And now that he was inside, she wanted to hug him like the rescuer he was.

Eventually, she rested her forehead against his, and they just breathed together. He sounded as out of breath as she felt. Her lips throbbed, unused to being so deliciously bruised.

Her stomach growled.

He pulled back with a smile. "I knew you were hungry. Eat. We must leave soon."

"We're not waiting?"

"We can return more quickly under the water now that you will be able to transform."

Yes. Okay. She was entering a whole new world. Maybe now, with his kiss, the elixir would activate and she'd be cured. She held the Sea Opal to her chest and tried to feel reborn.

He squeezed the can opener, but his thumbs slipped off. He handed it to her roughly.

"It's okay." She pocketed the Sea Opal, took the opener, and cracked the can. "I've had years to practice. You'd figure it out."

"I understand, but I cannot..." He darkened with frustration.

Danger tightened her chest. The film was still too close.

She stirred the contents. Stews were always worrisome as they mixed too many ingredients. "So to transform, what do we do?"

"You will dive into the water. We will swim easily, and when you feel confident, then we will dive. The first time a bride changes, it can be unpleasant. They feel like they cannot breathe, and..." He looked away.

"Tell me."

He looked worried. "It feels like drowning."

"Well, I know what that feels like." She gulped the stew. "It will be nice to ease in. I liked swimming as a kid. Even though the chlorine is kind of bad for my already sensitive skin."

Her mouth started tingling again.

That was weird.

She crunched something and spat it out. It was a peanut or some other kind of tree nuts.

No.

Red marks bumped up on her arms.

Transforming had *not* cured her.

Oh, no.

"It's happening," she wheezed. "Allergies."

Gailen took her hand and forced her to stand. "There will be no time for easing."

She clapped a hand over her closing throat.

"I am sorry, Starr."

The world rotated. Her view narrowed and receded like she was looking down a periscope.

Gailen jumped with her over the railing. They plunged into the ocean.

Gush.

The water closed around her body like a plastic bag. Gailen's fingers sank into her biceps.

It was supposed to get better. She was supposed to transform.

But there was only blackness and thrashing and panic. Her heart thudded in her ears. Gailen's worried face flashed across her vision. Panicked, just like she was.

It didn't work. Nothing worked.

The world receded into blackness.

SIX

Starr thrashed in Gailen's arms.

Her soul grew darker and darker.

He tore off her shirt and pressed his palm to the flat of her back. No gills. She was not transforming.

Her mouth flopped open and closed. She fixed on him with terror.

But she resonated. She drank the elixir. She was his soul mate.

"Starr, listen to me."

She writhed in his arms. Her fingernails scratched down his chest as she clawed to get free. She could not hear him vibrating.

He clapped her cheeks and pressed his mouth to hers. "Feel our resonance."

Her struggles grew weaker, and her lashes fluttered. Her eyes rolled back into her head, and her lids came down.

A sharp pain stabbed the center of his chest. "Starr!"

She went slack. Little bubbles in her parted lips drifted for the surface.

No. Impossible!

This could not be. How could...

Her soul abruptly flared like a nova. Whatever had stopped them from connecting before was gone. Her soul swirled within and around him, surrounding him with reassurance. Her mouth opened, and her body fully relaxed. Her color improved. Gills emerged in her lower back.

She had transformed.

He pressed his forehead to hers, dotted kisses to her brow and her cheeks, crushed her to him, and then pushed her back to double-check once more that she was still alive.

She was. Very, very much alive.

Relief drained him. He would never ask for another thing, because she was okay right now.

He folded her carefully into his arms against his chest. She was unconscious, heavy with the weight of deep sleep.

Precious weight.

And unwieldy.

He couldn't afford to leave his trident, but he also couldn't leave her.

Gathering his strength, he vaulted onto the deck with her in his arms, all his muscles shaking from the recent fright. He scooped his trident from the deck and rolled into the water once more.

She vibrated a moan. Then she nestled more securely against him.

Good.

He tucked her to his chest and his trident to his elbow.

And then he turned and very carefully kicked into the currents to take them back to Atlantis.

———

Starr awoke with a gentle swish of wind through her hair. Distant fairy lights twinkled. Ambient music played.

She'd fallen asleep at her computer again.

Her cheek ached from pressing into the hard keyboard. Any moment now, her back would creak from pulling yet another all-nighter hunched over her screens.

But bad guys weren't going to stop themselves, so she did what she had to do.

She squeezed her eyes shut and stretched.

Gailen's voice rumbled beneath her chest. "You are awake."

Oh.

She opened her eyes again.

Her face was resting not against a desk, but his hard shoulder. The granite was muscle and bone, and those beautiful tattoos swirled over his skin. And the light breeze wasn't the hum of her computer fan firing up nor her air-conditioning cooling the server room, but an actual breeze. No, not a breeze. A current.

"Gailen?" Her back and sides weren't warm from slumping against her armrests, but because she was comfortingly contained by his strong arms. "Where am I?"

"The fastest current back to Atlantis."

Underwater?

She pulled back. The blue sky wasn't blue. It was clear, see-through, like air. The air had a texture, but it stretched beyond the limits of her focus. If she squinted, she would see into the great sparkling infinity of the sea.

Then... She'd shifted?

She didn't remember shifting. All she remembered was blackness and panic.

Fear zipped through her.

"Starr, do not retreat." The long toes of his fins stopped kicking, and he lifted her chin to look deep into her eyes. "Stay with me. Let our connection flow through you. I will be your strength if you will let me."

"What happened? Why can't I remember?"

"You suffered an allergy on the boat."

Yeah, she remembered that. "I knew my allergies wouldn't be cured. They're a natural process gone rogue. Not an illness."

"It is more than that. You closed yourself off from me. That should be impossible because our souls are linked."

"Maybe you made a mistake."

"I am not wrong. We are linked." He pressed his lips to hers. Stirring heat flared through her, flooding her veins.

Reassurance and a hot, aching need throbbed in her body.

His tongue caressed hers, filling her mouth and overwhelming her. Her blood pounded into her feminine core. She clamped Gailen to her, skin to skin, and it wasn't enough.

His cock pressed hard and ready against her waist. She wanted to curl her fingers around him just to hear him groan.

"You see?" Amusement tinted his vibrations, echoing in her chest, while his lips remained on hers. "This is our soul mate bond."

Yes, she saw.

He kissed her more gently. "But when we entered the water, you remained an ordinary human. I felt your life drain out of your body. It was the worst moment I have ever experienced."

"I died?"

"You fell unconscious. The substance coating your soul washed away. Your soul connected with mine, and you shifted."

"Is that normal? Shifting when you're unconscious?"

"No. As you become accustomed to shifting, you will be able to exert greater control, but in the beginning, you should shift naturally."

Except she hadn't. "That's distressing."

"And yet, our souls are connected." He pulled back and pressed her to his chest. Then he continued kicking. "Brides learn to shift their fins and develop their queen powers over time. But breathing, seeing, and communicating are automatic. Shifting ability flows from the Life Tree and is channeled by a bride's powerful soul."

"So I have a weak soul?"

"No, Starr. Somehow, you can close yourself off from the mer. You can close yourself off from the Life Tree. You can close off from *yourself*. That is a level of control that no one else has."

"It's not control if it's not conscious."

"Something is conscious," he insisted. "Because it only operates when you are awake."

The protective film wavered on the edges of her consciousness.

She knew exactly what the problem was. It had driven her to therapy, but she'd never fully resolved the issues, and in the end, she'd declared a sort of truce. Like with her allergies, she'd arranged her life environment to be less affected by the problem.

Now, twenty thousand leagues under the sea, the truce was broken. She had to overcome the problem, and fast.

"The mer have been around for thousands of years," she said. "I can't be the first person to have this issue."

"The archives are closed to us. And although we have received many new warriors, since Balim left, we do not have an effective healer."

Bad news.

Her brother-in-law was part of the reason she was determined to end the terror of the Sons of Hercules.

"We will ask Queen Elyssa." Gailen kicked with new confidence. "She healed King Kadir and saved his life. And she has helped many queens develop their powers. She will know what to do."

Starr hoped Gailen was right. Elyssa had once been an ordinary woman too. She'd helped others who'd come to Atlantis, including Bella.

Her stomach growled.

A tiny fleck of seaweed glimmered in his waving brown hair. She pulled off the flake. "Is this okay to eat?"

"It is woody and requires a large amount to sate hunger. Eat it with denser foods."

She put it in her mouth and sucked on it.

It tasted a little peppery, like a dandelion she'd once tried to eat as a kid, or like the white part of a blade of grass.

But most importantly, it didn't make her throat close.

Did fish suffer from allergies?

"You seem unharmed from this seaweed," Gailen noted. "Should I acquire more foods for you to try?"

Her worries clashed with her desire to test out her new abilities. "Only if it doesn't slow you down."

"Feeding you will only give me strength." He snugged her close. "Because my soul is stronger with yours."

That was...

That was such a nice way of saying she was no problem.

And Starr was really, really used to being someone's problem.

Mostly her own.

He flicked his wrist. His trident snapped forward, spearing a small yellow-striped silver fish, killing it instantly. Without breaking his swimming stride, he juggled his trident back into his elbow and used the knife at his bicep to gut his food, then cut her sashimi strips. He seemed frustrated by the uneven cuts, but she doubted that she'd be more precise with a blade even on land—and certainly not while still swimming hard with a somewhat helpless woman in her arms.

"Usually, raw fish is more dangerous than cooked," she vibrated while chewing on the strip. "But look. No hives."

He rubbed her hand. "Very smooth."

"I can finally be one of those cute geek girls who loves Japan and sushi."

He hummed deep in his chest.

She ate her fill and relaxed with a heavy belly against him. But a lingering emptiness warned she wasn't really done, as if she'd been hungry her whole life, not just for the past week, and she needed to fill everything. Her heart, her body, her soul.

A wondrous world opened around her.

Great shimmering schools of fish darted and wove in synchronicity like magnificent flocks of birds. Clear jellyfish and other strange, see-through creatures swirled around them with odd appendages like the weird life inside a petri dish. But those creatures gleamed and sparkled. The entire ocean glimmered like a glitter bomb. And music came from all the animals. The ones closest to her added a bass beat. Farther away, the shimmering schools of fish darted and wove like interlocking pianos doing different scales. And far away, much larger creatures like whales added songs.

And she was in it. Not looking through a virtual

reality headset, but swimming inside, seeing it with her naked eyes. She wiggled her toes dangling between Gailen's long, graceful fins. She'd wanted to go outside and see the natural world for so long, and now she finally could.

But it wasn't all glitter bombs and rainbows.

"Look." Gailen pointed out a distant cluster of snarling, heavily armed mermen. "They are from the All-Council."

A sliver of fear pierced her. "Are we in trouble?"

"They hold back because they see you."

"Me?"

"They sense your powerful light and know that you have the potential to destroy them."

How great would that be? It was good to identify the terrorists who hurt her family, but to actually stop them with mer magic would be a superpower.

"Good thing they don't know the truth," she vibrated quietly.

"The truth is that soon, this will be normal for you." Gailen swam hard, but his vibration tone was cheerful. "We will marry at the Life Tree. You will channel its power. And after we have united souls and bodies, you will claim your queen powers, and these dark thoughts that plague you will disappear."

If her dark thoughts disappeared, she wouldn't need therapy anymore. She'd be cured.

A deep pulse of belief filled her.

Once she truly united with Gailen, she *would* be cured.

All they had to do was marry at the Life Tree and unite their bodies.

And their souls...

Wasn't she a mermaid right now? Swimming in the arms of a gallant merman? Anything was possible.

Starr rested her head against Gailen's shoulder once more. "Did you meet your friend while I was unconscious?"

"No."

"Are you concerned?"

"I will protect you, Starr. Although I am not perfect in my form, please believe in me."

Oh. "No, I meant for your friend. Do you think the All-Council might have gotten him?"

He glanced down at her in surprise. "He sensed them before I did, and he rescued me. I think he would not be captured."

"I wonder where he went."

"Yes." After a moment, he rubbed her back. "Thank you."

"For what?"

"Believing in me."

"Sure." Although why was her belief surprising? He was a native to these waters, with a dagger and a trident. He knew what he was doing.

His thumbs jutted away from her.

Oh. Wait, had he taken offense to her question about his friend because he thought she was critical of his thumbs?

The other warriors couldn't make that big of a deal out of it, could they?

Gailen dove, and they ghosted over the seafloor. The barren rock changed to being dotted with bits of coral and more fish. They approached a shadowy tower. From a cave beneath it came a creaky, groaning static noise.

"This is the ruin of ancient Atlantis, where I spend much of my time."

"What's that noise?"

"The static? A giant cave guardian named Octopus

Kong. He is the savior of Atlantis, but do not make him angry. He dislikes loud noises and rowdy visitors."

A shout echoed across the landscape.

"The patrol. Finally." Gailen slowed and waved. "Starr is here. She has returned."

"She has?" A stunned warrior pulled up and stared at them. He was nude and carried a trident in a defensive attacking posture. Multiple daggers were strapped to his biceps and legs with seaweed sheaths. "Where is the rest of the search party?"

"I did not see them. We passed All-Council raiders."

"Lieutenant Diras has been tracking several groups. He thinks they are searching for..." The warrior darted his gaze around and lowered his vibrations. "Come. Much has happened since you left."

More nude, heavily armed warriors flocked around, excited to see Gailen, and he returned their greetings easily. He seemed well-liked and had far more friends than Starr did. They swam toward the gleaming heart of new Atlantis.

The area turned into a vibrant coral reef screen saver. The barren rock was covered in a thick mat of coral teeming with colorful reef fish and busy crustaceans. The castles of the mer looked like a forest of gigantic bull kelp surrounding a single glowing flower.

No, not flower. A beautiful glowing tree radiating peace and light.

A strange yearning filled her.

If she could only reach that flower—the Life Tree—and bathe in its light, all her questions would be answered, all her ills would be cured, and she would be complete.

But Gailen followed the other warriors to the massive cement anchors in front of the city. Cables like thick metal sequoias stretched up the infinite distance to the surface.

They clanked. A submersible was attached to one of the cables, and it made a mechanical hum that interrupted the peace. Bubbles drifted up, super-compressed at these depths.

She'd never looked upon a piece of machinery and felt unease, but going back into that tiny space after the infinity of the ocean made her throat tighten.

Gailen stroked her soothingly.

But he also led her to a group of warriors right beside the submersible.

A warrior with a broad jaw and a permanent frown stared at them in shock. "Warrior Gailen, you have returned."

He threw back his shoulders. "Lieutenant Diras, this is Starr. She is my soul mate."

"Welcome, bride Starr. You have survived an incredible journey through the ocean. And all alone. It is a miracle you have survived."

Gailen stiffened, but said nothing.

How unfair.

"I wasn't alone," she vibrated. "I had Gailen."

"Yes." The lieutenant's frown deepened. "I meant without the usual escort. An impressive feat, Gailen. Queen Elyssa was right to choose you for the search party."

Gailen's shoulders relaxed. "Starr needs to see Queen Elyssa right away. We are eager to marry."

"Queen Elyssa is not here. The fighting has begun." Lieutenant Diras compressed his lips. "The All-Council army finally clashed with our warriors guarding the platform. Queen Elyssa arrived in time to heal the injured, so we suffered no deaths, but it is only the beginning. The leaders of the All-Council are coming."

"They are?" Gailen's vibrations took on a tinge of awe. "It is confirmed?"

"It is. They discovered the news before we heard it: enough kings have sent direct representatives to the platform opening ceremony to forge a new covenant."

"A covenant without the All-Council," Gailen murmured.

Lieutenant Diras nodded. "A covenant created on the mer-human platform surrounded by sacred brides and protected by queens."

"Protected from the mer," Starr vibrated. "Queen powers don't work above the water, and I'm proof that you have a security problem."

"Yes, which is why there is no time for a marriage ceremony. You must surface and secure the platform now." He motioned to the other warriors, and they brought over a harness. "The future of the mer depends on it."

No time...

Her yearnings twisted into a sharp, almost physical ache.

She didn't want to leave this behind. She didn't want to return to the surface with its allergens and dangers and enclosed spaces.

If only she could go to the Life Tree, everything would be okay...

But that wasn't to be.

Starr drew back into herself. Unfilled wants, aimless cravings, going without...these were familiar sensations. She knew how to deal with them. Just shut herself away from the longing. Close herself off from the possibilities, from the pain. Put herself into a small white room, shut the door, turn the key. Sherlock had a mind palace? Starr had an isolation chamber, and inside it, she was free of bothersome desires.

Although suddenly, that no longer seemed very free…

Enough.

"Okay." She reached for the harness.

"And Gailen will remain in Atlantis to prepare for the coming kings."

SEVEN

"I understand," Starr said coldly as she put on the harness.

"I do not," Gailen protested. "Starr cannot go to the platform unprotected."

"Of course she will not rise unprotected." Lieutenant Diras motioned to the bright star of a queen leaving the city behind him. "Queen Hazel will surface with you and drive off any dangers."

Everyone seemed satisfied with that answer.

How could this be acceptable?

Gailen pushed. "But what about on the platform? Our enemies already attacked Starr once."

Lieutenant Diras rubbed his forehead. "King Kadir agreed that human enemies will face human justice, not mer justice."

"Until they are captured, we cannot leave Starr without protection."

"The humans will protect their own."

"Starr is not a human anymore. She is my bride."

She floated in her harness, distant and subdued.

Lieutenant Diras looked at Starr. "Do you wish for mer protection? Or assistance in your work?"

She shrugged. "My work is pretty self-contained. But I don't want to underestimate my opponents again, so sure, I could use a hand."

"Very well." Lieutenant Diras pointed at the warriors beside her. "Isag, Xemil. Surface and obey Starr's commands."

Frustrations surged in Gailen as the warriors chosen to protect Starr surrounded her.

He would not be with her. Was she okay with that?

She looked okay with it.

Calm, cold, and okay.

And yet, that filmy substance coated her soul.

The lieutenant called him away from others. He lowered his vibrations so only Gailen could hear. "Where is Iyen?"

"He did not return first?"

"No."

Gailen described the last place he had seen Iyen. Lieutenant Diras started to call to Isag and Xemil, but then he stopped himself and rubbed his forehead. "We cannot send away any more warriors. The queens are already spread too thin. If the All-Council sees weakness, they will try to cut down the Atlantis Life Tree, and everything we have worked to protect will be for naught."

Queen Hazel's bright soul lit the ocean, resonating with her sleeping young fry and stealthy husband, Lotar.

Starr's warriors donned their harnesses and clipped her onto the cable.

"Say farewell to your bride," Lieutenant Diras ordered.

Gailen gripped his trident, his heart pounding. "A bride should never separate from her warrior."

"You are not married yet." Lieutenant Diras softened his vibrations. "Queen Elyssa's last order was for you to protect the Life Tree. A queen's words in Atlantis have the same meaning as the king's."

Frustration compressed him so hard, it felt like his muscles were squeezing out of his skin. Starr was still in a fragile state.

"I do not want to part from my bride," Gailen finally ground out.

"She does not share your feeling."

Starr watched them coldly.

It hurt that the lieutenant's vibrations rang true. "I could still assist."

"I have seen how they operate the machinery in the submersible. Starr's work requires pinching and twisting with fingers."

"But—"

"You know your place, Gailen." The lieutenant rested a hand on his shoulder. "Say farewell to your bride. She will return soon."

The hot refusal surged in his veins. Just like in Aiycaya when he knew that the old ways were wrong and he would not return quietly to his castle, surprising everyone since he was usually so agreeable. Even now, the lieutenant turned away, expecting without a doubt that he would do as he was told.

And how did things turn out in Aiycaya?

The rebellion seeped away, leaving bitter recriminations.

He thought he'd never part from his soul mate. He thought she would want to be with him as badly as he wanted to be with her. He thought they would understand each other without even speaking.

He had been wrong about a great many things.

Gailen kicked to Starr. She looped her thumbs in the straps of the harness. Such a simple action that he could never do.

She spoke to him with a flat vibration and an unchanging, dim soul. "Did you work things out with the lieutenant?"

"We shared information." He checked the harness closures, seeking any potential risk or weak point.

She watched him. "So are you going to search for your missing friend now?"

"We cannot spare the warriors. I will go to the Life Tree and wait."

"Wait?"

"Yes, for dignitaries to arrive or for enemies to attack."

"Seriously?" She cocked one eyebrow as he traced the harness clips leading up to the cable. "You're just going to hang out and twiddle your thumbs?"

"Twiddle my thumbs?"

She demonstrated. "It means to be idle. Do nothing."

"Since I cannot even twiddle, I will do less than nothing." The harness was secure. Starr would not be ripped away by a rough current. He faced her, but he could not paste a smile over his aching face. "I will await your return."

Her mouth opened and closed.

And then her soul light burned through the film. She grabbed his hand. "Is this is about your thumbs again? Do you want to come with me?"

"You are my bride, Starr. I only want to be with you."

"Then come."

His chest lifted.

"Gailen, release Starr." Lieutenant Diras motioned for him to move back.

"She wants me to go with her," he said. "And she is a future queen of Atlantis, so her word is worth as much as the king's."

The lieutenant shifted his focus to Starr. "You should surface with warriors who can pinch and twist your machinery."

"I want Gailen."

The lieutenant looked over the group and ended with a silent appeal to the newly arrived Queen Hazel. "Queen Elyssa requested for Gailen to guard the Life Tree."

"Oh yeah?" Queen Hazel secured her sleeping young fry between her body and Warrior Lotar's. "I'm fine with whatever. Hi, Starr! You've always been a mysterious voice on the other end of the secure line. It's nice to finally meet face-to-face, although I never expected to do it under the sea and naked."

Starr flashed a smile.

"Anyway, we're ready to go when you are." Queen Hazel flexed her hand, and a white shield, much like an iridescent bubble, floated around their group.

"That's amazing," Starr murmured. "It's a literal superpower."

"You can have this power too," Gailen replied. "You will develop it quickly after we join."

A ghostly frown marred her lips. Longing that was quickly cut off.

He tightened his grip around her.

"All aboard?" Queen Hazel nestled in Lotar's arms. "Let's go!"

Lotar kicked freely, not harnessed, keeping pace with the rising group. Queen Hazel's shield protected him from the currents, and not being harnessed to the cable gave him the flexibility to respond to an enemy's attack.

Lieutenant Diras watched them leave.

Gailen's guts twisted.

Starr turned away from him to communicate with Queen Hazel. She kept one hand on the cable as they rose. The strange film was back. Her inattention felt so cold, just like when she had been fine with leaving him behind.

And yet she had said she wanted him...

He needed reassurance.

The reassurance of connecting with her soul. And yet it was denied him.

———

"Oh my God, I'm so glad you're here," Hazel vibrated to Starr as they ascended the thick cable. "This party was my idea, and it just keeps growing out of control. It was supposed to be a simple grand opening with a ribbon-cutting, you know? And then I thought we should invite the traditionalist cities that keep making war on Atlantis so they could see what they were missing. Now kings are coming, and they're going to rewrite the ancient covenant? The last party I was in charge of basically blew up, and if this one goes wrong..." She buried her head in Lotar's shoulder. "I'll have to exile myself in shame."

Gailen vibrated a protest.

"Do not," Lotar told her sternly. His voice was quiet and deadly. "King Kadir will not exile you for a mistake. Only for deliberate sabotage."

"Oh, I know. I was just... Oh, Starr. I didn't mean to bring up bad memories about your sister. Sorry."

Well, she hadn't been thinking about it until Hazel said that...

The Sons of Hercules had kidnapped Starr's nephew

and blackmailed Bella into carrying poison into Atlantis. It was designed to destroy the Life Tree, but she'd refused to use it, and so instead, it had destroyed her castle. She and Balim had been unofficially exiled, and now they lived in upstate New York.

Starr would stop the Sons of Hercules.

They ascended, pausing at various heights to let their bodies adjust to the changing pressures.

"Normally, the mer swim on currents like fish and ascend more slowly," Hazel told Starr conversationally. "They don't shoot up and down a cable. But it's more efficient."

Gailen seemed uncharacteristically quiet. The few times anyone spoke to him, he didn't smile and engage as he'd done during their triumphant return to Atlantis.

Maybe he was nervous about what they would face on the platform.

"When we're shifted as mer, we have a different mix of gasses in our bodies," Hazel continued. "We're not going to get the bends or anything, but I feel a little light-headed when I go up too fast. Going down is fine. You don't have to hold the cable, you know. I've got you in my protective bubble."

Starr kept her fingers lightly on it. "Have you ever noticed anything attached to the cable?"

"Aside from the random barnacle or squid?" She checked with Lotar and the other warriors. "Not really. I guess the All-Council hasn't figured out how to sever it."

"Mer weapons cannot cut this metal," Lotar confirmed. "And our frequent movement prevents the All-Council from mounting a concerted attack."

"We have to watch out for sharks, though. The All-Council raiders whip them into a frenzy and then drive them at us. But between my shield and Lotar's shark sense, we'll be fine. So long as they don't figure out how to set a real beast after us, like the kraken, we can handle it."

The kraken was a mega-squid. It was like a moving underwater mountain with three beaks and a hundred tentacles, and when it turned too fast, it could start an underwater tidal wave. The estimate for underwater damages it had caused since it had been released from its prison was edging toward a billion. "The kraken could come here?"

"Oh, Dannika says she hasn't been seen in weeks. She might have finally returned to her home canyon. The red mirror stones are all broken, so she can come and go when she wants. We always expected her to go home someday."

Hmm.

The platform and this grade of cabling were rated to withstand most underwater fauna and violent weather patterns, even the most massive hurricanes to beat this region, but it was probably not rated to withstand the rage of a mythical hundred-tentacled beast.

But that wasn't her problem right now.

One thing at a time.

At the three-quarters mark, another queen, Nora, met them. "General Giru was seen in the area, so I'll take it from here."

"He did not leave after you and the other Atlantis warriors repelled the attack?" Lotar vibrated in surprise.

"King Kadir thinks he wasn't part of the attack. Which was smart of him." She cracked her knuckles. "It's okay. I'll catch up with him one of these days. His time is coming."

"Queen Nora is General Giru's soul mate," Gailen vibrated to Starr softly. "But he still serves the All-Council."

That sounded complicated.

"Okay, I'll turn it over you to. But have you heard any updates on the brides?" Hazel asked. "Are the same numbers coming? Are they all okay that we pushed back the date so Starr could safeguard the platform and we could make sure we escorted all the late-coming kings?"

"As far as I know." Nora nodded at Starr. "We've been kind of distracted ever since you went missing. Dannika hasn't said anything important because she doesn't know who's listening in."

That seemed wise.

"I'll just hyperventilate until I hear the news." Hazel's child, Tal, made a sleepy cry in her arms. She bounced him. "Starr, you're the only one who can save us now. Do your thing."

No pressure.

Cool, almost choking calm tightened around her neck.

Gailen rubbed her back.

She leaned against him, and the choking sensation eased. "Will do."

Hazel waved goodbye and descended with Lotar. Nora led them up.

The water felt thinner, and the surface of the ocean wobbled. The great floating platform appeared.

The cable connected to the repurposed oil rig, and multiple other structures anchored to it, creating a huge ring. The ring acted like an artificial reef, creating calm waters several football fields long. A deep fishbowl of glass bobbed near the old rig like a dark marble, and around it, smaller marbles interconnected.

Fish flocked under the shadows. The water tasted of metal and different kinds of fluids that they used in their machinery. The hum of propellers kept the platform centered over Atlantis.

Angry sirens, like bomb shelter warnings, filled the ocean. "What's that noise?"

"Sharks," Gailen vibrated. "It is dangerous near the platform. When you enter the water, you must have full control of your powers. Never enter it alone."

Noted.

They passed the struts and underwater walls, and the wild currents calmed. They left their harnesses with the patrolling warriors and Nora. Gailen pulled Starr into his arms and swam around the curved glass of the fishbowl. The interior was hazy, but it looked like dry land with chairs and tables. Possibly a restaurant? They continued around to a long, wide ramp that sloped up to shallows coated with pool tiles and then a set of wide, low stairs. The waves were much smaller here, and she stumbled against Gailen out of the water.

He shifted easily, his gills sealing into his lower back before her very eyes, and his fins shortened into human feet.

She didn't have it so easy.

Gravity smashed her to the rough tile, and she purged seawater so violently, it made her eyes water. Strength leeched out of her body. She slipped to her knees, then collapsed on trembling elbows.

Gailen knelt beside her. "Starr?"

She held up a hand. She just needed a moment. Or maybe a lot of moments.

"It gets easier." He helped her up and pressed her chilled body to his. She breathed slowly, leaning against him, her legs shaking. "You are breathing. I promise."

She coughed and sniffed. Her throat felt rough but usable. "It's been a while since I felt this weak."

"You need food." Gailen led her to a tub of oversized Bermuda shorts and T-shirts. The other two warriors had already pulled theirs on. She struggled into the T-shirt, which went down to her knees, and fished out the skinniest pair of boxer shorts.

The sounds of construction—saw blades screaming through metal, cracking air-assisted nail guns—echoed over the water. Seabirds wheeled overhead. The morning sun looked pale through threatening gray clouds, and an ill wind gusted, blowing through her clothes and hair like cold claws.

Above water, the site was enormous.

The old oil rig soared to the sky. It was all metal and scaffolding, hard and cold and echoing.

The connecting ring clanked as waves pushed the pieces in close and pulled them hard apart. The top was solid and wide enough to drive a dump truck around the whole oval.

They faced the glass structure. Beneath the surface, it was a fishbowl, but above the surface, it was a futuristic glass pyramid. A wide walkway encircled it, big enough for several full-sized trucks, in a sculpted pavilion. Smaller circular disks floated like empty teacup saucers, although in this case, each saucer was the size of an apartment.

Gailen stood beside her.

She was here to do a job.

A construction worker in thick boots, a hard helmet, and a bright orange full-body suit and jacket crossed the pavilion, and Gailen announced them.

The worker eyed their tridents and daggers. "Those aren't allowed on the platform."

"We will carry these until the enemy who endangered Starr is taken by human justice." Gailen's normally friendly tone brooked no disagreement.

She leaned against him.

He focused on the worker.

Which was good, but... Something felt wrong.

Maybe he was nervous.

Fine. She couldn't focus on this now. She needed to do her job.

Calm descended on her.

Gailen's frown deepened, and his grip on his trident tightened. "Take us to your leader."

The worker gestured for them to accompany him into the glass pyramid. "The site manager's having his breakfast with the old owner's son."

This company, Ryerson Deep Water Construction, had been founded by a man named Cal Ryerson. He'd died before the mermen ever appeared, and his son, Merrit Ryerson, had...well, not taken over, exactly. He answered to a board of directors and an executive team. But he was in charge of the mer project and touched every single part of the platform.

They followed the worker into the sheltered glass. The wind died, so she could finally pull her hair out of her eyes.

Inside, the ground sloped into the bowl. The empty tables and chairs were washed in blue.

The worker turned away and followed a ramp up the interior of the glass pyramid to a loft restaurant. Hot food steamed in an open kitchen, where a few people help themselves to what looked like steaks, shrimp, and mashed potatoes. When the sun was out, this would probably be bathed in light, but for now, the threatening clouds gave everything a stormy cast.

The workers looked at her and the warriors. Conversation died.

That wasn't creepy or anything.

Their gruff guide pointed up the ramp to a third level. "In the VIP lounge."

He remained behind with the silent workers.

In a private alcove—although there were plenty of empty tables and chairs up here—three men sat at a far table with a 360-degree view of the platform area. Nearby tables were arranged around them with maps and plans.

One miserable-looking old man leaned back in his chair, ankles and arms crossed, face pinched. He wore an orange suit, and his coat was slung across another table. That must be the site manager. The other two wearing ordinary business suits were Merrit Ryerson and his assistant.

Dannika thought one of these men headed the Sons of Hercules.

Which meant that any one of them could be trying to kill her.

Or possibly, all three.

Starr studied the three men who had life-or-death control over the platform.

And, apparently, her.

The site manager gazed miserably out the windows. "Even if the weather holds, it's going to be nasty work to reroute that plumbing. Nastier, of course, to marinate in offal."

"I won't have my city smelling like a sewer, Bob Haskins." Ryerson followed his gaze out the windows away from them. "Everything must be perfect for—"

His assistant, a quiet man with square glasses, tugged his sleeve.

"What?" Ryerson followed the man's gaze and saw her with the warriors. He froze and then took a deep breath. A smile forced itself across his broad face. "Starr Langley, back from the dead!"

All three men rose.

Ryerson put down the roll he'd been eating and wiped his hands. "Ryerson. Merrit Ryerson. So good to—"

"No, no, no." Bob the site manager waved irritably at the

warriors. "We have a rule on this platform. No weapons. Take those out of here."

Gailen rested his trident against the ground. "You failed to protect Starr. Until the criminals face human justice, we will protect her with our lives."

"Protect her with your lives, but take those blasted tridents out of here. They don't fit in our halls. You can barely pass with a pool cue, much less one of these. Bad enough you carry around the daggers. We have rules."

"When will you capture the humans who tried to kill Starr?"

Bob squinted.

"Kill Starr Langley?" Ryerson chuckled and opened his hands. "There seems to be some kind of misunderstanding. Until I received a message from your lovely head match-maker, Dannika Evers, I wasn't even aware you were coming. Most visitors to my floating city come on the regular supply ships. If only you had done so, I would have personally taken care of you."

And why did that make her shiver? "The next supply ship was going to arrive too close to the grand opening."

"Ah, but it departed early. And the grand opening has been pushed back as you must know."

Starr kept her tone neutral. "I didn't want to wait."

"I could have arranged a flight. Or at least a more reli-able boat."

"Reliable boat?" Bob held up his hand. "Who are you, and what are you all talking about?"

Ryerson glanced at his assistant, then tapped his finger-tips together. "With the burden of deadlines to complete my city, I didn't want to overwhelm you with rumors. I only know what I was told."

"Which is?"

Ryerson looked at Starr.

"I'm here to check your network," she said.

"The dropped calls?" Bob's weather-beaten face formed a permanent sour frown. "I reported it. Nobody told me about you."

She shrugged. He wasn't her employer. "My charter boat lost power. Then overnight, it lost the captain and crew."

"A tragedy all around." Ryerson folded his hands over his belly. "You should have told me you were coming, and I would have arranged everything."

"They left a crate of peanuts behind," she said. "I'm deathly allergic."

Bob tsked. "You're one of those."

"I am. And the charter company knew it."

"That is..." Ryerson's face reddened, and he cleared his throat. "Quite bad luck."

"Quite," she agreed. "But I survived, and here I am."

"Here you are. Yes, well, if only you had come on the supply ship." He curled a fist around the back of his chair. "It'll depart tomorrow. That's reliable transportation back to the mainland. Unless you intend to stay for the grand opening?"

"The network problems won't solve themselves." Most likely.

"Didn't you lose your equipment?"

"That just means I'll have to do it the old-fashioned way."

"How resourceful." Ryerson sat, picked up his roll again, and spread a pat of butter on it. The other two men remained standing. "I'd invite you to breakfast, but it sounds like I'd kill you. The guest cottages aren't quite finished, but never fear. We'll find a place for you to stay."

His assistant leaned down to murmur something in his ear.

Ryerson held up his butter knife to silence his assistant. "Bob Haskins will find a place for you to stay."

The assistant straightened. His expression was unreadable, and the light reflected off his square glasses, hiding his eyes.

Bob wrinkled his nose.

"After you freshen up, I'll give you the grand tour. You must appreciate the beauty of the first-ever floating city that my second-generation company, Ryerson Deep Water Construction, has brought to glorious fruition."

She didn't want to go off with this man. "I'm here to work. I don't need a tour."

"Nonsense. You must see the dream in reality. Bob Haskins?"

The site manager sighed heavily, grabbed his orange coat, and shrugged it on. "This way. But you're leaving those blasted eye pokers, or you'll be sleeping with the fishes. Your choice."

Bob led them out of the glass pyramid, past the floating saucers, and around the outer oval. The wind was back, blowing hard, but the walls provided a little shelter. A solid layer of cement coated the metal scaffolding.

"Ouch." She stopped and pulled a sharp rock out of her instep.

Bob didn't slow down.

Gailen handed his trident to Isag, scooped her under her butt, and lifted her, pressing her against his waist. "The ground is rough."

"Yeah." She grabbed his torso.

His biceps flexed like iron.

Her heart thudded. "Thanks."

He tipped his head but kept his gaze out, over the water, watching for hidden enemies.

Where the oval connected to the original oil rig, waves crashed and sprayed her. Gailen hopped from the oval to the metal grating of the rig and followed Bob inside.

Bob gestured down a set of stairs. "You know where the pokers go."

The other two warriors descended, and the ceilings were so low, Gailen let her down to stand beside him. The tight quarters of the old rig were a lot different from the spacious, elegant new construction. The scaffolding was dingy, and the cream paint on the walls was stained with rust. The warriors returned with one dagger each, sheathed to their biceps, and Bob grimaced but led them up more stairs to the crew's quarters. They passed through a noisy break room where workers played foosball and crunched popcorn.

Everyone abruptly fell silent and watched them.

Creepy.

They passed right by the snacks. Popcorn was safe, but what was in the bowl of mixed-texture snacks next to it?

She put a hand over her mouth. Nothing made her nose or mouth tickle. Maybe the saltwater was still keeping her too stuffed up. Or maybe...

No. She wasn't cured. Otherwise, she wouldn't have reacted to the stew on the boat. Right?

They continued into another hall, but it remained eerily quiet. Gailen and the other warriors padded barefoot behind her. Bob opened a door to reveal two bunks stacked with bedding and folded towels.

Starr opened the adjoining door. It was a tiny bathroom with a shower. "Just two bunks?"

"And you're lucky you've got that. I cleared this out for

new employees coming in on the supply ship. Which of you are actually working here?"

"Just me," Starr said.

Gailen stopped in the middle of the room, his brows pulled down.

"And him," she said.

"Good. When you're on the platform, you wear an exposure suit. It's easier to see you in the water, and it'll keep you from dying right away. Now they"—he jerked his head at the mermen—"clearly don't need it. But you, I've got to waste my time finding your size."

"I don't need it either."

He blinked and then frowned deeper. "Every human needs one."

"Ryerson didn't."

"I said 'human.' He's upper management."

She snorted.

He crossed his arms. "You didn't come in on a boat, did you?"

She leveled her gaze on him. "Is it going to be a problem?"

He glanced out of the corners of his eyes at the warriors and uncrossed his arms. "Fine. Saves me searching. Our meals are at set hours. Tell me about these allergies. Are you one of those who says she's allergic to gluten while eating a doughnut?"

"I travel with medically prescribed EpiPens."

"And where are they?"

"I used them all on the boat."

He grimaced. "You're going to die."

Gailen bristled. "Do not threaten Starr."

"Look, fish-man, I've got one job on this platform, and that's to tell you the truth. A nice lie is gonna cost you a million dollars a day. And if I knew then what I know now? You couldn't pay me enough to do this job."

"Why not?"

"I have my reasons."

There was a commotion in the hall, and a platform worker craned his neck to look around the warriors. "She's got a box."

Bob gestured for him to bring it in. "I hope it's food."

The worker thumped it on the floor. Gailen opened it for her with his dagger. Inside was a case of her favorite bars to replenish what she'd thought would be her snack supply. She tore one open and ate it while she inspected the rest of the contents. Her second-favorite case of tools in case she'd broken something in the first set, more cables, replacement batteries for equipment she'd lost on the charter boat, and a couple of new-in-the-box cell phones.

It wasn't what she'd prefer, but it was enough.

Her hair felt crunchy from dried salt. She picked up a towel from the bunk bed. "I'll grab a shower."

"You get ready, and then find me for the safety briefing." Bob went to the door.

"I already said I don't need a tour."

"Nobody stays on my rig without a briefing." He left.

The other warriors retreated and closed the door.

She was alone with Gailen.

There was a long awkward pause.

Funny how they'd been naked under the water, but now it felt weird.

They were soul mates. They'd almost gotten married. Were still supposed to get married. What was he expecting from her?

She backed toward the bathroom. "I'm going to take a shower."

He nodded, sat on the bed, and folded his hands. His thumbs jutted in the wrong direction.

Just like this awkwardness felt wrong.

Where was the eager, smiling, confident warrior she'd met on the boat?

She escaped into the shower and closed the door. It felt wonderful. She shivered as the sand and salt sluiced away. And the bar was a basic cheap unscented type which was usually safest for her skin. She scrubbed until she was nice and clean.

Gailen seemed down, brooding like he didn't want to be here.

Maybe he regretted surfacing with her.

She squeezed the smooth white bar of soap.

It wasn't nearly as comforting as Gailen's Sea Opal.

What had happened to it? She'd put it in her pocket just before her reaction and then awoke naked in the sea. Maybe Gailen had grabbed it. She'd have to ask.

Maybe when he was in a better mood.

It shook her just how intensely she noticed his feelings, his presence.

In surface time, she'd been lost over a week, but the time underwater had passed in a day.

How could so much have changed in a day?

But nothing had really changed. She had a job to do. She could think about this later. Now, she needed to focus.

She ended the shower, dried off, and pulled the damp, oversized clothes back on. When she emerged, Gailen stood.

A hopeful smile broke across his face. "You feel better."

Her heart squeezed.

She suppressed it. "Is that a question?"

His smile faded. He looked away. "No."

Again, things felt strange.

She'd gotten close to him so quickly that she didn't know how to be normal.

Or his feelings had changed.

Unease shadowed her heart.

Focus on the job.

She grabbed her tool kit and one of the new cell phones and opened the door.

Warrior Xemil handed her small boots and socks. "A human brought this for you."

"Great." She tried them on. The socks were too big and scrunched up, but they made the boots into a good fit. She wouldn't be running either way. "Where's the safety briefing?"

They consulted the first platform workers they found. The workers weren't rude, but they weren't friendly either as they directed them across the platform. The oval had opened to let in the supply ship, and it docked close to the oil rig by stored construction equipment and a helicopter pad, even though they were way too far away from land for any helicopter to reach them.

NINE

Gailen stood behind Starr, protecting her from the new humans who had landed with the supply ship.

And waiting to do something, anything, that was useful to her.

"Here's your safety briefing!" Bob shouted over the wind that whipped his orange coverings.

Starr's wet hair slapped her. She hugged a small box and put her shoulder to the wind. Gailen adjusted his stance to try to shield her more. The wind didn't bother him or the other warriors much.

"There's an emergency, we die," Bob shouted at the group. His soul light glowed brightly, showing his affinity for the sea. "If there's a fire, we die. If this platform sinks, we die. So, you see anything that you're worried about, you hit that alarm."

He pointed at a bright yellow button affixed to a post. The post was wrapped in blue-and-yellow tape that reflected dazzling light. These posts were ranged every few hundred feet all around the oval.

"It lights up and pages me. You use the intercom there to tell us the emergency—man overboard, fire in the galley, what have you. If you hear all the sirens, you get on your lifejacket, go to the nearest exit point, and pray to God that somebody's boat picks you up."

The humans listened soberly. Bob pointed out where to find things called first aid equipment, an AED, fire extinguishers, and chemical showers. Everyone nodded as if they knew what those things meant.

In the end, he dismissed the new workers and turned to Starr. "Scared yet?"

She raised a hand.

"What? Questions?"

"Can we go to the network room now?"

He raised a brow. "You're focused."

She did not respond. The film covering her soul separated her from him with cold precision.

"This way." He walked toward the old oil rig.

She followed him without a backward glance.

"Is bride Starr well?" Isag growled softly to Gailen. "She seems dimmer, and she dismisses us. Have we angered her?"

"No." But hearing the other warrior echo his concern solidified that it was not in his head. "She is not angry, I think, but I will ask her."

"And why did the human Bob say that no one survives going into the water?" Xemil asked, following into the quieter interior of the oil rig. "Humans can survive a short immersion."

Bob snapped over his shoulder. "Because if we don't drown or freeze, then one of your warriors picks us off."

"A queen patrols. Enemies will not cause you harm," Gailen assured him.

"Then we're back to freezing or drowning. And if someone falls off the wrong side of the walls? They'll be half a mile away before we can even start the rescue boats."

"Why do our warriors not respond to your alarm?" Gailen asked. "Isag or Xemil know it now. They could tell the others."

"I asked ages ago. You don't have the manpower."

"We do not have human men, but more warriors have joined Atlantis. Many patrol here now. And a queen."

Bob stopped just outside a small room. Starr passed him and examined the tangled cords leading to different human machines. Bob turned on Gailen with narrowed eyes. "All right. You tell your warriors. They hear that alarm, they need to move. We have a light system that shows where a person falls overboard."

"Xemil will explain the system to the patrol."

"And we'll see if it does any good." The man grimaced, but his soul brightened. Like Starr, his feelings were not well reflected by his face. He leaned into the small room. "The cable from your city comes up here. The control room for the rig is just above. This is all company property, but I just got a notification that we're supposed to let you do anything you want. Somebody has a high opinion of you."

"Cool." Starr set her box on the floor and opened it. It seemed to be a collection of tools plus a smaller box.

"Dinner's in a half hour." Bob frowned. "But I guess that doesn't matter to you, does it?"

"Nope."

He harrumphed.

"Bob." She looked up at him coldly. "I didn't want to say it where I thought I could be overheard, but one of the men at the safety briefing resembled a crew member from the ship that abandoned me."

"All those men came in on the supply ship. If they'd stopped to pick up your crew, someone would have said something."

She returned his gaze unflinchingly.

His lips pinched. "Which one?"

"The one in the orange jumpsuit."

"Very funny. Hair color? Ethnicity? Build?"

"Brown hair, white male, medium build."

"You just described most of my crew." He blew air out from between his lips. "We haven't issued ID badges on this rig, but with the influx of new service staff to prepare for the grand opening, maybe it's time."

He left with Xemil.

Isag stationed himself outside the door to guard the narrow hall.

Star sat cross-legged on the floor and dug her fingers into the plastic covering the smaller box. It would not yield to her short nails.

Gailen knelt and offered his dagger. "You should have told me. I would have confronted that male."

"I barely interacted with the boat crew. I didn't expect to need to pick them out of a lineup. But if they've snuck onto the supply ship, they have a lot more friends than I'd like." She took Gailen's dagger and unsealed the plastic. "I'd recognize the captain for sure."

And if they found the captain, Gailen would be happy to interrogate him. Very happy.

He flexed his hands uselessly.

Starr handed back the dagger and took out a shiny cell phone. "You can sit if you want. This might take a while."

He wandered around the small room and then did as she said and sat. She plugged one of her small tools into the cell phone and then opened a panel and plugged it in.

Lights flashed, and white text scrolled across her screen. She studied it with total focus.

The platform creaked and groaned. Mechanical noises growled and air fanned across his skin. Starr went almost invisible, her soul so coated in the film that she hid from him.

It felt cold. Like he'd been forgotten.

After a long time, she unplugged the device and traced the tangles of wires from the floor to the panel and out again, around the room. She strained to trace them up to the ceiling.

He stood. "What do you seek?"

"Something that doesn't belong."

"Which is?"

"I'll know it when I see it."

He felt so useless. "Can I know?"

"No." She studied the ceiling. "Ryerson was right. I didn't tell anyone in the company I was coming, and yet someone intercepted me. Only three people knew my itinerary: Mel at the mer-human foundation, Dannika, the head matchmaker of MerMatch, and Elyssa. We're certain communication between me, Mel, and Dannika is secure."

"But not to Atlantis?"

"Exactly. That's why I traced the cable up from the submersible. It's hard to imagine a listening device planted down there, but I wanted to be thorough."

He remembered her hooking onto the cable. He'd misinterpreted her touch for concern.

"Which means that the interception point is somewhere between this room..." She looked around one last time and then packed up her tools. "And the satellite."

He followed her out the door and down the hall. Her

eyes remained fixed on the wires along the ceiling. Isag stepped in behind them.

"I was under the impression that I would be on the hunt for a bug." She shone her cell phone light up at the ceiling walking with measured paces. "That's why we were careful to control the methods of contact. This line was supposed to be secure."

"When the mer send a message via the echo points, everyone in the ocean can listen," Gailen said.

"Yes, it's best to have that attitude. You only share what you're willing for your enemies to hear."

She followed the lines up the stairs and into a room with an open view of the platform. A worker sat at panels of glass and levers.

Starr played her cell phone across the interior of the room, then scooted a chair out of her way and dug under one wall. The worker rose trying to see what she was doing. Gailen blocked his gaze. He frowned and spoke a few quiet words into a phone.

Bob came in. "I said you could do what you want, but do you have to tear the place apart?"

"Yes." She scooted out with the metal covering in her hand, wires exposed. "The communication line goes through this terminal and then out to the antenna."

"It's there." He jerked his thumb at the ceiling. "And that means?"

"I'm running out of line to investigate. The ten-thousand-dollar piece of equipment that would have let me do this without taking anything apart is currently on a dead boat floating in the middle of the Atlantic."

He grunted. "So that's it, then? The gremlins that disconnect our phones are going to carry on?"

"Not at all." She rested on her heels. "Now I know this wire is secure. I'll investigate the terminal."

He pulled his lips to the side, glanced at Gailen and Isag, then jerked his thumb at the panel. "You're going to put that back?"

"When I'm done with my investigation."

He sniffed and exited. The worker watched them.

Starr turned on the terminal, then plugged in her cell phone and clicked the keyboard. Human text scrolled by. She was so unreadable.

"Can I help you?" Gailen asked softly.

"No."

That was a clear answer.

He flexed his thumbs.

Outside, the sun descended to cloudy darkness. Rain lashed the windows, and the interconnected metal clanked. Wind rattled and gusted down the hallway, and workers clomped in and out, passing Isag with frowns. Xemil returned, wet and dripping, and exchanged places with Isag.

Gailen's stomach growled.

He informed Xemil of his plans, exchanged his clothes for his trident, and hunted in the stormy ocean for the fish that he knew Starr could tolerate. He would not injure her by eating the wrong foods and breathing their dust on her again.

The seaweeds and smaller fish were not dense, but they were enough.

After stowing his trident and pulling his clothes back on, he collected a bottle of water for Starr. She had gone even longer than him without sustenance and had not complained.

When he returned, she'd scooted under the terminal again. Xemil knelt at her tool kit.

"Hand me the hex," she said.

He gave her the bent metal piece as if he'd been assisting her for some time.

Worry churned in Gailen's gut. He had been here all along, but she had not chosen him to assist her. As soon as he left, she chose a warrior with thumbs.

Xemil saw him, blanched, and jumped to his feet. "I will guard the door."

He could not unclench his jaw to thank the warrior. He did not feel thankful at all.

"And done." She scooted back. The wires were now covered again with the metal. She tossed the hex tool onto the others, got back in her chair, and continued typing. "Hey, Gailen."

"Xemil helped you." He tried to keep the hurt out of his voice. "He was very useful."

She typed. "Yep."

The coldness grew in his chest.

He should not have this feeling around his soul mate. He should be close to her, knowing her mind.

But she was so closed off from him.

Was that her mind?

He offered her the water bottle and a food bar.

She took both without looking at him. "Thanks."

He sat again.

She ate the bar without taking her gaze away from the screen, then she crumpled the wrapper, swigged the water, and continued to watch the text scroll by, occasionally clicking.

The night deepened.

Finally, she sat back, rubbed her eyes, and twisted,

cracking her shoulders. "Nothing."

He sucked in a breath and leaned forward. "Nothing?"

"The terminal's clean."

"Then there was not a listener on this line?"

"I can't say that yet." She slouched into her seat. "I haven't investigated the final length."

He looked out the window. It was hard to see through the opaque stormy rain, and cracks of lightning split the sky. "The antenna?"

"There too." She sighed. "No, I meant the connection from the antenna to the satellite."

"Is it not just air?"

"Yes and no. I'm not going to explain about radio waves right now, but..." She frowned and straightened. "When did it start raining?"

"Hours ago."

"It's just as well. The next task requires us going out on the walkways, which I'd rather do in the daylight." She packed up her tools and stood. "We should turn in."

Gailen stood. "Turn in what direction?"

She flashed a grin. "It means sleep."

And just like that, her soul brightened. She had been so dim for so long that he'd barely seen her soul, but now it flared, open and bright. Xemil did a double take as they walked past, and he followed them down the hall.

His surprise mirrored Gailen's discomfort.

He'd been beside his soul mate for all these hours, but she had reacted to him as if he were a rock.

She had said he could be her assistant.

But she hadn't needed his assistance at all.

As they approached the sleeping room, her soul light began to dim again.

He'd always thought that once he found his soul mate,

their souls would resonate with such force that he would never doubt his place again.

But now, those doubts welled up and threatened to crush him.

TEN

Gailen was being weird.

When she'd suggested turning in, his smile had echoed hers and then swiftly faded.

He seemed so unhappy.

Why?

Again the unease returned to her. They were ignored by the few workers they passed on the walkways up to her cabin. Xemil stationed himself outside their cabin door.

She let herself in.

Gailen waited in the doorway.

"Are you coming?" she asked.

He entered and stood in the middle of the room.

She didn't have much to do to get ready. Normally, it was a regimen of medicated face wash to stop food-related eczema, medicated lotion to combat the drying effect of the medicated face wash, and so forth, but all she had was a set of hotel toiletries, so she brushed her teeth and made up the lower bunk bed.

He watched her silently.

She crawled into the lower bunk. "Are you going to sleep standing up?"

He rested a hand on the upper bunk. "Do you want me to rest here or with you?"

Oh.

Huh.

The fact that this was a question for him made her have to reevaluate some things.

He said "rest." As in just resting, not in doing anything more.

When was the last time they'd kissed?

When was the last time he'd looked at her like he wanted her?

It was one thing to hold off on getting naked together in a shower, but it was another to want to sleep separately and not even snuggle.

"Whichever you want," she said distantly.

He dropped to her level squatting in front of the bunk. A deep frown wrinkled his forehead.

She drew up her knees and hugged them.

He studied the post of the bunk bed and scratched his finger against the hard metal. "Did you wish that you had not brought me?"

Her chest squeezed. "I was going to ask the same thing."

"Why would you wonder that? You are my soul mate, Starr. I always want to be with you."

"Well, why would you think that I wouldn't want you to come with me?"

"Because I cannot help you. I do not understand what you do, and the few things that I do understand, I cannot help with." He gestured with his thumbs.

Oh. "I already told you that doesn't bother me."

"You waited for me to leave and then asked Xemil to hand you tools."

What? "I finished the deep scan and was at a good point to replace the panel. Xemil said you went for food. Which I thanked you for, by the way."

He frowned at the floor. "You did not look at me."

"And right now, you're not looking at me."

He focused on her. "When I look at you, I see a soul that is darkened. A soul that shuts me out and does not want to entangle with mine."

"But you know why." Her heart thudded. Sweat prickled her armpits. "I can't help it. You have to listen to my words, not just my soul."

"You told Lieutenant Diras you did not want me to surface with you."

"I didn't say that."

"You agreed that you did not need me."

"I was just trying to be flexible. There's so much to get ready for this grand opening, which is now looking like it's going to rewrite mer history, and it sounded like you were needed somewhere else..."

His face fell. "So. You did *not* need me."

"Well..."

He flinched like he'd been kicked. "Why ask me to come?"

"Because." She squeezed her knees. "I couldn't stand to see them treating you like you were unimportant because of your thumbs."

"And now you see it is true. I have done nothing of use here. I am unimportant."

"You're really important." She dropped her knees and scrubbed her face, trying to calm herself before her disorder took over and forced her calm because that would only hurt

Gailen more. "You've guarded me, gotten me food, and revised the rig safety system so that the mer can help if someone falls in the water."

He rocked his head like he disagreed.

"Look, you're right that I didn't fight the lieutenant. I didn't want to stop you guys from doing what you needed to do."

"Soul mates should never be apart."

"You said that, but when he reassigned you, you didn't argue."

"I cannot argue. He is my superior."

"I thought the whole thing about Atlantis is that you *can* argue. It's different from the other cities where you're supposed to obey the chain of command in lockstep. Isn't that right?"

He stilled.

"I'd have been happy to argue on your behalf, but I thought maybe you'd changed your mind. Maybe you didn't want to surface with me. If someone forces me to do the wrong thing, I could die. And I get asked to do the wrong thing all the time."

His voice lowered. "Then being together with me is the wrong thing?"

"No." They were going in circles. She dropped her hands. "If you're needed somewhere else, then you should go there. I can handle this. This is what I've trained for."

"Very well." He stood. "Lieutenant Diras was right. Xemil and Isag will protect you."

"No, wait." She rested her feet on the floor. "I feel like we're saying two different things. I don't need you to do my job. But if I have to go in the water again, or if I get sick, I don't want to be with anyone else. The only person I want to be with is you."

He hesitated.

"You can see souls." She pressed her hand to her chest. "Can't you see the truth in mine?"

"No." He rolled onto his heels. "You have retreated from me this whole time. From the moment we surfaced, your soul disappeared. I feel like you aren't even here."

"That's how I've lived my whole life." She dropped her hands to her lap. This was so crazy. "I don't have any real feelings."

"Each second you live this way must hurt."

She snorted. "Not at all."

"You cannot shift or grow your queen powers with a closed soul."

"Right now, I have a job to do. It's easier if I get through it without thinking about my feelings."

"Then I should go, because I am making your work harder for no reason."

Well, he was.

She'd sought therapy because she felt something was missing from her life, but when she found out what it was, she had mixed feelings about doing the work to tackle it. That was one reason she'd made a truce.

Honestly, it wasn't a bad way to live.

Isolated and distant from everyone, untouched by their feelings or emotions. A single ship floating in a vast dark sea.

But she'd already been there in real life.

And it had nearly killed her.

Gailen stood before her offering another choice. Her small isolation didn't only hurt herself. It hurt him and drove them apart.

She stood.

Her knees wobbled from the long hours hunched over the communication terminal.

She steadied herself against the bunk. "You're right that I don't need you. I don't need this life that you're offering. So much of my past has been survival and endurance. I didn't even realize it was possible to choose a deeper feeling."

He nodded slowly.

Even from here, she could *feel* his heart breaking.

"But Gailen." She held out her hand. "You changed that. And I do want it now. I just don't know how to ask for it without shutting down and shutting both of us out completely."

ELEVEN

This was the most vulnerable Starr had ever allowed herself to be.

Even with her therapist, she'd been guarded. She hadn't said that she wanted to change, only that she needed ways to work out the coldness and develop friendships. Her therapist had told her that she needed to resolve her depersonalization disorder first.

And now Gailen stood before her, poised on the precipice.

Warriors could look into the truth of one's soul. And he'd always seen beneath her shield.

"What do you want me to do?" His voice was low and rough.

"I think I want..."

His presence loomed so much bigger in this small space than it had in the boat in the open air.

This wasn't her first time reaching intimacy with a man. She'd once pursued a man as reserved and uninvolved as she was. Their first sexual encounter had been awkward, but an acceptable start. He'd disagreed. It was too much effort to be with her.

Gailen was nothing like that man.

He stood before her totally vulnerable, and she couldn't do the same for him.

No, she *must* do the same for him.

She held out both hands. "A kiss?"

He slowly leaned forward, his gaze darting over her face, giving her every opportunity to pull away. Her body throbbed before they even touched. And then his mouth covered hers. Dizzying heat filled her veins, and even though she expected it, the sudden combustion made her swoon into his arms. His big hands slid around her back, powerfully containing her, and he seated their lips more perfectly, meshing their bodies into one. She opened her tingling lips to his liquid possession, and...

Tingling?

Oh no.

Her chest squeezed.

It was not an allergy. She was *not* allergic to Gailen. It was just excitement.

Excitement that triggered panic and wrapped her in cool, emotionless plastic.

Gailen pulled back. "Starr..."

"I know. I'm sorry." She pulled back, puffed out in irritation, and grabbed handfuls of her hair. "It's my disorder. Whenever I feel too strongly, it's triggered. And you make me feel strong emotions."

He stood, agonizingly beautiful, in the center of her room. "What do you want me to do?"

"I'm sorry."

"Do you not want me?"

"I do. But I can't jump in. I need to..."

"What?"

She felt her way to a possible answer. "Ease in? I think that will help."

"What you want me to do?" His favorite question.

But it forced her to be the one to lead.

He wanted to love her the way she needed to be loved. She could lean on him, physically and emotionally, and he accepted her weight. It made her heart ache for him even more.

The aching was risky. She wobbled, in danger of shutting down.

But he just waited. If she shut down for an hour, he would wait as he had on the boat. If she shut down for a day? Same. If she shut down for an eternity?

Yes, he would wait even for an eternity.

She was worth an eternity to him.

And so she was able to breathe through her fears and return to solid ground. "Just stand there."

He stood. A proud warrior. The soft T-shirt fabric stretched across broad shoulders, muscular pectorals, and fell gently to his tapered waist. The curve of his thick cock made a rugged male seam against the Bermuda shorts.

He was beautiful and strong. Powerful and broad. And so patient.

Her heart swelled.

The protective film slipped around her.

But she pushed it back. *I don't need you.* She wanted to feel this. Feel him.

That was the problem with the shield. It never let her choose.

But still, he stood waiting for her to find her way back out of the maze she had created in her own mind.

She reached out and touched the back of his hand.

He turned his palm to link their fingers.

"No."

He released her again.

She trailed curious fingers over his flexible wrist, up his taut forearm to the bony elbow, and over the bulging muscles of his biceps. Swirling orange lines interlocked and captured her with vivid fascination. He flexed, and the lines stood out in sharp relief.

"You're so strong."

He wiggled his thumbs. Bitterness flashed across his face before being replaced by acceptance. "Only you think so."

"Don't mermen heal? The Life Tree sap runs through your veins." She rested her hand on a small scar at his shoulder. "Am I wrong?"

"You are right." He watched her fingertips touching him. His irises glimmered with iridescence and the intensity of his feelings. "Most warriors do heal, but sometimes the injuries are too severe. Another warrior, Faier, suffered from terrible scars until he met his soul mate."

"So now that you've met me, you'll heal."

Gailen frowned. "My thumbs are already healed, just the wrong way."

"Have you ever considered cutting them off?"

His eyes widened. "Cutting them off?"

"If the bone sets crooked, a doctor might rebreak it so it can heal right. Since mermen can regrow missing limbs, why not?"

"Then I could not help the warriors during their time of need."

"You already feel like you're not able to help them, though."

"I am not the one who..." He darkened. "Do they bother you?"

"No, of course not."

He lightened. "We have been attacked several times, and although I do not have the same abilities as the other warriors, I have managed to fight back. That is enough for now."

And the other warriors thought he wasn't fit? How could they?

But then she remembered him shutting down, going still and silent, and all the hours they'd wasted on this platform. All because he had swallowed his words.

"It's okay to feel how you feel," she reminded him. "You should tell others what you think, Gailen."

He frowned.

She trailed her fingers over the bulges of his shoulder to the thick column of his neck, and the thought of teasing him there made her nipples tighten. She rested her thumb in the hollow behind his firm jaw and then followed the tendon down to his shirt collar, then tugged the hem. Using one hand, he pulled it over his head and dropped it on the floor, baring his torso.

Acres of rippled muscle stitched with iridescent orange dominated her with hard promises.

He would pleasure her for hours.

She splayed both hands across his broad pectorals. He flexed, and his flat male nipples moved beneath her hands. He was a living creature, a gorgeous male, and he invited her thorough exploration.

Her one other experience had been quick, awkward, and uncomfortable. Gailen was none of those things, and her experience with him wouldn't be either.

She traced the dusting of light brown hair from his

bellybutton across his flat abdomen. Over his pointed hips to where the shorts were slung low against the hot ridge of male need for her.

It stole her mind.

He started to pull the shorts down.

She stopped him. "I just want to concentrate on this."

He released the band.

The lines of his tattoos flared in patterns. Tribal shapes. Bright orange, like a pepper, one of the few foods that she could eat.

Turning him around, she followed the tattoos up every vertebra to the base of his neck, where his short, dark hair crested.

And then she pulled off her T-shirt and fit her braless bare chest to his back.

He sucked in a breath.

She closed her eyes and throbbed for him.

He was much larger than her, and yet she could still wrap her arms around him. He was a warrior, and he smelled like masculine spice, musk, and sea salt. She took a deep breath. Delicious, spicy, sensual. Sex.

Yes.

Gailen smelled like powerful gentleness, passionate worship, male sex. His scent in her nostrils made her damp pussy quiver.

He rested his broad hands over her forearms.

Gailen was fun. Safe. Heady.

She squeezed. Her body was sensitized, as if she'd gotten into a bath that was too hot at first, but then became a comfortable temperature. Tingling streaked to her center. And she ached.

It was a good ache.

His voice rumbled low. "Starr."

She moved around his body. Her sensitive nipples slid over his shoulder blades.

He turned and enveloped her in his arms, and she let him. Their bodies pressed together again, chest to chest. Every part of her trembled. She walked a wire between far too much and not nearly enough.

He cupped her cheek. "Can I?"

She nodded.

His lips brushed hers in a sweet, sensuous, loving kiss.

———

Kissing Starr changed everything.

Her mouth moved, sweet and sexy and hot and all that he wanted.

When she touched him with such openness, such fascination, he did not feel like there was anything wrong with him.

He only felt what was right.

The more they pressed their bodies together, the brighter her soul glowed with certainty and wonder.

All his past disappointments and struggles were worthwhile. His embarrassment, his shame. They had all led to this kiss.

She opened her hot mouth to his. He invaded, and their tongues hooked and tangled, stroked and soothed.

Her small breasts pressed against his chest, and her slim hips undulated with sensuous moans. He needed to lay her on the bunk, pour his cock into her eager wetness, and unite their souls for all time.

She followed his lips, biting and sucking.

He flooded her mouth with his desire, crashing into her like the waves of the ocean against the barrier. What was the film that threatened her soul? It was nothing. In a thousand years, the ocean wore the mightiest wall down to a pebble. With her encouragement, his love would do the same.

She pressed her soft vee against his swollen hardness.

He was ready, so ready. He palmed the small of her back, urging her closer, needing so much more than he'd already received.

She wavered.

Ah.

He reined himself back.

This kiss was for her. She was doing so well. Her soul flared with passion. Every moment was good.

And the tide of passion receded within her.

She pulled back, licked her lips, and studied him with bright eyes. Color spotted her cheeks, clearly defined and adorable, a natural human tattoo against her pale skin. "I think if we do this enough that someday, I will be able to focus and break free."

"Your soul is already much brighter, Starr."

She smiled, sat on the bunk, and patted the cloth. "Sleep with me."

He folded himself around her and into the bed. She pulled on his shirt, leaving her bottom tantalizingly uncovered. The bunk was too small, and she lay against his shoulder with their knees and legs interlocked.

"It's different, isn't it? Being nude under the water and on the surface."

He brushed his fingertips over her rounded derriere and to her mid-thigh where his shirt ended. "Yes."

"I feel cozy and safe for the first time in a really long time. If I had this every day, then I think that I could give up the shield and become normal."

"You can have this every day. As much as you want."

She hooked her thigh over his and sighed.

This was the weight of his soul mate. Her body, peaceful and healthy, pressed against his. This was how she must always be.

This was how he would be if he turned away from the bitterness. Turned away from the unfairness and regrets of his past.

Have you ever considered cutting them off?

"What if they did not grow back?" he murmured.

"Hmm?" Starr roused with a yawn. "Your thumbs?"

"Or what if they twisted the same way?" He flexed his misaligned thumbs, and they moved uselessly toward his wrists. "Perhaps this is my destiny."

"Mm. That fear is what drove me to therapy." She splayed a hand across his chest. "But I haven't taken a full deep breath in as long as I can remember, and just now I realized something miraculous. I can smell you."

He tried to lower his arm so she did not rest her nose close to his armpit. "The queens have spoken of this body odor. It is a surface problem the mer are unfamiliar with. I am sorry."

"It's different when it's someone you really like." She forced his arm up, nuzzled his ticklish armpit, and giggled. "It's a whole new world. Shifting to the mer and seeing the huge ocean world with my own eyes was so overwhelming that I don't think I really took it in. But suddenly noticing this small change and realizing what I've gone without for years has filled the black-and-white lines of my life with color."

"Because of the odor?"

"Because I can breathe. It's like suddenly realizing I'm not angry, or realizing I'm not scared. It happened so slowly,

I didn't notice it until it hit me. I didn't think I changed when I drank the elixir and kissed you, but this is big."

"You have changed."

"And I have to want to embrace it. What new miracle will happen when I let more feelings into my life?"

Her question echoed in his mind. "When you come to Atlantis and become my bride, you will get all of your powers and more. You'll be able to do anything you want. Defend the city, control your powers."

"You've seen so many queens, it probably feels ordinary to you."

That was partially true.

You should say what you think, Gailen.

He had almost left her tonight because he thought she didn't want him. Being useful and obedient was ingrained in him. He wanted to get along, no matter how much it hurt.

That had to change.

He spoke to the inner feelings. "Do not worry that this is only new to you, Starr. You are changing me too."

She glowed brighter in response.

He *was* so used to having broken thumbs that he forgot what it was like to have full use of his hands. And he was so used to being frustrated by all the things he couldn't do that he forgot to be satisfied with what he could.

Starr opened his world too. He had more options than he thought. She thought he could change any time he wanted. And if he didn't? She thought he was worthy even with these thumbs.

"Tomorrow is going to be a big day." She yawned again. "I can feel it."

"I do not know how I can help, but I will try."

"You help me just by being here and existing." She hugged him.

It made his chest ache.

Because they were both so broken in their own ways, but together, they were able to fill in each other's cracks.

"You are going to help me so much tomorrow." She lowered her voice to a whisper. "Because tomorrow, we're going after the last connection point. And if I'm right, it's the reason someone set me adrift and tried to kill me."

He'd guard her with his life.

Their hidden enemies would not dare to try again.

TWELVE

For the first time in years, Starr woke rested.

In Gailen's arms.

She'd told him she needed his presence, but that wasn't nearly enough. She needed him so much more than she could express.

Waking up in his arms was like discovering she had a best friend and that person had also chosen her.

She snuggled in, cozy and safe.

And that hint of masculine spice struck her in the heart. The glimmer in his iridescent eyes made her feminine areas clench and all of her body come alive.

He didn't just want to be her friend. He wanted more. A lot more.

And she wanted it too. Even though it was so dangerous.

She only allowed herself a little bit of delicious morning kisses and touching of his electrifying rock-hard body, and he was so accommodating for her, even gripping her hips and grinding his shudderingly hard cock against her thigh until her pussy clenched and she wanted nothing more than to arch and take in every delicious inch...but soon. Once she was sure the film was under control and she wouldn't hurt them both by shutting down.

And then she rolled out of bed and onto the floor, pulled on yesterday's clothes, and checked her phone.

She'd missed a call from Dannika.

Starr checked the time difference and then returned the call. "What's the emergency?"

"Oh, Starr." Dannika blew out a long breath into the receiver. "Bella let me know you'd texted her last night, but I just needed to hear your voice. We never should have asked you to go. I knew that there would be risks, but I never imagined that you'd be so endangered."

She flashed a smile that Dannika couldn't see. "It's been a journey."

"How's your investigation?"

"Unfinished."

"Then you may want to pause. I know better than to tell you anything sensitive, but I want to emphasize that *nothing you're doing there will have any effect on the investigation that is already taking place. The FBI already has all the materials they need.* Do you understand?"

"Sure. I'll stop investigating and just be a tourist."

"Great." Dannika sighed again, knowing that Starr was just accommodating her for any potential eavesdroppers. "The week you were missing was agony. You don't know how many sleepless nights I've had. And not only because the kraken is also missing and my son is going through a phase."

Starr pulled on her socks. "Bella used to tell me about baby Jonah. Kids are bad at that age."

"I can't tell if he's bad or if I'm just getting old. I have no idea how Angie went through this. At twenty she had two children and at forty she had another five."

Starr couldn't imagine seven kids. That was a sitcom, not the life of an ordinary person. She had trouble picturing more than two. Or one. "Sounds exhausting."

"You understand. Now if we could only figure out where a giant squid the size of Mount Fuji could be hiding..."

That seemed like a difficult thing to misplace. "Is she not in her underwater canyon home?"

"I've just heard a report from the Luscans living at the cliff of the canyon. They don't believe she's passed."

"The ocean is vast and unexplored."

"For humans. The mer think they have a handle on most hidden depths."

"She'll turn up eventually. Or she won't."

Dannika laughed. "How prosaic, and yet comfortingly true. Thank you, Starr. I won't keep you. Have fun being a tourist."

Starr hung up and laced her boots.

Gailen angled out of the bed and stretched. His muscles flexed in sharp relief, making a gorgeous masculine profile from the sculpted curve of his shoulders to the points at his hips and his bulging thighs. She loved the hard jut of his jaw and the roughness of his cheek when he covered her with his possessive kiss.

Her pussy throbbed again.

Soon.

He leaned over her and glanced at her phone screen. "Dannika wishes you to stop investigating?"

"No." She borrowed his dagger, which he'd left on the upper bunk, to open the second new cell phone package.

"She wants whoever's listening to our calls to think we're going to stop."

"Then will your actions make it clear that you lied?"

"I hope not." She went through the second cell phone setup process. "Anyway, it's not all a lie. The way some people never forget a face, Dannika never forgets a voice, and so even though the early recordings of the Sons of Hercules leader were distorted, she told me what markers she was listening for. Her evidence must have convinced the federal investigators. She has highly placed friends."

He watched her finish the setup and fit the phone into a waterproof case.

She handed it to him. "Last night, we checked the interior, so now it's time to go outside. Are you ready?"

"I am." His smile sent dangerous waves to her heart.

She left the room and greeted Isag, who must have switched in the night with Xemil, then asked for directions to Ryerson's office, and she got passed around by the workers until she ended up in front of Bob.

"What do you want with Ryerson?" he asked sharply. The bags under his eyes suggested he was long overdue for a morning coffee.

"He promised to give me a tour."

"Oh, yeah, he'll love that." Bob pointed to the stairs. "His office is up there. Fair warning, we're expecting some sort of call from corporate at any moment. I have the cryptic order to 'keep him in sight.' So don't take him out of it. Got it?"

"Noted." She started for the stairs.

"Starr."

His tone made her pause.

"I don't really have time for this, but I'm still working on those badges." He drummed his fingers on his cluttered desk. "When you get done with your tour, come find me."

She nodded.

His gaze flicked over the warriors and rested again on Gailen's dagger—securely attached to his biceps—and waved for her to carry on.

She climbed the stairs, her warriors a comforting presence behind her.

Dannika had told her two markers for identifying the leader of the Sons of Hercules based on the many voice recordings her sister, Bella, had gotten during his blackmail, extortion, and kidnapping of Jonah.

One, the leader had an odd verbal tic of using both the first and last name of whoever he was addressing, as though he'd been taught it to win friends and influence people, or to shore up a flawed memory.

Two, he used classical mythology, but mixed characters up.

"How could the leader have chosen Hercules for his mentor?" Dannika had demanded more than once. "Yes, he slew a sea monster as one of his trials, but he was only doing the trials in penance for having murdered his innocent wife and children."

"Funny how that got left out of the Disney movie," Starr had commented.

"Oh, don't get me started on Disney." Dannika's tone had grown incensed, as much as the serene, encouraging matchmaker ever expressed an emotion like anger. "But they are celebrating a man who was cursed with fits of madness! I supposed it's poetic, actually. They would have had a much less problematic hero in Perseus, who, while better known for slaying Medusa, also slew a sea monster."

Poetic or not, the leader of the Sons of the Hercules had a lot to answer for, and Starr had her own prime suspect.

Gailen followed close behind her as they reached the next level. He seemed so much steadier today. He met her glances warmly. It was no longer awkward, and that was wonderful.

Ryerson's office was pretty obvious. Unlike the more functional areas of the platform, his door was framed with wood trim and had his name in gold. His door was ajar, and as she approached, his voice rose.

"And that is why I told you not to do that!"

Another voice spoke more calmly.

"I didn't authorize anything," Ryerson snapped back loudly. "We have a tight deadline. One week's extension is nothing for what we're building."

Starr stopped outside the door. His office was dark and wood-paneled, with books, gold sconces, and large upholstered captain's chairs with clawed feet.

Ryerson slammed his hand on his desk, causing the gold lamp, a stack of books, and an inkwell to jump. "You fix it. You fix it right—ah." He straightened and faced the door. "Starr Langley. To what do I owe the pleasure?"

She pushed the door the rest of the way open. "You promised me a tour."

"So I did."

His assistant stepped back from the side of Ryerson's desk. He bowed his head, subdued, and strode quickly out the door and down the hall.

"Ah, forgive my assistant. Not all of us are raised to handle the stress of presiding over a multibillion-dollar company." Ryerson pulled on a bulky orange jacket and pristine yellow hard hat. "Now, let me unveil how art has met engineering in the groundbreaking new city my company has envisioned to safeguard the future of mankind."

"And the mer," Gailen said blithely behind Starr

"Yes, yes. Of course them." Taking on the role of the unstoppable tour guide, Ryerson led them through the oil rig droning on about how this was an investor's dream. "Sea homesteading has eluded us for centuries. Once all the land was taken and the unknown territory conquered, what next? Turn to the sea. Build an island, set your own rules, enjoy the ultimate freedom."

He led them out the doors and across the windy open area. "Once construction is complete, this will be our grand dock."

She got out her cell phone, recorded a few minutes of video, and then snapped pictures. "And what's the highest point?"

"You would think it would be the oil rig with all those antennas, but you would be wrong." He lifted one hand and showed off what was clearly his proudest feature. "The friendship pyramid is our design figurehead. It's slightly larger than the glass pyramid at the Louvre."

"How would I get to the top?"

"Yes, yes, that's part of the tour." He walked back to the oil rig and around the oval to reach the pavilion, dodging rumbling construction equipment and talking as he went. "This walkway will be finished with Moroccan tile."

"What are the saucers?"

"Saucers? Oh, you mean the foundations for future modular homes." He stepped up to the edge. The foundations bobbed gently. "We had hoped to finish at least one model home by the grand opening. These biological concrete pontoons will support the weight of a modest condo. We patterned it off the failed ocean community in French Polynesia."

She snapped a photo.

"We have perfected where they went wrong and have gone further. Come."

He led them into the glass pyramid. It was abruptly quieter, and her boots echoed as she followed him down the ramp into the blue fishbowl.

"Behold our glory." Ryerson gestured expansively at the glass theater.

It was like the inside of an aquarium, but she was the fish in the air while the ocean surrounded her.

"This is the largest one in the world, even larger than the restaurants under the Maldives. Here, people can watch in comfort as marine life swims in its environment, safely separated by three feet of glass. We first tried clear aluminum, but…"

Starr touched the cool glass.

She'd been in that water so recently. And yet, it felt like a lifetime ago. Several dull gray fish gaped at her. She couldn't see their lights or sense their music as she had in the water, and she could barely see through the dense blue.

How funny that when she'd been in it, she'd seen an infinite distance, but now she could barely see more than a few feet.

A drip sounded close by, and a little stink like seaweed tickled her nose. Apparently, there were downsides to getting her smell back.

"We're still working out the kinks." Ryerson scratched at a rust stain trailing down an inner wall from a bolt the size of his fist. "At this scale and distance from shore, the logistics of the project have defied any feat of engineering humanity has ever tried before."

"The ancient ruin of Atlantis is many times this size," Gailen said. "We are still unearthing it."

"Yes, well, such a feat is beyond your engineering now. Who were the original builders, anyway? Perhaps aliens."

"What are aliens?"

"Another time." Ryerson cleared his throat. "Are you finished, Starr Langley?"

"Almost." Something moved in the blue just beyond her vision. A warrior. But not one she'd met. Violent red tattoos slashed his broad cheeks and heavily marked his body. He fixed on Gailen, and his upper lip curled in a sneer.

The hairs stood up on her forearms, though she wasn't cold. "Gailen, is he a friend of yours?"

"Huh?" Gailen ambled to her side.

The warrior darted back into the dark water.

"Hm. I could be wrong..." He motioned to Isag. "Find Xemil and alert the rest of the patrol."

Isag jogged out.

"Was it an enemy?" she asked.

"I hope an enemy would not penetrate our safe zones so easily."

Gailen and Starr followed Ryerson to the main level and then up the ramps. Past the area where he'd been having breakfast the previous morning, Ryerson led them out onto a balcony with stairs leading up to a very windy crow's nest.

"I hope this puts your fears at rest." Ryerson rested both hands against the chest-high wrought iron railing at the pinnacle. "This company and everyone employed by it are dedicated to its success. There's no other reason we would come here for months of our lives in the isolation of the cold, surrounded by sharks and creatures who are worse than sharks, if we didn't truly believe in the future of mankind being furthered by sea homesteading. My city will be the first of many. It's the new railroad, the new diamond mine, the new lithium. Our future skyscrapers will be seascapes. And Ryerson Deep Water Construction will be the first. Here."

Her cell phone security app picked up a rogue signal. She walked along the railing to triangulate it.

"I find your lack of response a little disheartening," Ryerson said. "I know the rumors. I know what you must suspect me of."

Oh, did he? He sure was nonchalant about it. "What do you think I suspect you of?"

"Being the leader of..." He glanced sideways at Gailen, perhaps accurately understanding that if Gailen suspected him of being the Sons of Hercules leader, he would challenge him to deadly combat. "I know you think I'm the root of your friends' little problems. But ask yourself: Why would I mean you harm? Why would I want to cause a problem with the customers who gave me a start?"

Such a reasonable question. And such interesting candidness from a crafty businessman.

"This"—he gestured at the massive multibillion-dollar construction—"is my legacy. We all know that climate change is going to accelerate. We might not get *Waterworld*, but every billionaire is taking money out of coastal real estate and putting it into floating real estate. This is demonstrably the future. And I'm at the forefront, leading the change."

"Your business is an oil company." She knelt and reached under the railing. Her hands closed around a small black box affixed to the underside. She could see it through the grating, but there wasn't an easy way to dislodge it.

"My father's business was an oil company. I've single-handedly pivoted to something much more lucrative. There's a reason that I'm here and not the CEO or the vice president."

"Not the actual owner," she said.

He gritted his teeth. "I still have plenty of stock. Despite the baseless rumors, I'm one of the good guys, and it hurts to know that your foundation no longer believes in me. I'm just like Calliope, who had visions of disaster and no one listened to her."

She managed to pry the box apart enough to reveal the contents to a cell phone picture. "That was Cassandra."

"No, it wasn't."

It wasn't her job to argue with him, and she really didn't care if he agreed with her not.

He saw that deadened look in her eyes and quickly backpedaled. "Oh, what does it matter? The point is that if I can see the future, I can change it. Mold and shape it. When global warming takes out the land, I'll have the sea, and the poor, doomed mermen are paying me to build it. So I ask you again, why would I do anything to risk my own future?"

That made a lot of sense and was very believable.

Except it wasn't true.

The low growl of a distant plane echoed across the sea.

He squinted up into the sky as a jet modified with pontoons circled, coming in for a landing within the oval. It took a skilled pilot to clear the low wall and land without plowing into the oil rig, but they managed it and bobbed over to the dock where Bob was waiting.

"Someone is trying to destroy the platform," Starr said. "The same way that someone found out I was on that boat and tried to destroy me."

"Well, it wasn't me." He made a circle around himself.

"I have my spies. I know what's circulating back at the home office. But you and your goons can poke around all you want. Nothing near me is even a hint of a problem."

"Nothing, huh?" She flashed the picture of the box at him. "Then why is the top of your design figurehead fitted with a jammer?"

He squinted at the picture. "Jammer?"

"Great for knocking out communications between boats, oil rigs, cell phones." She glanced at the suits emerging from the pontoon plane. "Airplanes."

"I didn't place that." Ryerson straightened. "That wasn't me."

The phone in his pocket rang, and he held it to his ear. Bob's voice was loud enough to be heard even over the wind. "Ryerson, these gentlemen want to talk to you."

He turned and waved at the distant men, then pocketed his phone and loomed over her. "You try anything, little girl, and I'll destroy you."

Her heart thudded, and the film descended around her, wrapping her in stillness.

She should fight it, but...

Gailen stood behind her.

She didn't need the film. Gailen's protective presence was enough.

And just like that, the film melted away, returning her to a normal state of equilibrium.

She sensed the responses Gailen wanted to make as if he'd said them aloud, but his glare drove Ryerson back as quickly as any audible threat.

"Legally, of course." Ryerson fixed the same broad smile as always upon his face. "I'll prosecute libel and slander to the fullest extent of the law because I am a very innocent man. Excuse me. We'll continue the tour after I deal with something."

He descended the steps, leaving them alone on the roof.

Gailen pulled her into his arms. His own trembled.

She rested her head on his shoulder, taking great strength from the contact. "You can say what you want, you know."

"I do not like that man. His soul glows brightly, meaning he has a great affinity for the sea, but I do not believe his words are honorable."

"Agreed."

Ryerson crossed the pavilion beneath them and circled the oval, dodging construction equipment. His assistant met him at the old oil rig, but Ryerson waved him off and continued to the suits. A hose delivered liquid—possibly fuel—to the airplane. Ryerson was escorted directly onto the plane. Its engine started, and it flew off into the gray sky.

She watched it go. "But I think he's about to face some consequences."

Across the oval, both Ryerson's assistant and Bob watched the plane from their separate locations. First Bob, then the assistant focused on her and Gailen at the top of the pyramid.

She shivered.

"Good." Gailen linked their fingers, his thumb jutting the wrong way. "What are you going to do now?"

"I'm going to tell someone about the jammer." She descended the stairs into the sheltering glass. "And then I'm going to search for that stingray."

THIRTEEN

"Stingray?" Bob sat back in his heavily cluttered office and wiped his sweating face. Losing Ryerson seemed to have massively stressed him out. "What in blue blazes is a stingray?"

"A type of flat, cartilaginous fish that soars across the ocean," Gailen told him helpfully.

Bob blinked as if he didn't know whether or not to believe Gailen.

Starr snorted. She hadn't laughed this much in years, and it certainly helped that her prime suspect for the Sons of Hercules leader was currently on a one-way flight back to the United States in the custody of his company's lawyers—who were probably even more motivated to keep him contained than the FBI. "It's a device used by the military for phone surveillance. It mimics a cell phone tower or, in the case of this platform, a satellite connection. Once local devices have connected to it, it forwards their transmissions up to the satellite eavesdropping on all data."

"And that's why, starting a couple of weeks ago, my phone wouldn't hold a signal?"

"It's one possibility, if the stingray had fluky power or a bad signal location."

He sighed. "All right. Where is it?"

"Somewhere hard to access."

"Great. And it wasn't this jammer thing?" He poked at the box, then got out his phone. "Hey, Search Bar. What's a stingray?"

"Searching..." his computerized voice assistant said in a melodious tone.

He'd sworn a blue streak when she'd told him about the jammer and sent some workers to pry it up. They'd said there was something else glued up there with it, but they'd had to go get better tools to reach it, and by the time they'd gotten back, the second mystery device was gone.

Which was...not good, honestly.

"It might have been the mystery device," she said.

"A stingray is a flat, cartilaginous fish related to sharks in the... Searching... Searching..."

"Ah, there goes my phone. Signal lost." He tossed his cell on the crowded desk and jerked his chin at Gailen. "Yours too?"

Gailen held up the cell phone Starr had given him.

"But not yours." Bob squinted at her.

"I didn't know whether a stingray was in use here, but I prepared for the possibility." She held up her encrypted phone. "I can use our devices to triangulate the signal. If it was the mystery device, I worry about who might have moved it."

"And you want me to back you up."

Starr linked her hand with Gailen's. "Humans prefer human justice."

"I really don't have time for this. You didn't identify the charter boat captain or crew in the pictures I found for you.

But somebody moved that mystery device." Bob lowered his leaned-back chair to the ground with a thump. "Let's go."

She headed back to the pavilion, her starting point, and set up the app on her and Gailen's phones. Bob stood with them for a few minutes, hands deep in his pockets, another gray storm threatening. He was barely there a minute when one of his workers ran up and he was needed elsewhere.

"I'm coming right back," he shouted over at her through the wind. "Don't do anything stupid."

She would try very hard not to.

"How does this work?" Gailen asked.

She showed him how to operate the program. "The nearest satellite should be over twenty thousand miles from here. If you stood on the other side of the oval from me and drew a triangle from my cell phone to yours to the satellite, we'd look like we were on top of each other. But if the stingray is collecting our signal from, say, the top of the glass pyramid, then we'd look several football fields apart."

"Our triangle is fatter," Gailen said.

"Yes, exactly."

"Your work involves small machines and interesting puzzles." He frowned. "My work in Atlantis has no machinery or puzzles. Will you regret descending with me?"

"It will be refreshing to do something different," she assured him. "I've always wanted to go out and dig in the dirt and make something grow. Now I think I could actually smell roses and lavender and honeysuckle. Things I've only read about and never thought I would know what they were really like."

"Queen Elyssa has described 'smell' many times. I do not think the mer have that sense."

"That's okay. You can see forever and hear the music

and light of animals—and humans. I'm sure you have other things that are just as wonderful."

He brightened. "Yes, and now that you say so, we do have machinery and puzzles. We still have not solved the mysteries of old Atlantis, the cause of the Great Catastrophe, or how to lift the ruin. I still do not know what plant attacks the structure."

"Well, if it's an invasive vine, maybe it will at least have pretty flowers."

"Or maybe it will smother the new city." He looked grim, but then he lightened again. "If these puzzles interest you, then you will be fine."

"I have a lot to look forward to, I think."

He grinned.

Suddenly, she couldn't wait to find the stingray and be done with this project. The Atlantis Life Tree had beckoned her like a promise. Her destiny awaited beneath the sea.

Ryerson was on his way to being arrested. Bob was on the lookout for the captain and crew that had stranded her. Once they got the stingray, the platform would be secure and she could go with Gailen and discover just how far her new abilities stretched.

"You stay here," she told him. "I'll cross to the other side of the oval."

"On foot? No. I will swim."

"Keep the phone as dry as you can." She double-checked the case. "It's only waterproof for a few feet."

He shucked his T-shirt and Bermuda shorts, dropping them on the damp pavilion. Unlike the workers who wore thick jackets, he seemed immune to cold. And she was pretty comfortable in her own thin T-shirt and boxers, come to think of it. First a clear nose, then cold hardiness? She really had changed.

He strode down the steps, nude and unashamed, and entered the water with barely a ripple. The inner lagoon was choppier now that the wind had come up, but Gailen held the phone above the waves and crossed easily, then climbed the scaffolding on the other side. Together they performed the tests.

Huh.

The data located the stingray device in the glass pyramid. But not at the top like she'd expected. Somewhere inside.

That could explain a bad signal.

Wherever it was, she wouldn't be stupid. She'd wait until both Bob was back and Gailen was with her to search.

"I did not get it wet," Gailen called cheerfully as he neared her side, lofting the cell phone like a torch. "Although if a case is waterproof, does that not mean it is immune to water?"

"Yeah, they all say they're waterproof, but then you drop them in the toilet and suddenly they're not." She walked along the railing as he swam to the lip of the artificial shallows.

A dark shadow moved beneath him.

Gailen frowned. "Starr, I—"

He thrashed and disappeared.

Something had dragged him under the water.

Her heart kicked.

She raced to the steps. Waves splashed her boots.

The waves folded over and smoothed.

Gailen was gone.

Bob jogged up to her. "What was that? Where did he go?"

"I don't know." She searched the water. Her heart thudded faster and faster.

Isag and Xemil had never come back. They were supposed to find each other and the patrol. *But they'd never come back.*

She gasped for breath. Her lips tingled.

Too much excitement.

The film came down, wrapping her in calm.

No!

She fought against it, dropping her cell phone and tearing off her clothes. She pulled her feet right out of her socks and boots and shoved them all at Bob.

Bob gaped at her. "What are you—?"

"I'm going after him." She waded in. The water wasn't cold, exactly, but it was shocking, and she couldn't stop her gasp.

"Starr?" Bob shouted. "You're not armed. Starr!"

She was a mer.

Gailen had transformed her.

She could breathe through her nose and smell for the first time in decades. She could swim in the mid-Atlantic during a brewing storm and feel no cold.

Starr paddled out beyond the lip of the steps and ducked under the water.

It was wet and cold, and currents rushed around her, dragging her to and fro. How had it felt so calm in Gailen's arms? This wasn't calm. She was falling and gasping and gulping. Water filled her throat. She choked. The glass dome skidded past her face. She cracked her wrist on a jutting strut.

Pain lanced her.

She hugged her wrist to her chest with a desperate cry.

I transformed. I transformed. I transformed.

Starr managed to kick in the direction the vicious currents were dragging her.

The ocean opened. Light flooded the darkness, and bright spots of fish glimmered.

She had transformed!

In the distance, Gailen struggled as a crowd of deadly warriors dragged him into the abyss.

Xemil zoomed past her. Others were swimming in from different directions, but like Xemil, they were too slow.

They couldn't reach him in time.

Neither could she.

Losing Gailen like this... No, she couldn't lose him like this!

The film surrounded her and tightened. She couldn't breathe.

Without him, she couldn't breathe.

Gailen's final vibration echoed. "Starr..."

Xemil wheeled. Shock transformed his features. The warriors who'd been chasing Gailen veered to help her.

No!

Darkness closed her eyes.

But a great coldness froze her heart.

No one was going to save Gailen, and it was all her fault.

FOURTEEN

Gailen fought the All-Council warriors who dragged him away from the platform.

In the distance, Starr's panic dimmed her soul. They were connected, so the strength left his muscles.

He forced himself to fight harder. If he could only hold her in his arms. "Let me go!"

"The general requires your presence," the violent red-tattooed leader snarled.

He elbowed the leader in the gut.

The leader grabbed Gailen's hand and forced his arm behind his back. The pressure crushed his thumb.

Pain shot up his arm.

He screamed.

In the distance, Starr spasmed and went limp.

The Atlantis patrols surrounded her, tridents out.

They would protect her.

He was on his own.

The small raiding party stole Gailen's dagger and bound him with unbreakable bolas, and the leader dragged him into deep water. And yet, when they approached the tip of the All-Council army, it seemed far closer than it should be.

"General Giru." The leader saluted a pale warrior with an unusual chest plate. Dark purple tattoos tangled across his face like thorned vines. "I collected the orange-tattooed warrior."

"Did anyone follow you?" General Giru asked in a gravelly tone.

"They were distracted, but they will come."

Representative Rikoy smirked. "That cripple attends the Life Tree. See how he clutches his injured hand? He is deformed, and yet they trust him. They are asking to have their Life Tree cut down."

The general eyed the representative from the corners of his cold eyes. To the leader who had captured Gailen, he murmured, "Return to the army. Take Rikoy. Tell no one."

"Yes, General Giru." The leader swam to Representative Rikoy with as much deadly intensity as he'd shown capturing Gailen.

"Leave?" The representative recoiled. "But I am the one who knows this cripple. I was his city's representative. I can tell if he is lying."

The general flicked his fingertips in dismissal.

The leader escorted Representative Rikoy away.

The general ordered the rest of the unit to spread out. Only one harsh, heavily tattooed warrior remained—Viren, General Giru called him, and Viren made a good show of ignoring them.

Gailen twisted in the bindings. His crushed hand throbbed.

The general studied him. "You tend the Life Tree? Truly?"

"If I say no, will you let me go?"

General Giru rested the longest blade of his trident against Gailen's throat. "The warrior who tends the Life Tree knows every dissident who joins Atlantis."

He stilled. "I know them."

"Tell me about a mer. Ulio."

"Who?"

The general's blade nicked his throat. Just the skin. The pain was hot and sharp. "You know of the warrior Ulio?"

Flowing blood pumped from his veins, and he tasted it in the water. His ears roared. "I know nothing."

The general traced his blade down Gailen's chest to his abdomen. Stinging salt attacked the shallow but long cut. "You must."

"I have been at the platform."

The blade paused at his thigh.

He tensed. "If you have kept us under surveillance, you know."

"Ulio arrived before you rose to the platform."

"But I was..." He'd been rescuing Starr. "I was captured by Representative Rikoy then. I was not there."

"The truth."

"That is the truth!"

The blade hovered above his cock.

Gailen arched away. "I do not know this warrior. Have I seen him? Describe him."

The general's eyes made slits. "You would know."

"How?"

The blade rested against his male sac.

Bitterness welled in Gailen. He wanted to snap, *This, again?* He had endured torture in Aiycaya, but it was worse now, crueler because he had met Starr.

You should say what you think, Gailen.

No. He needed to return whole and help her become

strong so that they could begin their family together. If the general unmanned him here, in addition to the pain and loss, he would be too weak. He'd be attacked by predators and sharks. And that assumed the general let him go with his life.

He could not antagonize this male.

Being once more in this position, desperately trying to placate someone who was implacable, made his guts burn, but he had to endure. "No warrior by that name has joined Atlantis."

"By that name?"

"King Kadir welcomes any warrior who asks to join Atlantis. He does not require proof of their standing in their home city."

General Giru glanced behind him at Viren.

The heavily tattooed warrior nodded. A silent answer to a silent question.

General Giru returned to Gailen and lifted the blade to his jugular. "Should we go together to Atlantis? Perhaps your king will tell the truth if you truly have any value to him."

Being unmanned in front of the king would be even worse. It would agonize everyone and damage Atlantis.

"And when that warrior Ulio is *not* in Atlantis, what will you do? Accuse King Kadir of lying?"

"If I find out that any of you are lying, I will—"

"You will what?" Gailen lifted his bound hands, the impossible fury building, an unstoppable force. "Break my thumbs again, like the warrior who brought me to you? Cut them off? Beat me, unman me, leave my body for the sharks? Leave my bride with no husband when our race is so desperate for young fry?"

The general moved his lips to the side, clearly irritated

by Gailen's outburst. "You chose to rebel against the All-Council."

"And you choose to serve them even when it dooms our race."

"That is my duty."

"That is your excuse!" Bitterness flowed through him like a raging current. "You know why the kings gather here. And you choose to murder the warriors trying to save our race because 'it is your duty.' Someday, King Kadir will rule, and you will obey him. And on that day, you will look at me and shrug. You will forget your devastation and feel smug because you claim to have honor."

"I do not claim to have honor," General Giru growled. "But I will follow my duty into death. Or worse."

"That is how you are smug. You know what the All-Council has done. What you have done for them."

He lowered his chin with haunted eyes. Each word vibrated like chips of ice. "I followed orders."

"Orders that threaten brides and young fry. Exactly who the All-Council is supposed to protect."

"They... I will never feel proud of the... It was necessary to stop Kadir's vision before rebellion consumed the ocean."

"Rebellion has already consumed the ocean."

"The head of the All-Council, Sirak, explained..." He glanced back at Viren and hardened. "I obeyed orders."

"Why?"

"One dishonorable act can stop something worse."

"What is worse than hurting brides? Will you obey an order to kill Queen Nora?"

His grip on his trident tightened. "That will never happen."

"The All-Council attacked our queens. Why not yours?"

"General Giru!" One of the warriors darted to them. "Atlanteans are coming."

General Giru tore his gaze from Gailen. "How many?"

"Five warriors, two queens, one young fry."

"Move the army. I will meet you at the rendezvous point."

All but Viren swam hard.

Distant souls moved swiftly toward them.

The general pointed his trident at Gailen. "Every day I wish I was not cursed by my improper connection to a modern bride. I would cut out my own heart to serve the All-Council."

"How honorable," Gailen sneered.

"I sacrificed honor long ago, before I became a general. So do not say that I will feel smug when this battle is over. I know what the All-Council has done, and what I must do. We will destroy whatever we must to preserve our race."

"To preserve the All-Council, you mean."

"It is the same thing."

"If the All-Council acts without honor, then what are you preserving?" Gailen demanded. "When you have killed all the rebels' brides and young fry, who will be left to carry on the race?"

The general stared for a long moment with no answer.

"General Giru, they are coming," Viren reminded him.

The general turned away from Gailen, and they kicked hard.

"Who really preserves our race?" Gailen called after them.

The general did not look back.

Gailen struggled in his bonds. His heart continued to thump, and anger mixed with fear, but also a new emotion. He had released his deepest thoughts, the ones he had wanted to throw into the faces of his tormentors in Aiycaya. It felt good.

The cuts stung. His thumb throbbed.

Perhaps not.

He turned and wriggled, ankles and wrists still bound, toward the Atlanteans.

Queen Nora led the way. Queen Elyssa and King Kadir swam together, with Prince Kael just behind her.

His kidnapping had summoned his king? At this busy time?

Shame washed through Gailen. He should have fought the kidnappers harder. He should have taken more care.

The Atlanteans converged on him.

"My king, queens." Gailen tried to salute, but the bindings prevented it, and pain lanced his thumb. "General Giru retreated that way. The whole army was just moved."

"Scan the area," King Kadir ordered the other warriors, who quickly dispersed. He released his serious young fry and sliced Gailen's bonds. "You are injured."

"Not badly."

"Oh, Gailen. I'm so sorry. We were chasing him and then we lost him, and you got hurt." Queen Elyssa put his crushed hand between hers. She closed her eyes, and white light glowed from her fingers.

The pain receded, and warmth tingled up to his wrist. Queen powers were amazing.

"Was Starr okay?" he asked.

"Pretty much." Queen Nora peered where the general had fled. "She passed out, but the patrol returned her to the platform, and she's under guard. What did Giru want?"

"He asked me if a warrior had joined Atlantis. Ulio."

"Ulio?" King Kadir frowned, and his son mirrored him. "He could not have meant the head archivist, Ulio."

"But if he did, that would explain the rumors Lotar overheard." Queen Elyssa opened her eyes and patted Gailen's hand. "Someone pretty high up in the All-Council went missing. It's got them upset."

"It could not be Head Archivist Ulio. He knew of ancient Atlantis and threatened to expel me if he caught me straying to research it again. Had he been working that night I discovered the ruin's location, I would not have escaped. And I would not be here now."

"People change." Queen Elyssa took her son into her arms. "What secrets do they not want us to know?"

"Perhaps we will find out." King Kadir addressed the warriors, who returned empty-handed. "When we return to the platform, summon Lotar. I have a mission of the utmost importance."

Gailen flexed his injured hand. It was much better now that Queen Elyssa had infused it with her healing powers, but still sore and useless.

Queen Nora glanced at his thumb. Guilt crossed her face. "Did Giru do that?"

"No, another warrior."

She brightened in relief.

"He did this." Gailen indicated the shallow cuts marring his torso.

Queen Nora winced. "The one time I leave the platform, he shows up. I won't leave again."

"Maybe you should. I do not believe he will stop the All-Council from targeting you."

"Bring it on." She cracked her knuckles with a cocky grin. "When it matters, he'll choose the right side."

"When?"

"When what?"

"When will it matter?"

She blinked. "I don't know what you're saying."

"General Giru was here. He hurt me. He's hurt other warriors and will again."

"He's obeying orders."

The rage flared.

No, Queen Nora was his ally and he didn't wish to make her sad.

But...

You should say what you think, Gailen.

Unleashing his true feelings on General Giru had broken something free within him. He needed Queen Nora to hear his truth. "How can you be satisfied joining with a warrior who has hurt so many? Who may soon make us dead? Because of orders?"

Queen Nora rolled her head to the side. "Well... He hasn't killed anyone yet."

"Yet." Gailen lifted his thumbs, even the one Queen Elyssa had healed, which still jutted in the wrong direction. "After the fighting passes and Atlantis emerges triumphant, and you join with your new husband, what then? Will you wave to us injured warriors, damaged and pained, with a smile while you swim by with your chosen husband? Will you carry his young fry? Will you smile to us as you give him the happiness stolen from us by his trident?"

"I'm sorry," Queen Nora vibrated faintly. "I don't want him to do these things, and he doesn't want to either. It's complicated."

"It is not complicated for the warrior who is dead. And all your patrolling, all your talking, all your patience has not made him deviate from his path. He may know his actions are wrong, but he will do the wrong actions and hurt many more warriors. Maybe kill them. All in service to his All-Council. If you think he will change, you are naïve."

Queen Nora turned to Queen Elyssa. "Am I?"

Queen Elyssa hugged her young fry. "Gailen isn't wrong. But you also know General Giru better than anyone. So, you're probably not wrong either. And if you're both not wrong..." She shrugged. "Whatever you think is best, I'll support you."

Queen Nora stared in the direction the general had fled. Her soul shone with beauty.

General Giru was foolish. Queen Nora was his soul mate, and so she could sense his presence deep inside the same way that Gailen could sense Starr.

"I was supposed to stay by the platform as a deterrent, but maybe it's my turn to be a hunter. At the very least, if Giru has to keep running away from me, he won't be stalking and kidnapping you guys. I'll give him something else to think about."

She swam off with determination.

A small flare of hope lit in Gailen's chest.

Then, worry.

He'd been containing his anger about the general and Queen Nora for so long. The cathartic release of getting the words out energized him. But at what cost?

"Did I do the wrong thing?" Gailen asked. "Have my words sent her to face an enemy she cannot defeat?"

King Kadir returned his gaze, sober. "I trust in my warriors and my queens."

Was that really enough?

Oh. These sorts of thoughts must cross King Kadir's mind all the time, whereas, for the first time, they crossed Gailen's.

Queen Elyssa entwined with the king. "A lot has happened, I think. But you know, no matter how you feel about yourself, your love for your soul mate is purer and more honest. And no matter how much General Giru fights it, no warrior would ever sacrifice his bride."

Even though she was a human who could not see souls, she understood.

"I defied your orders to go to the surface," Gailen recalled.

"Oh, Gailen, that was another misunderstanding. I would never ask you to go against your soul mate. But I do look forward to meeting her in person."

As a unit, they swam to the mid-ocean platform and were accosted when it was just in sight.

"My king." The patrol greeted them with excitement. "Queen Lucy has escorted the first group of princes and kings. They're now ascending to look at the platform."

King Kadir's soul brightened. "It begins."

Queen Elyssa nestled against his side. "We'd better go meet them. Gailen, let Starr know we'll be back shortly."

They veered off with their unit. He swam with the remaining patrol to the platform. Eventually, Queen Elyssa's light dwindled and disappeared.

Nerves squeezed his belly.

How many surface days had passed? Starr must see Queen Elyssa very soon for healing.

He only hoped this incident hadn't destroyed her wish to shift and live with him beneath the sea.

FIFTEEN

Three days had passed since Gailen had been taken.

Starr sat in the cold, damp glass fishbowl and hugged her knees.

Now, he was coming back.

For the first time since he'd been taken, the muscles in her spine relaxed. She slumped over. Her body ached.

The panic in the water had been horrible, and then she'd passed out and awakened on the platform in the dark, with Xemil and Isag standing guard.

An uneasy Bob had been kept back by their sharp tridents, but he'd had no sympathy. "You're awake? Savages attacking savages."

She'd dragged herself back to her room, lain on her bunk, and shut down.

The earth had rotated and the sky had lightened. She'd eaten the rest of her snack bars, drunk her bottled water, and closed her eyes.

Bob had called updates through the door that she'd been expecting but which he'd shared with a tone of disbelief.

"Ryerson was arrested. They say he's the leader of that terrorist group, the Sons of Hercules. The company's gone through a purge and sent a few of the new employees home. I've got their photos if you want to see."

The pilot that operated her body had replied, "No."

"You sure? It's a crazy world out there. He called himself the king of the oceans, and all along, he was plotting against us. You never can tell with people."

Yes, it was funny. People could be heroes in public and villains behind closed doors.

The mer-human foundation had accepted bids and chosen Ryerson Deep Water Construction to build this platform, and then Merrit Ryerson had squeezed in and made himself a key figurehead. He clearly liked power. And he had sounded so plausible on the top of the pyramid, but he'd used the same phrasing as the man who'd kidnapped her nephew from a hospital. Dannika had identified him, and it looked as if law enforcement had as well. So he was both, somehow. A champion who honestly thought the ocean platform was the future and a villain who would do anything to stop mermen from rising and claiming their mates.

But there was one man who didn't have two faces.

And if she'd been stronger, she would have been able to stop him from getting kidnapped.

Her therapist had walked her through how to handle the depersonalization. She was supposed to internally address her shield and say, "Thank you, but you don't need to protect me right now."

But she couldn't thank this mechanism. It worked great when she was all alone and she needed not to cry. But it worked terribly when she was in a life-or-death situation like when the warriors had stolen Gailen.

When she needed to act and the film wrapped her up in invisible cables, how could she say thank you? She'd tried on her bunk, silently mouthing the words, but the straitjacket had just tightened more.

After another day of lost time, Starr had regained control and begun the steps to dismantle the film. Unite her halves. Repersonalize herself.

It would be easier if she had something to focus on. Something like Gailen's Sea Opal. She still had to ask him about it, but at least she knew the truth inside her heart.

Gailen was out there.

And she was suddenly certain that he was returning to her.

She'd forced herself to get up, shower, and eat. Then she'd returned phone calls, including Dannika's, which confirmed what was already public knowledge—that Ryerson had been formally charged, gone in front of a judge, and been fitted with an ankle bracelet. He was on home arrest in one of his many mansions awaiting trial.

"And all his traffic will be monitored," Dannika had told Starr with glee. "These are only the first charges. They can add more as they investigate. I hope he incriminates himself even more."

"What's the response from the local chapters?"

"Well, mixed." Dannika's good cheer had deflated. "I've just gotten the report from Mel. Some can't believe he's the leader, others think he's a decoy, and yet others are worshipping him as a hero. How someone could worship two domestic harassment charges and three restraining orders, I don't know."

Even though Ryerson had been caught, the foundation was playing it safe. Mel would remain in the Florida office, always available for any emergency. Dannika was preparing to sail from Sanctuary Island in the Caribbean to the platform by yacht, staying above the water so she would be available at any time.

"Others are doing the same," Dannika had said. "Aya, for example, is leading the brides gathered in Europe on the boat—"

"Don't tell me," Starr had said. "This phone should be secure, but I still haven't dismantled the stingray."

"Oh, yes. Right. Don't worry, I've been vague on my communications with the city." Dannika had sighed. "It's demoralizing that the Sons of Hercules were so deeply entrenched. Right on the platform! But we've almost put this behind us, and soon, we'll enjoy a new age of peace."

Yeah. Sure. That sounded nice. "Dannika?"

"Hmm?"

"What happens if this isn't the end? What if the Sons of Hercules aren't done?"

"You just have to neutralize the stingray, right?"

"I don't know."

Dannika had been silent for a long moment. "We've talked about it amongst the queens. What if the All-Council figures out how to sever the cables or jams the turbines centering the platform over Atlantis, or, heaven forbid, sinks the platform altogether."

Exactly.

"There comes a point when you must choose what you want and ignore any obstacle. *Any* obstacle. These brides have been waiting for years, and we already delayed once. They might be at the point of no return, or they might give up."

That would be awful.

"It depends on how badly they want it," Dannika had

continued, subdued. "And everyone must answer that question for themselves."

Starr had ended the call and sought Bob, but he was busy, so she'd left a message. She'd passed Ryerson's assistant sitting in an isolated corner of a crew snack room, typing quietly into his laptop. He'd looked up and watched her walk by. Xemil and Isag had followed her, protective shadows.

Gailen was coming back, and she'd wanted to meet him, but going in the water... No she couldn't go through that again.

Starr had entered the glass pyramid, glancing around in case a breadbox-sized stingray device just stood out, and descended into the fishbowl. Xemil and Isag had guarded the entrance, watching the construction workers who took their dinner until the mealtime ended and all had turned quiet.

The evening shadows lengthened overhead, but the sky, as much as she could see from the distant entrance, was a clear gray melting into a red sunset with no storm clouds.

She watched and watched.

Darkness fell. Small emergency lights glowed on the ramps, but she was somehow able to see into the shadows.

And then...

In the dark water...

Fish scattered.

He was coming.

She crawled forward on her hands and knees and rested her fingers against the glass. It was too thick, like aquarium glass, to fog. A shadow emerged from the blue, then a shape, and then it solidified into Gailen.

He floated on the other side of the glass. His hair waved, and the reflection of the restaurant's light made an iridescent shimmer across his pepper-orange tattoos. His body, fully nude, was whole.

He was okay.

He'd survived just fine.

Relief gushed through her.

But as soon as she felt anything, the film squeezed her so tight, she couldn't breathe. So many emotions thrashed to get out.

Gailen kicked his long, beautiful fins. In a few short strokes, he circled the curved glass and disappeared.

Get up. Go to him.

Her body was stuck, just like before. Her pilot held her in a holding pattern. The emotions were too strong.

Please.

Her legs stayed glued to the glass, but she looked up at the doorway.

Gailen appeared in the doorway, dripping and nude. He returned Isag and Xemil's relieved greetings and left them behind, pattering down the stairs and crossing to her with sure strides. He pulled her to her feet and enfolded her in his arms. "Starr, it is okay. I survived."

Her chest hitched.

The film tightened.

"It is okay," he repeated.

But it wasn't okay. She splayed her fingers across a fresh line of scabs. He'd been injured. "I'm so upset."

"I know. I failed to consider the dangers."

"You didn't fail. It was my own body again." She was so frustrated by it. This shield had protected her once, but no matter how she tried to let it go, she couldn't. "This was life and death. I could have saved you if I'd channeled the powers the other queens have, but instead, I collapsed. Why did I jump in?"

"You did not think."

"Right, but I always think. If I hadn't jumped in, the warriors patrolling here would have stopped your kidnapping." She sounded so flat to her own ears.

Gailen squeezed her tighter, hearing the crushing regret and soul-shattering sadness in her cold, emotionless tone. "I was kidnapped by experienced warriors who had planned for resistance. Yes, you could have saved me if you had used queen powers, but the Atlantis warriors were already too far away to help me."

"I don't think I can ever be a queen."

"With time and practice, you will be." His voice brooked no argument. He believed that from the bottom of his soul. "You must release this film, Starr."

She wanted to but she couldn't.

She just couldn't.

He cupped her cheeks and lifted her chin. The iridescent orange threads gleamed in his warm brown irises. "We will tear it away together."

His mouth descended.

At the last moment, she forced herself to tilt her chin up, to meet him.

Their lips touched and meshed. *Yes.* Exultation burned in her. She'd done it. He always heard her through her distance and helped her to connect to her core.

Gailen's arms went around her, crushing her to his bare chest. His full, hard cock pressed against her thigh. Everything they'd done in her room returned in an instant, and she throbbed for him.

He heard all the words she wanted to say.

But she couldn't vibrate with her chest when she was on the surface. She pulled back her mouth just enough to form the word against his lips. "How?"

"Come with me to Atlantis." He dropped hot kisses on her mouth and then up her jaw to her ear and tugged on the lobe. Sweet desire drizzled through her. "Marry me in front of the Life Tree. Imprint your essence upon my castle and join our bodies. Entwine your soul, your future, your destiny with mine. "

This was the life she wanted to embrace. A life that she'd thought was beyond her.

But she had to pass out to shift.

The film descended to suffocate her.

She gasped and jerked back. "I think it would really help if... Gailen, where's your Sea Opal?"

He frowned and then nuzzled her. "I gave it to you."

"I put it in my pocket on the boat and woke up naked underwater."

"I removed your coverings to expose your gills." He compressed his lips with chagrin. "I am sorry, Starr. I feared you would die and did not think about anything else."

It hurt.

She felt angry and disappointed.

The stone had been so beautiful. A little piece of him, and she'd lost it without any chance of getting it back, just cast it into the deep. If she'd known what little time she'd get to enjoy it, she would have treasured it more. Guarded it more preciously.

But they'd been so focused on her allergies that they'd lost the Sea Opal. It had simply slipped away in the panic.

What was Starr losing right now? What other precious things were slipping away without her even realizing it?

She pulled back and pressed his broad palm to her chest. "We have unfinished work here."

He winced and repositioned her grasp.

Another bruise. Another injury.

He traded hands and linked their fingers, his thumb jutting away. "Then we will complete it. And when you are ready, we will descend together."

She would overcome this. She would conquer the shield and claim her power. Then she would channel her powers and protect him.

They walked up the ramp to the main level.

Isag stood at ease near the door. In the strange not-darkness of her mer-enhanced night vision, the oval walls were shadowed, with light gleaming from the regularly spaced emergency posts. The former oil rig was well lit for twenty-four-seven operations, including the docks.

The modified pontoon plane bobbed against the dock.

"When did the pontoon plane come back?" she asked Isag.

"Not long ago," he vibrated. "Before full night."

And it was full night now, assuming that meant it had arrived before dark. A company executive must have come.

"That's funny," she said.

Gailen turned. "What is?"

She told him about Ryerson being arrested and charged. Even though the pontoon plane was used to fly high-level management, Ryerson couldn't be here. They had him on home arrest, and if he tried to leave, he'd go straight back to jail.

"Human justice." Gailen flexed his fingers. "I hope it is swift and decisive."

She did too.

Starr got out her cell phone and scanned for the stingray while Isag brought Gailen a pair of shorts, and then Gailen released him. He, like Xemil, had gone a couple of days without food or rest watching over her, and she hadn't noticed because she'd been inside her isolation bubble.

"That means you've gone without food or rest too," she said.

"It is different underwater. My body as a mer is not subject to the same rhythms." He flashed her a smile.

Gailen's confidence was so encouraging.

And addictive.

Walking around the interior of the pyramid trying to trace the signal on her scanning app was exactly what she needed. The normalcy put her back onto an even emotional plane.

Her phone led her around the cafeteria counter and into the clean, tidy, dark kitchen. There was an emergency button striped with yellow and blue on the outer wall between the cafeteria and the food-prep area. Gailen opened cabinets and peered at the bulk boxes of ingredients.

"Careful," Starr said. "I know it's only been used a few times in practice for the grand opening, but we could still disturb an allergen."

He closed the cabinet carefully.

Her phone led her beneath the counter wall. It looked solid but thin, and she poked the flat wood framed by decorative moldings.

The wood panel moved.

Gailen knelt, pushed until a corner popped out, and then wedged in his fingers. "This is when I regret losing my dagger to the All-Council. Ah, there it comes."

The thin panel popped out. Styrofoam packing peanuts cascaded around her booted feet. She jumped back.

Ha-ha, what a joke. Packing peanuts? That almost felt like a message.

He looked up at her. "Are you okay?"

"Yeah." She waved the white dust away from her face. "It's just Styrofoam."

"No." He held up a small brown lump. "Peanuts are mixed in."

She dropped her phone as she stumbled back, raced around the counter, and jogged halfway across the cafeteria, gulping for air like a fish out of water. Her lips tingled.

The film came down.

Her panicked heartbeat slowed, and her breathing evened out.

No reaction?

Huh. She must not have gotten a whiff...

No. She could still smell the cloying mess of stale nuts.

Gailen stayed back a safe distance. "You are okay?"

"Yeah. But I feel no reaction. I just feel..." She touched her throat and her nose, still filled with the stale smell. "Nothing."

Warmth filled his face. "You are cured."

"I don't know if I'd go that far." Sometimes an allergen didn't cause a reaction at first, and then later it did. But she hadn't had a lesser reaction to peanuts before...

And she *had* swallowed the magical elixir and activated it...

"I'm going to stay here just to be safe." She sat at a table in the middle of the cafeteria. "Can you see the stingray?"

He disappeared behind the counter. "There is something."

"What?"

He emerged a moment later with her dropped phone. He'd learned to take pictures the other day when she'd taught him how to use the scanner app.

She peered at the photos. Inside the panel, among the remnants of both types of peanuts, was a small device that matched the general shape and buttons of a stingray. Like the jammer, this particular model had no batteries and was designed to be wired into a power source. So, if someone shut off the power to the kitchen, say, when it wasn't being used, that would shut off the stingray and cause everyone's phones to lose signal until they connected to the real satellite. The same when they turned the power on again—it would force everyone's phones to reject the satellite and connect to the closer stingray again.

But attached to it was some other device. One with several long blocks of putty wrapped in black tape. Cylinders poked out, and exposed wires led to a pager.

That looked like...

Oh, no.

God, no.

All the strength left her body.

"You're going away from me again," Gailen said.

She pushed against the film wrapping around her hot, thudding heart. Yes, it was good to stay calm, but she couldn't go comatose now of all times.

"What is it?" he asked.

She forced out the words. "My experience in this mostly comes from movies and TV. But it honest to God looks like a bomb."

"Actually, it's the control center for a series of bombs planted all over the platform." Ryerson, jailed leader of the Sons of Hercules, breezed into the cafeteria as if he'd never left. "And you, Starr Langley, are going to dismantle it for me."

SIXTEEN

"You're supposed to be in jail," Starr gasped, her soul darkening behind the thick substance.

Ryerson laughed. "Rich people don't go to jail, Starr Langley."

Gailen moved in front of Starr. His empty hands clenched for his stowed trident, his stolen dagger. "You dare return here? You are the leader of the Sons of Hercules."

Ryerson did not break stride. He wore dark coverings and carried a large bag. "That has yet to be proven in a court of law."

"You attacked my fellow warriors. Atlantis. You tried to hurt Queen Bella's young fry."

"I cured him."

Behind Gailen, Starr stood.

"Sit down." Ryerson kept the table between himself and Gailen and stopped outside of easy reach. "If you want to save the rest of them, we haven't much time."

The impulse to attack—to avenge the injured and exact mer justice—made Gailen's muscles twitch.

Starr curled her hand around his forearm, stopping him. "What are you talking about?"

"These bombs are all over the platform." Ryerson opened his black bag, unrolled a large map, and jabbed at the markings. "This is the brain. Take it out, and the rest will deactivate. You can have your grand party, and no one will be any the wiser."

Starr stared at the map. "So many. You'll destroy the whole platform."

"After the company provides me with qualified immunity, I'll bring in my team to remove them."

Gailen growled. "You will remove them now."

Starr tightened her grip on Gailen's forearm. "Why?"

"What do you mean, why?" Ryerson asked.

Gailen knew about bombs. The Sons of Hercules had first appeared when they bombed the Sea Festival of the Azores several years ago, targeting the warriors of Dragao Azul. "Why are you doing this? Why do you hate mermen?"

Ryerson rolled his eyes. "I couldn't care less about mermen. I promise you."

Starr took a long, deep breath. She seemed to be taking strength from Gailen's presence, and that was the only reason he didn't leap across the table and destroy this dishonorable man. "This one controls the others? Okay. How do I turn it off?"

Ryerson pulled a smaller leaf out of his bag. "Here. This is a diagram of the control box."

Starr stared at it. "No. There's no pager."

"Oh. It's this one." He put a different leaf on the table.

She blinked rapidly, then smoothed the curled edges. "You didn't plant these."

He hadn't?

Ryerson opened his hand and waved it in a gesture for her to hurry. "That much should be obvious."

"But you *are* the leader of the Sons of Hercules," she pressed. Her soul was still wrapped tight, but the masking substance seemed thinner, as if she was regaining control. "You kidnapped my nephew and blackmailed my sister."

"Eh, I was going through a phase." He gazed up at the pyramid and around the glass. "This city is my legacy."

Starr's tone flattened, but her soul burned brighter. "Kidnapping my nephew was a phase?"

"A very lucrative phase. If you thought companies would pay anything for Sea Opals, you should see what you can get away with in government contracts."

"You worked with the government to kidnap my nephew?"

"The research physician thought he was a fine test subject." Ryerson tapped the diagram. "We have until the end of the fifth meal. Disarm it."

She studied the papers, then centered her phone camera over the diagrams.

"Ah, no." Ryerson waved his hand. "No photos."

"I have to send this to someone who has experience disarming bombs."

"No, they're monitoring all communications."

"They?" Gailen repeated. Frustration from facing down his race's greatest enemy and not being able to do something about it made his throat tight. "Who are they?"

"I'll be happy to tell you once we've come to a legal agreement over my cooperation. But don't send photos. They'll see that you sent it and blow us up."

She lowered her phone and looked up at Gailen. Again he got the sense she was anchoring herself to his presence.

Then she faced Ryerson. "I don't understand what you expect me to do."

"You're a hacker. Hack in."

"To what? This isn't a computer."

"It has one attached. Use your brain, Starr Langley, and hack the computer."

"The pager? I can't even root the pager without downloading a utility."

"How do you know?" He gestured at the distant wall by the bomb and stingray. "You're not even looking at it."

"I'm as close as I can get."

"Nonsense."

Gailen stopped him. "The bomb was hidden with peanuts."

"That's proof!" Ryerson brightened. "He put those there because he knew you could dismantle it. Just like when he spread the peanuts around your ridiculous charter boat."

Anger burned hotter in Gailen. "You know the male who tried to murder Starr?"

Ryerson's certainty wavered. He stepped back with his hands up. "I told him not to hurt her. He wanted to delay her until after the grand opening, and we were always tracking the boat to pick her up later. She was never supposed to be in any real danger."

"Leaving someone adrift is very dangerous," Gailen snarled. "Surface currents and weather patterns are deadly."

"I could have died," Starr agreed flatly.

"And when he had to make it personal with the peanuts, I lost plausible deniability." Ryerson nodded as if they agreed. "I'm the angry one. But don't you see? He created a bomb you could disarm. This is a sign."

That sounded odd. When a warrior left out a trap, he lined it with many types of blades, nets, and poisons to incapacitate any target.

Starr must have agreed. She bit her lip. "If we can activate the jammer, that will interfere with any signals the pager sends."

"The pager is a backup. It's wired into another cable. And anyway, the jammer has been packed to send to the mainland as evidence against me. *Me.*" Ryerson arched his brows. "I'll have you all for slander."

"Okay, then, is this the kind of bomb that will deactivate if we unplug it? Is it on a closed loop and if we remove anything, it will go off? Or—"

"Can't you tell from the diagram?"

"No." She folded her hands over her phone. "I know as much about explosive devices as I do about medicine and law, i.e., I have no domain knowledge."

"What kind of a security expert are you?" He got out his phone. "Look, it can't be that hard. Dismantle...a...bomb..."

She stared. "Are you honestly googling how to disarm a bomb?"

"This is my legacy, and I refuse to let terrorists sink my city."

Starr's gaze dropped again to the schematics. Her soul light fluctuated.

This man was supposed to be defeated. He affected Starr deeply and Gailen didn't know how to protect her except to challenge him.

"You are the leader of the terrorists," Gailen growled.

"Oh, please."

"You embrace fear and hate."

"You want to know how it happened?" He chuckled as if he'd been wanting to share for some time. "I posted a meme. Some college kids picked it up, and the next thing I know, I'm getting contacted by crazies across America willing to give me a platform." He lowered his phone and laughed incredulously. "And the more outrageous my claims, the more money rolled in. Department of Defense, international security forces, mercenaries across the planet. All wanting to know how to deal with this oceanic threat."

"You posted a meme..." Starr murmured.

"And built an empire! Then your foundation selected my company. Even better, I'm right at the source to sell exactly what sells best: fear."

Gailen's rage flared. "You shot our warriors. Blew them up. Now this platform."

"No, I told you. I would never blow up my great city. The grand opening is going to be a success. My security contracts will only increase as I build islands. And real estate moguls will invest, invest, invest." He sighed over his happy future, then frowned and refocused on his cell phone.

Starr slowly stood. "So you take no responsibility for what happened to the warriors? What happened to my sister and nephew? What happened to me?"

"That was...mm." He shook his finger at her and tapped his closed lips. "Immunity. But rest assured, none of it was my idea. I would never hurt anyone."

"With your own hands."

He laughed. "How many degrees of separation do you require? Every American who wears name brands, eats chocolate, or buys an engagement ring is responsible for child slavery, drought, and mass murder. Do you care about that? No, you enjoy the highlife perfectly free of guilt over all the corpses that are feeding your need. It's already the same with Sea Opals. No one cares what happens to the mer."

"People care."

"You think about children on cocoa plantations when you bite into a chocolate chip cookie?"

"I'm allergic to flour, and chocolate gives me a migraine."

He narrowed his eyes. "We're more alike than you think, Starr Langley. My team has been hunting you for at least as long as you've been hunting me. We're both used to being alone and even prefer it. Much better company is to be had in an empty room than when surrounded by the idiotic masses. The difference is that I embrace my singular genius, whereas you still feel like you owe something to the world."

Starr frowned, and her soul light dimmed.

Gailen wove his fingers through hers.

You are nothing like him, he silently promised her. *And no matter what happens next, you will never be alone again.*

———

GAILEN WAS one insult away from attacking Ryerson. And Ryerson, in his "singular genius," seemed to have not yet figured it out.

She squeezed Gailen's fingers, trying once more to keep him close to her when she felt like her internal organs were going to fly off in all directions.

"We're more alike than you think," Ryerson repeated, scrolling through search results on his phone.

Actually, she did think they were alike.

He'd started a terrorist organization with a meme. He made money off both sides. And the only reason he acted now to stop the destruction was that it threatened his bottom line.

He was so separated from human emotions that he might as well be wrapped in plastic.

"How...to...disarm...a...pager...bomb..." He shifted his weight from one foot to the other, then slammed his phone on the table. "Here. You're the security expert. You look it up."

She didn't take the phone.

"Go on," Ryerson ordered. "It's almost the end of the fifth meal. He's going to know he was compromised. The destruction will be your fault."

This was such a beautiful city, even clanking and unfinished and imperfect.

If it blew up, what would happen to the brides? Would they give up?

She was supposed to save this place. Dannika, Hazel, even Bella thought she could do anything. She had a small reputation for being a hero, and she wanted to keep it.

But a bomb wasn't a computer. If she hit the wrong button, they all might die.

And his unnamed accomplices might blow them up first.

"Why aren't you taking the phone?" Ryerson demanded.

"Why are you so certain yours isn't compromised?" she asked.

"They know not to scan mine. I'm their leader."

"Your subordinates didn't listen when you said not to kill me."

"I'm off-limits. Just google what you need to take care of it. ... Starr Langley, do you want to die? Rephrase." Ryerson rested his palms on the table and stared into her eyes. "Do you want all the others on this platform, the innocent workers sleeping in their bunks or playing foosball or video chatting with their wife and kids, to die?"

That was the difference between them. "No."

He smiled broadly and straightened. "All right."

She pocketed her cell phone and stood. Squeezing Gailen, she tugged him with her to the wall between the cafeteria and the food prep area and pressed the emergency button.

The pyramid lit up, blue and yellow lights reflecting through every pane of glass.

Ryerson shrieked. "What are you doing?"

Bob's voice crackled over the intercom. "Control."

"There are bombs planted all over the platform. They could blow at any moment. I'm not sure where it's safe to evacuate." Starr rattled off the bomb locations she remembered. "Two on the old rig. They're in rooms marked A11 and N225 on the map."

"N225 is my office, and I'm sitting in it right now. I don't see anything out of place in here unless you count the new...hold on. Is that..."

The intercom shut off. Emergency lights flooded the walkways, lighting the whole oval and shining beacons into the stormy darkness.

Isag raced across the outer pavilion.

"Tell the warriors patrolling the platform," she murmured to Gailen, crossing the cafeteria past the still-frozen Ryerson. Starr sent photos of the bomb and the schematics to an internet friend as she walked. "They might be able to help us evacuate, but then they have to get as far away as they can. I don't know how big the explosion will be."

He released her and jogged to Isag at the entrance. They exchanged tense messages, and Isag raced away.

Gailen returned to her side. "There is a problem."

"What now?"

Bob's voice echoed across the platform from the external speakers. "Evacuate. All platform personnel must immediately evacuate."

"The All-Council army has the platform surrounded." Gailen blocked her from heading after Isag into the water. "Queen Elyssa and King Kadir are trapped below. They cannot help anyone with the evacuation. We cannot dive to escape the bombs."

SEVENTEEN

The All-Council army has the platform surrounded.

Starr struggled to take a calming breath. Panic was rising. All she wanted to do was retreat.

But there were bombs on the platform, an enemy army beneath it, and nowhere to go.

Gailen waited for her to tell him what to do.

"Maybe we can disarm it," she said faintly.

They returned to the kitchen, and he walked around the counter with her. She braved the peanut dust—at this point, it honestly felt like the least of her worries.

How crazy was that?

The stingray was wired to the bomb. She took a few more pictures for her online friend, BomberDude22.

Looks like a satchel charge mashed to a pager trigger, BomberDude22 texted back.

Is there an easy way to shut off power? Or...?

The answer returned with a swift ping. *Not unless you know there's no deadman switch.*

How do I disarm this?

BomberDude22 sent a laughing emoji. *Evacuate a city block and call in the robots.*

Well, she'd already done step one.

Or catch the bomber and make him do it.

"You've ruined everything," Ryerson moaned in the middle of the cafeteria. "It's over now."

She straightened. "There's still a chance to stop this."

"My reputation... How can I deny my involvement? Why must everyone disappoint me?"

"You have to convince the bomb maker to disarm it."

Ryerson's face blanked, and then he laughed dryly. "And how to do you propose I do that? How do you propose I convince a tin-hat red-pilled crazy man who has wired up my entire future not to press the button?"

Gailen stood beside her. "The same way you convinced so many humans that the mer meant you harm."

"Convincing someone to fear their own shadow is ridiculously easy. Convincing them otherwise?" Ryerson sobered. "Here's a tip. If you see them before they see you, run."

It sounded like running was their only option.

Starr held Gailen's hand as they started across the cafeteria again.

Outside, platform workers in orange exposure suits hurried toward the dock ships.

A group in military fatigues too calmly crossed the outside pavilion and converged on the pyramid.

Bad news. The platform didn't have an organized security force. Especially not in camo.

Starr pivoted and raced with Gailen up the ramp to the shadowed upper balcony. How crazy that only a few days ago, Ryerson had been up here eating breakfast like it was just another day, when the whole time, he knew the platform was wired to blow. They could maybe get to the outside balcony and slide down the glass to safety. She pushed the outside door.

It was locked.

Oh, no.

She rattled the door. Where was the lock?

Gailen worked on the door. She crept around the dim cafeteria, seeking another exit.

From the floor beneath them, voices rose as Ryerson greeted the military men with friendly chiding. "Gentlemen, gentlemen. What is this? I leave for a few days, and the whole place falls apart."

"You betrayed us," a quiet voice replied.

Starr peered over the edge to see just how much danger they were in.

The voice belonged to Ryerson's assistant, the nondescript man who wore square reflective glasses and business suits.

He looked completely different in fatigues. The clothing emphasized his compact frame, and the patches and pins on his breast suggested he knew how to use the stuff attached to the tactical belt around his trim waist.

"Frank Williams, please." Ryerson's tone turned wounded. "You're the one who betrayed me. How could you stab me in the back?"

This was not going to go well.

And there were no other exits.

Gailen pushed on the glass door, but it was stuck tight.

They were trapped.

———

GAILEN TRACED the door edges while the Sons of Hercules argued below.

The glass was thick, but breaking it would make a lot of noise and create jagged edges that could injure Starr.

"This is crazy." Ryerson's dryly incredulous voice echoed Gailen's feelings but did not sound convincing. "Look at what you're doing here. Blowing up expensive real estate in the middle of the sea? Is this the kind of statement you want to make?"

"You know it's not," the male, Frank, replied softly. "We agreed to wait until everyone gathered at the grand opening. The jammer would have taken out communications. They would have been helpless to call for rescue when the timed charges went off."

"Timed?" Ryerson's voice flattened. "I thought you had it wired?"

"I changed it. We would have gotten them all at once: the mermen, their human sympathizers, and the female breeders hidden in plain sight. We all agreed."

"We didn't agree to anything. Look, this is a big misunderstanding. Take down the bombs and I'll get you a nice, quiet room at the VA."

"Something you don't understand, sir, is that you may leave the military, but the military never leaves you. When the president learns what we've done, we'll receive medals. We can't stand by while mermen flood our cities."

"No one is flooding anything."

"The coast guard can't patrol the whole coastline. We have to stop the monsters now before they convert all our women to breeders and unleash a tsunami on our cities to drown the men."

Starr glanced back at him with a grimace.

Gailen shook his head. A merman couldn't control

tides, unleash tsunamis, or even physically react to a woman who was not his soul mate. In fact, a tsunami was just as dangerous to mermen because it could smash them into submerged objects and terrain.

"The mermen want *Waterworld*, Ryerson. They want us huddled and broken on these floating cities they tricked you into building so that when they hunt the fish out of the oceans, they can spear us on land. We're land fish to them. We have to stop it now before the cannibalism begins."

"It pains me to hear these words come out of your mouth," Ryerson replied. "When you were with me the moment I made them up."

"You had an insight. An epiphany. The fish are disappearing out of the oceans and the tides are rising. You saw the truth. We're the next fish."

"I was pandering!" Ryerson barked a laugh. "Do you think I can get money from conspiracy theorists using ordinary reasoning? It's all made up."

"But it makes sense."

"No, it doesn't."

Frank's tone turned resigned. "You've led so many others to the light, and yet now you back away from the truth."

"Because it's not true!"

"And that's a shame." Frank's voice lowered as he moved away. "Arm the satchel."

"No, no, no. Wait. We can work this out."

"That's something a human sympathizer would say. You know there's no negotiating with fish-men. We need air to breathe. They don't."

"But that... Be reasonable. Please. Don't arm the..." Ryerson changed from desperate pleading to abject fury. "You're a fool. The absolute worst assistant anyone ever had. I regret every moment I worked with you. Just being in your presence makes me stupid. You're fired. Do you hear me? You'll never work in this industry again."

Gailen renewed his attention on the door. There was a hinged side and an open side. A small gap appeared at the bottom and at the top... Ah. A long rod anchored the door to the metal frame. He pulled it up.

The wind tore the door open, and it banged against the outside glass.

"What was that?" someone asked.

Starr raced with him out the door. He helped her clamber over the railing and lowered her down the sharp incline. The wind pushed her, and she slid and landed hard.

Gailen slipped down the glass and landed beside Starr, then helped her up.

A boat motored to the pavilion and sidled close, its turn causing a wave to break over the narrow walkway between the glass and the choppy water.

Bob leaned out a hand. "Get on!"

Starr's soul darkened, and she contracted.

Sharp cracks sounded behind and above them. A man leaned over the balcony. An object made of human metal glinted in his hand.

Gailen hauled Starr into his arms and leaped for Bob. The site manager fumbled them with surprise, and they all toppled onto the slick deck.

Pings ricocheted off the railing.

Bob shouted at the man inside steering. "They're shooting at us! Go, go, go!"

The engine snarled, and the boat veered away, spreading more wake over the platform and knocking the running Sons of Hercules off their feet.

Bob's boat raced for the oval, which was now open to

the ocean. Just as the stormy sky erupted with rain, they passed into the massive swells of the Atlantic.

They motored far from the platform. Inside the boat's shelter, Starr shared her photos of the bomb.

Bob's jaw clenched. "And we worked on top of this for months? Savages."

They came alongside several other boats at a safe distance. Bob confirmed head counts over the radio. "Stay alert, everyone, because if I understand what Gailen told me just now, our mermen are going to be too busy to help if anyone falls overboard."

Gailen peered down at the opaque swells hiding and then revealing the distant platform.

"Hmph. Now, we wait." Bob set his feet, crossed his arms, and stared out at the platform.

Starr pushed back onto the stormy deck and wedged herself between the secured equipment and the shelter walls. She declined Bob's offer of an exposure suit and life jacket. Despite her shivers, she promised Gailen she wasn't cold.

"Not outside cold." Her teeth chattered. "I'm trying not to be overwhelmed. Yeah, I was scared, but more than that, I still feel like I should have been able to stop this."

Gailen looped his arms around Starr and hugged her close, her back to his front, and rested against a solid barrier.

Her shivers stopped. "Hey, how did you get the door open?"

"A rod secured the top."

She snorted. "Wow."

"Hm?"

"If I can't even open an unfamiliar door, it's just as well I didn't try to defuse the bomb. And yet..." She stared into the night with him. Time, for the surface, crawled. "Do you think Ryerson talked them out of blowing it up?"

A bright light flattened the black clouds, and then several smaller flashes blinded them. The assembled humans gasped and pointed.

"No," Gailen said.

The explosion roared across the water like a multi-headed monster, and the boats rocked in violent swells despite the great distance. He braced them against the ship's walls.

Starr sighed, her soul darker than ever. "I should have done more."

Gailen nuzzled her. "You saved all these humans."

"What about the mer? Explosions are usually worse underwater."

"I think the queens can shelter them from this." The booms continued, and smoke billowed up into the sky. "The explosion is strong, but they are stronger."

"And now there's no place to meet the brides. What will happen to the kings and princes? Will they still make a new covenant without the All-Council?"

That was a true problem. "Without the brides, they will not see value in a new covenant. We will have to try again when another platform is built."

"Another five years, then."

His long scar itched. Could they endure this war another five years? It was tearing the mer apart.

Starr's cell phone rang.

"Dannika." Starr heaved a great sigh and answered. "Hey. We're okay. As far as we know, nobody except maybe the Sons of Hercules died. But I failed. I didn't stop them. The whole platform is gone. It's a burning wreck on the water."

"I know. I heard." Dannika's voice sounded tinny from Gailen's angle with the phone pressed to Starr's ear. "I also heard you evacuated everyone safely and didn't get shot, so that's a win."

"Yeah. But Dannika, there's nothing left. I couldn't save it. There's not even a dock, a place to anchor. Gailen thinks the kings are going to leave."

Her voice broke.

It echoed the pain in his own heart.

Now the brides would stay away, knowing the mer could not protect them. The dignitaries would disperse. The All-Council would win.

"Don't let them leave," Dannika ordered.

"How can we convince them to stay?" Starr sniffled and rubbed her damp face.

"You must find a way."

"But everything's ruined."

"Everything is ruined, and yet, we're undeterred. Tell the kings to hold fast to hope. This is not our darkest hour." Dannika's tone deepened with regal promise. "The brides are coming anyway."

EIGHTEEN

Starr's heart stopped.

Behind her, Gailen tensed as if the same thing had happened to him.

She'd misheard. "What?"

"I discussed it with the other queens. Their brides are unanimous. At the appointed time, weather allowing, we will embark from our corners of the world and converge on whatever's left of the platform."

Her ears started ringing.

This was unbelievable.

"The loss is a setback," Dannika said. "But at the end of the day, it is an obstacle, and we are resolute. The Sons of Hercules will not stop us from reuniting with our husbands, sons, or grandsons. No, we are coming."

Gailen slid her around in his arms until they were facing each other. She'd expected his shock would be as great as her own, but she hadn't expected his chin to wrinkle or redness to rim his eyes. He swallowed hard and let out his breath in a ragged gust. "We have to tell the kings."

"You do." Dannika must have heard him. "The mer invited us. Now, they must prepare for our arrival."

Starr checked a few more logistical details with Dannika and then finished the call. The waves were still violent and orange-tinted from the distant raging fires. "How do we get to them?"

"Dive."

"Even if we're surrounded by enemies?"

He stripped. "We must risk it."

Her stomach rolled.

If he was wrong...if she had to watch him get ripped away from her again while she did nothing...

"They will not attack you." He drew her into his arms again. "You are a queen."

"With no powers."

"They do not know that. Your bright soul will hold them back."

"Except my disorder makes it look dim."

"Do not let your disorder win."

Her guts twisted.

He linked their hands with a silent squeeze. He knew exactly how hard this was for her. And he was willing to do whatever she needed to help her take the next step.

But it had to be done. She hadn't saved the platform. She had to try to save the new covenant of kings.

She went inside and handed her cell phone and their clothes to Bob, then staggered across the stormy bow to where Gailen stood at an opening in the railing. The platform still burned. The wind lashed her with rain and the spray of massive waves.

"You will never shift with this deadened emotion." Gailen hooked one arm around the railing and pulled her against him. His hard, nude planes compressed her soft ones. "Open yourself to me, soul to soul. And open to yourself."

That was exactly the problem. She could open to him. But to accept all the fears and failures, lost wishes and forgotten dreams for herself? Even now, she felt like she had to sneak up on what she really wanted. How could she be radically honest and totally fearless? Embrace her sadness, her happiness, her fear, her strength?

Her life had been full of frustrations. She had wanted so many things, and just wanting something had never been enough. Look at how hard she'd wanted to save the burning platform. Now she wanted a life with Gailen as a mermaid that wasn't under constant risk from the All-Council.

Just wanting something had never been enough...

Gailen kissed her.

Heat and dazzling need filled her. She clenched his broad shoulders, soaking in his strength. What had her therapist said? *Do not live in the past or the future.* She had to focus on the sensations that moved through the impermeable barrier until they dragged her to the other side. The living side.

His lips moved against hers. "Let me in, Starr."

She wanted to.

She wanted to trust in herself. "And if I don't?"

"You will pass out. But do not fear. We will still get through this." He grinned. "I will bluff."

All she had to do was open to the rage, the fury, the terror, and the possibility swirling around life's great currents and hope for the best.

With Gailen? Maybe it was possible.

Starr took his hand. He released the rail and together they jumped in.

———

The water closed over them.

Gailen shifted naturally.

The undersea world opened. Warriors teemed beneath him, and as he'd feared, this area was no longer controlled by Atlantis. But the enemy warriors focused on a glowing white shield sheltering a group of warriors much closer to the platform. They looked up belatedly, surprised at his entrance, and then rotated tridents to face him.

Starr choked and panicked in the wild surface currents.

The enemy warriors formed up a unit to attack.

There was nowhere to go.

Gailen kicked down toward the enemy warriors as if he had no fear and tucked her to his chest. "You can shift, Starr. Trust in me."

Her eyes rolled inward. Her mouth opened and closed, and her all-too-human chest contracted.

"You have done this before. The power is within you." He barreled toward the unit. "You can shift or you can pass out. Either way, you will shift. Make the decision, or it will be made for you."

She tensed, fighting her own will. The sticky black substance coating her soul melted away, and her soul flared.

The eyes of enemy warriors widened.

She vibrated faintly, "Did I...shift?"

He pulled her close. "Yes."

Her inner flame brightened. She squeezed him and kissed him on the cheek. "Thank you, Gailen. Thank you."

Her soul flared like a queen's.

Their enemies scattered.

He swam through their formation into a deeper, easier-to-navigate current. A shout of warning rippled through the enemy units. The ones who turned to face Gailen saw her soul and zoomed out of their way.

His chest burst with the feeling he could do anything in the world, thumbs or no. He could drive off the entire All-Council, from one hypocritical, self-hating general down to the last miserable warrior.

Starr vibrated an incredulous laugh. They were connected, and she experienced the echo of his feelings.

He swam to the bright glow in the center of the All-Council army.

The bubble shielded a small contingent of the Atlantis army surrounding the visiting dignitaries and keeping them safe.

Endi saw him and Starr. He shouted, "It is Gailen. Drop the shield!"

The shield faded. Gailen darted through as the surrounding army reacted to give chase. The shields strengthened again, and the enemies bounced off, their tridents harmlessly skidding away.

The Atlantis warriors greeted him with shocked laughter, and many patted his shoulders as he swam through. Xemil and Isag waved from different positions within the shield. They both looked more tired and bloodied, and relieved to see him. Isag lofted his dagger, and Xemil had his trident.

He nodded for them to keep the weapons for now and continued to an open area where the dignitaries from the other cities gathered. Lieutenant Diras guarded them for extra protection.

Queen Elyssa and Queen Hazel floated on opposite sides of the bubble, their souls radiant and their fingertips white with energy. Their young fry floated near, closely monitored by Atlantis warriors.

King Kadir floated at the front edge. He parleyed with All-Council leaders on the opposite side of the shield.

The All-Council army stretched out to infinity, waves upon waves of enemy warriors. No General Giru or Queen Nora was visible, but a line of sight stretched through the endless army to the still-flaming remnants of the platform bubbling and boiling as chunks broke off and sank into the deep.

"And so you see, Kadir, this is the result of relying on humans," Sirak, the All-Council leader, was vibrating with a deep bass. "The All-Council knows this. As head, I tried to save you from exactly this kind of deadly attack."

Sirak looked younger than Gailen had expected, with bright blue eyes and yellow hair, and tattoos like blue fracture lines across his skin. What city had that marking style? Was it possible that despite his appearance, he was old enough to have come from one of the destroyed cities of the past?

"Now our greatest fear has come to pass," Sirak intoned. "The humans have once more lured us to the surface only to wipe us out. And you still wish to reunite our races? They will study us and use this knowledge to descend and hunt us beneath the oceans. You have doomed us, Kadir. And that is why you must be stopped, no matter the cost."

King Kadir appeared to have no arguments left.

"We have to tell him," Starr said.

Gailen kicked forward.

Lieutenant Diras swam from his position and blocked Gailen. "King Kadir confers with the All-Council. Your report can wait."

"But he needs to know—"

"Hark, everyone." Sirak raised his arms and rotated for his vast army. "The misinformed kings, princes, and first lieutenants tricked into this ill-conceived rebellion are dispersing. Do not attack. They return to their cities chastised, where they await our rule." He lowered his arms and grinned with sharp teeth at the dignitaries. "Pledge your loyalty to me, and you may pass. Refuse, and we will chum the water with your entrails."

The dignitaries kicked with stiff resignation toward the All-Council head.

King Kadir's shoulder's slumped, defeated.

The light from the queens' fingertips faded to allow them to pass to the area controlled by the army.

No, this couldn't be allowed.

Starr fidgeted. "Gailen."

He raised his vibration. "Wait!"

"Gailen." Lieutenant Diras's eyes flashed, and he lowered the flat staff of his trident to push them back. "Do not intervene in the matters of kings."

"But the brides are coming."

"To what? The platform was destroyed."

"I know, but— Stop!"

The dignitaries had reached the All-Council head, and the first one reached out to pledge.

"No, you cannot!" Gailen pushed against Lieutenant Diras's trident. He had been held back and constrained by the lieutenant in too many other less critical places, and with Starr's confidence affirming him, he raised his vibrations to project across the whole shelter. "Do not leave. The platform does not matter. You must stay! The future of the mer depends upon the new covenant."

The first dignitary slowed, surprised by his shout.

King Kadir frowned. "The platform does not matter?"

"The brides do not care about it."

Everyone focused on him. An uncomfortable heat

burned his ears and prickled his armpits, and bumps rose on his skin.

"So you have to stay," Gailen vibrated lamely.

"The platform was our meeting place, and now you say the brides do not care?" King Kadir repeated.

"Yes! Exactly."

"But you and Starr could not stop its destruction."

"Yes, but it does not matter."

"Who is this young fry?" Sirak rumbled. "This chaotic loss of discipline allows any warrior to have an opinion on matters he cannot understand. Your plot has gone down in flames. It is over. Admit defeat so you may yet survive."

"It is not over unless you leave," Gailen insisted.

The dignitaries floated uncertainly. The seething mass of the All-Council army surrounded them. A deadly muttering grew louder, like the growl of an approaching tidal wave. And he wasn't convincing anyone.

King Kadir held up a quieting hand. "Gailen. What are you trying to say?"

"He's trying to say that you guys are giving up way too fast." Starr floated to face the dignitaries utterly calm, utterly brilliant. "The platform doesn't matter because the brides are coming anyway."

NINETEEN

King Kadir blinked. "What?"

"The brides are coming anyway!" Gailen vibrated as loudly as he could, echoing across the shelter.

Lieutenant Diras lowered his trident and floated back in shock.

King Kadir frowned more deeply. "The brides are coming anyway? How do you know?"

"Queen Dannika told Starr on the human cell phone," Gailen vibrated. His heart thudded all out of rhythm.

King Kadir fixed on Starr.

As did the queens, the delegates, and all the warriors.

Her soul remained steady, and she did not seem bothered by the attention. "They've waited too long for this reunion, and they're resolute. Nothing will make them turn away."

King Kadir's face broke out in a smile, and his soul blazed. "Then we will not disappoint them. This reunion *has* been delayed too long."

"Madness. Utter madness." The All-Council head tried to grab the hand of the first dignitary.

He jerked back.

The army surged forward.

The dignitaries kicked back beneath the shelter of the brightening shield.

"Lies." The All-Council head glared through the impenetrable white shelter at Gailen and Starr, then focused on the dignitaries. "They have nowhere to meet you. Their land is on fire."

The huge oil rig shrieked and crashed into the water. The wave disturbed the All-Council army, forcing the closest warriors to regroup and making the rest scramble and struggle to remain in formation. Even Sirak had to maneuver around his closest warriors.

But the force flowed around the shield, not touching anyone within its shelter.

King Kadir focused with new radiance. "That does not matter. The brides are coming. They are resolute? Atlantis is also resolute. Our new covenant may be forged in the ashes of the past, but it will hold true on the waves of the future."

His regal vibrations set a new tone of hope. The others swallowed and straightened. Even Gailen felt a lump in his throat.

"And then what?" Sirak adjusted his ornate sheaths and smoothed his yellow hair. "Humans are creatures of air and land. They cannot dwell in the water too long."

"They're determined to overcome any obstacle," Starr vibrated, and because of the stillness of the water, her unexpressive tone carried.

Sirak pinched his lips. "They may visit you one time, but

that is not a future. It is a visit. You cannot risk your cities, your race, for one visit." He paced in front of the shelter, gesticulating for the dignitaries. "When you defy the All-Council, you lose our protection. We stopped the intercity wars. We hunted the honorless exiles and grasping raiders. We assembled an army to stop the horrors of the deep when they arise. And when you defy the ancient covenant, you defy the very core of the mer. For what? One. Visit."

Doubt cast a pall over the dignitaries, who murmured among themselves.

King Kadir turned on him soberly. "I would not ask our guests to risk their cities over one visit. When we forge our new covenant, we will not do so on the open ocean."

"You think floating boats can withstand the tempests that destroy even the largest human construction?"

"They will have an island."

The murmuring increased and extended outward through the All-Council advisers.

Sirak frowned. "What are you plotting, King Kadir?"

"Only that the brides' dedication has increased my own. If they are determined to reunite with us, I am determined they will have any land they need."

"And how do you expect to provide that? Raise the ancient ruin?"

King Kadir tipped his head. "Would it not inspire your confidence, All-Council head?"

The murmuring increased. Shock mixed with awe. Could he really do that?

Lieutenant Diras looked sharply at Gailen, but he subtly shook his head. He had no idea how to do this.

"You cannot turn back the centuries, King Kadir. The old city is dead." Sirak lifted his vibrations to the dignitaries. "This is your final chance to leave in peace."

No one moved.

Sirak curled his upper lip in a silent snarl, and he suddenly looked a lot older. "We will meet again. And next time, you will admit defeat, but no one will survive."

King Kadir said nothing.

Sirak glared at Gailen and swam into his army. The units formed behind him, swimming away, and the vast field of enemies swam around their shelter. Some jabbed their tridents at the shield and shouted insults so the queens flexed their fingers and the bubble expanded, forcing the All-Council warriors to scramble back.

Ha.

On King Kadir's commands, they descended to a current that would intersect with others to lead them to Atlantis. Despite the enemy units still trailing them and the events of the night, everyone relaxed, and vibrations rose with good cheer.

More warriors wanted to hear all the details about the brides and their adventures, while others speculated wildly about how they would come up with a new island in a week. King Kadir was surrounded by sober dignitaries, and Gailen wanted that answer too.

Queen Elyssa swam to Gailen and Starr and squeezed them in a hug.

"You two came at just the right time." She pulled back, her fingertips and soul still glowing to maintain the shield, and her kind eyes glimmered. "Hi, Starr. It's so nice to meet you."

"Starr!" Queen Hazel hugged her. Unlike Queen Elyssa's steady command of her powers, Queen Hazel must have stopped controlling hers, because the shield contracted on her side, drawing the warriors and dignitaries in with disgruntled surprise.

Queen Elyssa quickly pushed the shield out again, fully capable of maintaining it solo.

Queen Hazel wailed. "Look at what happened to my beautiful venue!"

"I'm sorry, Hazel," Starr vibrated quietly.

"I swear, every time I hold a party, something goes wrong. I'm going to find those Sons of Hercules, and I'm going to mace-tase them into another dimension."

"Uh, well, you might have missed your chance..."

Had Ryerson or his followers escaped? All the innocent platform workers had been accounted for, but they'd had no communications with the terrorists. Plenty of construction boats and life rafts had been left behind.

"Were you all okay?" Starr asked.

"Oh, yeah. Isag got the word to us just in time. We already had the shield up because of the army, but—oh." Queen Hazel lifted her hands, and her fingertips glowed. The shield brightened even more and expanded. "We moved away and tried to warn the All-Council, but you can see how that head guy listens. I don't think anyone died, but they're lucky the first blasts were higher up."

Lucky...

The current carried them past the communications cable. Although the oil rig had fallen into the ocean, the cable was taut, meaning it was still connected to something on the surface. But it drifted at an angle, so whatever remained was at the mercy of the currents and winds.

Queen Hazel's young fry squealed in the arms of another warrior, and Queen Hazel grabbed Starr's forearm. "Tal's awake this time, so come meet my baby. You can say whatever you want as long as it's 'Oh my God' and 'How did he end up so cute?'"

Starr looked startled. Then her soul light brightened. She looked at Gailen as if she needed permission.

He released her easily. Young fry were the pride of the mer, and Starr had not described many friends on the surface. Hopefully, that would now change.

The queens converged on young Tal.

Behind them, Lieutenant Diras focused on their trailing enemies. His gaze crossed Gailen's. He paused. Then he nodded slightly in acknowledgment.

Huh.

Across the bubble, the other warriors were alert, but in high spirits. But Gailen felt strangely separated from them, as always. The warriors he had spent the most time with had all become fathers or husbands, and the newer ones who'd arrived had formed friendships without him.

But for the first time, that was okay. The bitterness he normally felt with the awareness that everyone else's roles had changed and grown didn't come.

He was changing too. No longer trapped in only one version of himself while everyone else left him behind, he too was swimming out into the new ocean of becoming a husband, and perhaps soon, a father as well.

King Kadir broke free from the dignitaries and swam to Gailen. "You bride has made friends."

"She knew Queen Hazel on the surface." Gailen followed his warm gaze to where Queen Hazel demonstrated how to fold a baby carrier out of a long weave of seaweed, a trick she'd learned in her oceanic travels. "My king, how did you learn to raise the ancient ruin?"

King Kadir glanced at the dignitaries and other warriors, then lowered his vibrations to a deep murmur. "I am relying on you."

Gailen's jaw went slack. "Me?"

"I could think of no other way to disperse the All-Council army without bloodshed. Theirs," he clarified. "And we are so close to reaching a new covenant, one which even the All-Council will wish to join. An outbreak of violence helps no one."

"But you think I can raise it?"

"Reminiscing about Archivist Ulio reminded me of a small detail. When the time comes, your insight will be critical."

"*My* insight! But my king, my skill is with plants and castle gardens, not engineering."

"Yes, Gailen. You are my secret weapon. I am sure of it." King Kadir's tone changed. "Gailen, I would not ask another warrior this, but will you open your wedding ceremony to the other delegates to showcase the best of Atlantis?"

What a question! Gailen had always expected to have a traditional mer ceremony with his bride. The vows could be performed alone in front of the Life Tree or with all warriors of the city present, such as when King Kadir had married Queen Elyssa. Rarely were warriors from other cities present. To marry in front of visiting princes? Kings? Such things happened only in legends.

And now King Kadir asked Gailen to become a legend.

He barely knew how to accept the honor. "I must ask Starr."

"Of course. And we are waiting for a few more delegates to arrive, so if you preferred privacy, or did not want to wait, I respect your wishes." King Kadir glanced over his shoulder and then hunched in with a wince. "Elyssa is angry. She argued that I should not ask you because you would hide your true feelings to appease your king."

Ah. "Since meeting Starr, I have changed."

"Of course you have. Very good. Gailen, you will save us yet." King Kadir floated up to Queen Elyssa.

She folded her arms. He rubbed her elbows and looked chagrined.

Even a king could feel chagrin.

Starr finished with the other queens and descended into Gailen's arms. He cupped her against him as his precious hope. She felt perfect there.

"This is so much fun." She spread her fingers. Her soul brightened. "It feels like I'm flying."

He felt the same way.

Gailen shared King Kadir's request. Starr was fine with it, and they returned to Atlantis with higher spirits despite the incredible setback. And everyone they met in the city reacted the same way—devastated at the loss of the platform and then awed that the queens were coming anyway.

While they waited to start the ceremony, he gave her a tour of the coral forest growing from the seafloor beneath the Life Tree. She glowed like her namesake, powerful and bright-eyed, as he swam. "What are those long curved sticks?"

He veered closer. "The bones of the megalodon. It arose from the deep, and instead of defeating it, the All-Council lured it here to consume Atlantis. The queens destroyed it with their great powers, saving our city."

"Amazing." She paddled on her stubby human feet, examining the colorful corals that grew in ornate clusters.

"Gailen!" Endi swam down and laughed. "Are you boring your bride with what falls beneath the city? Does she not care to go to your castle and see the size of your Life Tree seed?"

The warriors patrolling with him flashed smiles, but quickly sobered as though they were worried Gailen really might be boring his bride, and only Endi was brave enough to make a joke about it.

Starr focused completely on neon nudibranchs and rainbow crustaceans weaving among the coral.

He answered, "She likes exploring."

"Are you sure? You do not want her to think rooting in the ground is all you do. You are a mighty warrior!" Endi and the rest of the patrol swam away.

Starr rested her hand on a bare patch of curved bone. "Fascinating."

He kicked to her side in one stroke. "Is it really? I once accomplished many more interesting feats as a warrior. I could tell you about them."

She took a long time to respond because she was thinking carefully. "I am so happy right now, it scares me."

"Scares you?" He pulled her closer needing her touch. "You are scared of joining with me instead of with a more capable warrior?"

"No." She rested her hand against his chest. "I've always wanted to walk through a field of wildflowers, lie back on the grass, rake leaves into a pile and jump into it, simply be outside on top of a mountain surrounded by nature. I wanted to have this experience"—she gestured to the vast coral forest —"my whole life. And these corals look like the most exotic wildflowers. These long rib bones make an amazing tree. This has been my dream for my whole life, and you've made it possible for me. Getting what I wanted after so long is scary because I'm afraid it will be taken away. I can't really have it."

Ah.

His sweet bride. He loved her even more now, and he'd loved her more than anything before. She validated everything about him. He wanted to give her everything right back.

Whatever she needed, he would provide it.

From now until they swam together in the blacknight sea.

"You can." He rested his forehead against hers. "This is only the beginning. I promise I will show you everything, even though I am not the most capable warrior."

She swallowed hard and hugged him so tight. "There is no more capable warrior. I want to experience everything with you."

His throat tightened.

A commotion electrified the city above, and warriors swam down to let them know that the other delegates had arrived.

Gailen grinned at her. It was time.

Lieutenant Diras was vibrating quietly to King Kadir and Queen Elyssa outside the Life Tree enclosure as they swam near. "My king, my queen. Do we have time for this wedding? The All-Council blankets our region, and we must also guard against sabotage by the visiting dignitaries. If anyone attacks during this ceremony, we will struggle."

"Lieutenant Diras, you are experienced in mer warfare." King Kadir squeezed his arm. "But you do not realize uniting warriors with their brides is an excellent battle strategy. Each union strengthens our city. Accepting her connection to Gailen will unlock Starr's queen powers, making her equal to a hundred All-Council warriors. So it is wise to hold a wedding even in the middle of the fiercest raid."

"It can't be any worse than giving birth during a mega-lodon attack," a very pregnant Queen Lucy vibrated as she swam close, glowing, with her husband, Warrior Torun, and her mischievous twin young fry.

Behind her trailed several kings, and Queen Elyssa and King Kadir formally welcomed them to Atlantis.

It was so hard to believe that all these important warriors were going to watch him, ordinary Gailen, wed his bride. And yet they all queued up to congratulate him. Like he was really someone. Even their gazes didn't seem pitying, and they didn't linger over his damaged thumbs. He could barely swallow his amazement and vibrate normal replies.

Starr was a centering presence at his side. She glowed, unaffected by the audience.

Queen Lucy stuck out her hand in a human handshake. "Congratulations, Gailen, Starr. I wish you a long and happy union and kids who are great sleepers."

Their female, Tory, grabbed her twin brother's hair and yanked. He screamed and attacked her. Torun sighed and separated them.

Queen Lucy raised her glowing fingertips. "This is going to be a nice wedding. Don't make me put you in time out."

The twins fussed. Torun calmed them with quiet competence.

Queen Lucy winced and rubbed her belly.

"Uh, is everything okay?" Starr asked.

Everyone was suddenly acutely attentive to Queen Lucy's state.

"Yeah. Just..." Queen Lucy rubbed harder. "I swear he or she is already taking the kids' side."

The Atlantis warriors chuckled. Even the visiting kings cracked a smile.

The visitors swam to the Life Tree dais. Since the Atlantis Life Tree was still so young, it should have been protected inside closed petal walls, but it had been battered and attacked. The protection had cracked, shattered, leaving only remnants around the scarred trunk and slender branches. And yet the Life Tree glowed on, young and strong.

It was time.

Gailen grabbed Starr's hand.

She curled her fingers around his, and even though he wished he could clasp her more fully with his broken thumb, this was enough. Whether their marriage was witnessed by one or many, all that mattered was each other.

Then her soul light dimmed.

Something was wrong.

He stopped.

Had Starr changed her mind?

In the last few—what, minutes? Time was so different underwater—Starr had met tons of delegates from the different cities. King Jolan of Sireno, King Kayo and Queen Fab of Aiycaya, Prince Lukiyo of Lusca. The names passed her in a friendly, somewhat surreal blur.

Floating with Gailen outside the shattered Life Tree enclosure, bathed in the tree's beautiful light, she'd felt at peace.

This was thrilling and what she wanted. All she had to do was settle in and accept.

And Gailen was so adorable. He had this amazing way of being kind, not only to her but to everyone. Warriors were drawn to him. Even the serious ones who had their minds on other things had a smile for him.

And then he glanced over at her, and her heart pressed against her rib cage, swelling with an ache. He had chosen her. How could things have finally worked out so well? After her failures, was this really how she was rewarded?

Atlantis was so beautiful, it was like a dream. She'd

spent a lot of time watching fantasy movies and browsing on DeviantArt and fan sites. Artist renderings of fairy villages or elven woodlands were the closest to what she saw here. Everything so natural and yet at the same time, so unearthly. Even the warriors looked beautiful and still masculine. Their tattoos glimmered with iridescence, outlining their muscles and strength. They were all armed with sharp, commanding tridents, and their lithe bodies were strapped with sheaths, making them capable and deadly.

This was indeed Rivendell with its ropey vines and glimmering gold leaves and shimmering fish that swam like flocks of doves. Beneath the city, spires of coral twisted like limestone statues, and small crustaceans that couldn't flutter still reminded her of butterflies.

And she wasn't stuck in a room hidden in a corner. No, she was out and in the world. Rolling on the grass and jumping into the leaves and finally living the life she'd only seen on TV and in other people's dreams.

She was in it, and yet...

The delegates had all gone into their positions when Gailen turned to her.

His expression sobered. He stroked her hand. "You are sad."

"I spent my whole life inside, mostly alone. I missed my sister's graduation, my graduation, my sister's first wedding, the birth of her child, all the important moments in our lives. And now, I'm here." She tightened her grip on his fingers. "I'm sorry I can't share this with Bella."

He held her close and silently gave her comfort.

How funny that this was enough. Just having him here, understanding her, was enough. Gailen did not tell her that she should be grateful she was outside, or that she should only be thinking of him at their wedding. He was generous and understanding.

Bella and her husband had been exiled because of Ryerson. She was even angrier at him for inspiring a movement that had tried to destroy this city and hurt her sister, because now that Starr had seen the light, how could she live her life separated from the Life Tree? She didn't want to go.

But if the All-Council got its way, the ancient covenant would prevail.

The other cities would reject modern brides.

And, in the worst-case scenario, Atlantis would be overrun. A traditional king would take over and undo all the changes. She'd be forced back to the surface after she gave birth to her and Gailen's child, cut off from her family and the mer forever.

But those were problems for after the wedding.

"I'm finally able to come outside and go out, and I can't be with my sister." She pulled back from Gailen. "I would love to share this experience with her."

"You will share many experiences with her." He brushed her lips with his. "As you continue to heal yourself and develop your queen powers, you will go to the surface many times. Perhaps we can even perform this union in a human wedding ceremony as other mermen do."

Huh. She'd put away images of herself in a flowing cream dress, a tiara of fall leaves in her hair, and carrying a cascading bouquet of copper and cream roses long ago. But Gailen was right. She wasn't as affected by environmental allergies as before. She could have that ceremony on the surface, and Bella and Jonah could be there.

Gailen turned toward the Life Tree and offered his hand once more. "Are you ready?"

She linked their fingers. "Yes."

———

Gailen led Starr into the center of the Life Tree sanctuary where all his friends and new family had gathered.

He straightened and pulled shoulders back.

King Kadir addressed the visiting dignitaries. "Today, a loyal hero of Atlantis unites with his soul mate. His bride will embrace their connection to become a queen. That is the way in Atlantis. With the new covenant we forge, it will become the future of all cities."

Loyal hero of Atlantis?

Gailen?

Heat burned his ears, and he reflexively contracted his broken thumbs. But his king looked at him with pride.

Starr was so serene, not because she held herself apart with the film, but because she'd opened herself to the Life Tree. She wanted to be with him. She wanted this life, and she had no doubts.

A new calm fell over him too.

Gailen had thought he'd wanted a bride. Any bride. But that was a mistake.

He passed before King Kadir, who lovingly embraced his Queen Elyssa and their young fry, Prince Kael. The other couples floated around the dais. They knew the same truth that he now did.

He'd always wanted his soul mate, who was Starr, and if he could only go back and talk to himself from the past, the warrior who'd so bitterly thought this moment would never come, he would say to wait. Wait just a little longer.

Endi and the other single warriors jostled awkwardly,

their expressions mixed between happiness on his behalf and anxiety on their own.

Just wait, he wanted to say. *Do not become bitter. Your bride is coming.*

But it wouldn't have helped him. Some things had to be experienced.

They crossed onto the dais, and he shifted his fins to feet.

Starr bounced lightly on the soft loam with him.

Little shards of Sea Opals glittered on the dais. The slender branches of the young Life Tree stretched toward the surface with hope, and the peaceful tinkling of its tiny resin gemstones tumbling through the branches filled his soul with rightness.

He knelt before the white trunk and placed his hands on the knotted scar. It had been cut down, and Queen Elyssa had miraculously regrown it with her powers.

"I, Gailen of Atlantis, present Starr as my chosen bride. Shower your blessing and healing on our union so she may give us a young fry."

He kissed the scarred trunk.

The Life Tree made a clear, happy chime.

He stood and bounced back. "Now you repeat the vow."

Starr knelt. Her soul linked to the Life Tree, strengthening her connection to it and to him. "I, Starr of Atlantis, present Gailen as my chosen husband. Shower your blessing and healing on our union so he may give us a young fry."

She kissed the trunk.

The Life Tree chimed a more metallic tridents-scraping-daggers sound. The visiting dignitaries murmured uneasily, but the warriors of Atlantis didn't react. It had happened so many times, it was no longer unsettling, just different.

Starr rose and went into his arms.

Queen Elyssa softly vibrated a human wedding song. The tree glimmered in reaction to her. The light of the Life Tree glowed over their gathering, blessing them and strengthening their community.

Starr looked up, and her smile intensified. "It feels like we're standing beneath a field of starlight."

He pressed her body to his. She fit against him perfectly, relaxing into his touch, and rested her head on his shoulder.

His heart swelled with protectiveness. He would care for her forever. And he would never let the sadness that had touched her when they first met return.

And there, in the upper branches, a tiny white flower unfurled.

He guided her to the blossom. She carefully plucked it and sipped the bead of nectar inside. This would make her temporary elixir transformation permanent.

Queen Elyssa's song finished, and then a guard at the front of the Life Tree signaled to King Kadir. Their joyous time was over.

King Kadir made the announcement. "All visitors, you now see why we fiercely protect Atlantis. Soon this happiness experienced by our warriors will flow over to everyone. United with modern, mainland brides, our race will once more thrive."

This was the vision that had united the warriors of Atlantis. The delegates glowed, touched.

As the others left the Life Tree, King Kadir rested his palm on Gailen's biceps. "Thank you for opening your ceremony. They will remember this longer than the platform destruction. Especially once our brides return and show the true strength of the soul connection."

His chest lifted again. Not just because he could marry Starr, but because it often seemed like nothing he did mattered, and yet, he'd finally done a lot. "Yes, my king."

Queen Elyssa swam close. "Congrats again, Starr. I wish we could hang out, but you know how things are."

Starr faintly smiled.

"We'll help you make your fins and figure out your queen powers. Do you know what they are yet?"

"No."

"Well, they could be anything. Healing or pushing or shielding. Sometimes people have a guess, but sometimes it's a surprise."

"I love the Life Tree and the gardens."

"Wonderful." Queen Elyssa glowed and pressed her hands together. "Gailen's battling a mighty weed right now at the ruin. Maybe you can figure out how to win. At the very least, you'll be surrounded by plants."

"I would like that."

"Oh, it's like you were meant to be together." Queen Elyssa grinned. "Soul mates."

"Queen Elyssa." Lieutenant Diras vibrated for her amid a group of other warriors. "They await your instructions."

She wished them well, and the royalty departed.

"I'd like to see this plant," Starr told Gailen.

Gailen rested his forehead against hers. "Can I tempt you to see your castle first?"

The water heated, and her body turned to his. Her lids half-lowered as she nestled against him. "Yes."

His heart sang.

He covered her mouth with his kiss.

She melted into him, opening her lips, and stroked his

mouth eagerly with her tongue. She wanted this wedding night just as much as he did.

His cock hardened against her soft body. The temptation to take her here before the Life Tree thudded with urgency.

But, as generously as he had shared their wedding, he greedily did not wish to share her passion.

He cut off the kiss and kicked with full power across the city to his bobbing green castle.

Through the long entrance into the interior of the sphere, he swam into the lush courtyard and ducked down a side tunnel. He gave her no time to look around at the gardens he had planted or all the details that he had imagined showing off to his new bride when he'd spent so much time creating them. Now that they were married in front of the Life Tree, all he wanted was to unite their bodies and fully meld their souls.

Starr's fingers brushed his back in feathery little movements. She explored his lower back and his sensitive gills. Shudders of arousal zipped up and down his spine. Her lips teased his neck with experimental nibbles along his flexing shoulder to his collarbone. Heat flooded his cock with pounding arousal. Once, she had been afraid to kiss him in case it triggered her illness. Now? She fearlessly tasted his body, curious and demanding.

He reached his safe hollow in the tunnel. Beyond this wall was the castle's heart chamber. Their union would open it, and then the castle would truly become theirs.

She covered his mouth with her kiss.

Their souls and bodies ignited.

She was gorgeous and slippery, sweet and bouncy, and oh so vividly alive.

He kissed down her chest, filled his palms with her soft

breasts, chasing her moans of pleasure. Her desperate mewls led him to pinch her hard nipples between his rough knuckles, and she arched with need. He put each in his mouth and sucked until she cried out, shuddering, with the first blinding flare of a bride's release.

His heart pounded with accomplishment. Even a warrior such as him could pleasure his bride.

She wrapped around him like a starfish containing a mussel, boring into the hard shell of his fears, embracing him with all her hunger.

He gripped her hips, struggling to contain her. "With this union, we will open our heart chamber. My release may even plant the seed in you for our own young fry."

She wiggled. "I'm not afraid of that at all."

"No? Are you not afraid that you could end up with a father who cannot hold his young fry?"

"You would be the kindest, most loving, and most supportive father even if you had no arms whatsoever." She stopped trying to hook his legs. Her hands descended and curled around his hard cock.

Pleasure spiked in his brain, and he thrust into her grip. "You are my dream, Starr. All I have ever wanted. The bride I chased. Do you understand what this means to me?"

"Yeah." She plunged her tongue into his mouth. "If you can think this much, I have to work harder."

"Work harder?"

"Neither of us can believe this is real." She stroked his hard cock. "And if I think about it too hard, I might wake up, so I want to stop thinking. I want you to lose your mind."

He rolled over in the water, twisting with her, and tore his cock out of her clever palms. "I cannot lose my mind because it is only filled with you."

She wrapped her thighs around his waist and canted her hips to take him.

His cock parted her sex, and he gently thrust into her.

She moaned and arched, urging him deeper. Her soft wetness encased him, squeezing him, joining with him.

Starr was chaos. Now and forever. And he was hers. So much hers.

Her chest vibrated with pleased moans. He thrust in, chasing her delicious cries.

And her softness broke and she tightened around him, shattering without a sound. Her orgasm gripped his cock and tugged hard. She went over and yanked him after her.

He unloaded his full release into her climaxing body.

She shuddered and relaxed, entangled in his limbs.

He held her close, so close, until his own shudders stopped.

A new doorway glimmered on the green wall. Their union had opened the heart chamber. He pressed their palms to the glowing green wall, and the chamber unfurled, letting them in and sealing behind them. Green sparkles zipped around the walls sheltering them so they could rest.

His world had fundamentally changed.

Starr was right that he needed not to think too hard. He needed to trust in himself, not give in to his fears or his darker urges.

She snuggled in his arms. "Are you still sad that everything had happened this way? Did you still wish that you'd stayed in Aiycaya?"

For the first time, he could honestly answer, "No."

It was worth going through everything to have this moment right here. Other times, he had doubted that, but not now.

She tapped her fingers on his collarbone. A restless movement? Pensive, maybe.

He stroked her sinuous back. "You do not wish to rest?"

"I'm used to pulling all-nighters. And you've just infused me with tremendous energy." She placed a serious kiss on his pectoral, then her contented smile flipped into a frown. "I'm so happy now that it makes me ask what I'm missing. We have to figure out a platform solution. And you have no idea what King Kadir expects you to do with the ruin? It's a puzzle."

An ordinary bride should be exhausted, but Starr was not ordinary. "We could visit the ruin as soon as there are warriors to convey us. Or if you are confident in your queen powers, we do not have to wait."

"Good point." She flexed her stubby human toes. "The Sons of Hercules got one over on me. If I'd realized early enough that the assistant had planted all those bombs, I might have been able to stop him. And I don't want to look back on this moment and feel the same way about the All-Council. If there's something we can do now, I want to do it."

She was a warrior.

And so was he.

Then she yawned.

Gailen entwined with her. "We are on the brink of a great war, Starr. I will describe the puzzle to you so that you may think about it as we rest. And when the insight strikes, we will be ready to fight."

She accepted that and went lax, falling asleep almost instantly.

So, she had been tired.

He held her a little longer.

Because this might be their last rest. If the All-Council

had their way, in a short time Atlantis would no longer exist, and everything, including this castle and heart chamber, would be gone.

And that would make them both so sad, just like on the boat when they first met and Starr had been wrapped behind a film of isolation.

He would never let her be hurt like that again.

TWENTY-ONE

Starr awoke in Gailen's arms in the heart chamber of their castle.

It was vibrant and green, like awakening in a caterpillar's cocoon. At any moment, she would stretch her wings and find out she was a butterfly.

She curved in his arms and faced him.

He was still asleep and so innocent, so beautiful.

But what she'd learned from last...night?...was that he was also relentless and focused on her pleasure. He must be exhausted now. She would let him sleep.

She stroked his rippled sides. His muscles were thick and fascinating. Even at rest, there was a hard strength to him. She traced his flat belly and down his abdomen.

His cock hardened.

Hmm.

She gently cupped him.

His eyes opened and fixed on her.

As she'd suspected. "Sorry. I didn't mean to wake you."

Without changing expression, he covered her mouth with his kiss.

He was hot and ready for her, and he wanted her just like she wanted him. The promise pulsed into her as his tongue thrust into her mouth. He would never get enough of her. Never.

And that healed a deep wound in her.

She was not too much effort for him.

Starr fit his cock to her throbbing pussy. He surged into her, thrusting straight into her pleasure spot. Waves of need crashed against her. He pulled back so that he could gaze deeply into her eyes. In the glimmering orange iridescent threads, his love shone.

This was not just one moment in pleasure, this was his forever. And her forever too.

He chased her until she climaxed hard, shuddering with fulfillment. Soul-deep satisfaction flooded her, and then a buzz of energy just like last night. Instead of jumping to get up this time, she pushed it into introspection.

How funny to live her whole life thinking things were going to be one way, and then in one instant, everything changed. She met Gailen, and her whole life shifted, goals reframed. All the bugs in her programming evaporated, and everything just worked. It was only going to get better from here.

And she wanted to give that to all the other women in the world.

Her stomach growled.

"Come." They disentangled, and he tucked her against him to leave the heart chamber. "Look upon your gardens and let me feed you."

Oh, right.

Food.

They flew through the sparkling green tunnels and burst into the vast inner courtyard.

The ground was blanketed in a massive garden. His small bean-sized Life Tree seed rested on a pedestal in the center. Trails cut outward in multiple spirals. He dropped to one and released her.

Her human toes bounced on the soft ground.

He led her through a maze of green paths carpeted with spongy seaweeds. Overhead, tall plants waved mystically and formed sheltered tangles. Against the wall of green, vivid pops of color fluttered: yellow and orange flowers or anemones. Grand rocks, mammoth shells with beautiful stones inside, and overturned bowls spilled purple flowers.

Gailen plucked a handful of lavender seeds. "They taste good, Queen Elyssa tells me."

The handful felt like peanuts.

"Nuts." She steeled herself. "My old nemesis."

He reflected warmth and confidence. "If you cannot eat this food, we will spear the fish you once ate, Starr. You will not starve in Atlantis."

And it wasn't as if she had to worry about anaphylaxis. It could be horrible, but it was no longer a death sentence.

The seeds grew heavy in her hand.

He cupped her elbows. "This is how you recede. Wait until your soul has grown bright again. Then try."

Right. Okay.

"I have just remembered that I do have some of the seaweed you ate." He entwined her and swam.

She fluttered her stubby toes, mimicking his long-finned strokes. They rounded the corner into another delightful enclave. Smooth coral spires held succulent-like plants in bright olive, dusky brown, and burnished red. Some leaves were frilled and some were smooth.

He gathered her seaweed. "This is a younger version of the one you already ate. It should be safe."

She tested the familiar seaweed.

It tasted brighter, crunchier, tastier than the woody pieces she'd eaten before. Yum. Her stomach growled again. This was one of those moments where she wanted to try all the things, but she was terrified too. And there was no way around it. She just had to go through with it.

She slipped one of the crunchy lavender seeds into her mouth. It tasted like how coffee smelled. Ooh, with a little kick of spice. She waited. No tingles? No, no reaction. She crunched the whole handful.

A small octopus lounged on one of the coral spires. It waved a tentacle as if to say hi.

She waved back. "Hey."

The octopus lowered its tentacle and lounged.

She got a chill octopus? Groovy.

Her stomach reminded her that she was still hungry. Things seemed to be okay, so she polished off the seaweed and tried a few more plants and some slices of fish steak. As her stomach filled, her anxiety switched from her the situation to the ruin.

Gailen sensed her mood. "Ready to solve puzzles?"

She was.

He swam her to the castle exit, which was a long tube burrowed through the thick green wall, and swam into the subdued city. A lot seemed to be happening and everyone was busy but friendly and surprised to see them so soon.

He collected his trident from Isag, then joined a patrol heading to the ruin. Passing the submersible still attached to the cables, they crossed the empty ground.

The ruin was farther than she'd realized, and they parted from the patrol at the base of the big tower of Babel. A dark cave emitted a scratchy noise.

"Octopus Kong," Gailen reminded her. "Savior of Atlantis."

The grumpy giant emerged from his cave and used his tentacles as though he were sweeping off his front porch. He turned his giant plus-shaped eyes on them as they swam overhead. And then he seemed to harrumph and retreated into his cave.

What an amazing world she was living in.

Gailen ascended through the layers of water. The patrols crossed below, looking much sparser here. They would get help if they called out, but it would take a while for help to arrive.

He quieted his vibrations. "We tried to elevate the platform, but the last stages were broken. We always planned to repair them, but then…"

Massive vines, like pictures she'd seen of trees overgrowing temples in Cambodia, clogged the inner tower. "This grew."

She reached out and rested her hand on the vine. It was so large and bulging. Unlike the white pure Life Tree, it was hellishly black and even had a reddish tint, like some sort of tentacle or living creature. "It's really taken over. Like a weed, huh?"

"A what?"

"A plant that grows somewhere you don't want it."

"Then it is very much a weed. If it were not here, I would like it much more. The vine might be useful for construction. It is hardy and interesting."

"Even the most beautiful flowers can be weeds. Most start as ornamental and then invade."

"This is a true invader. I have traced its roots as far as I am able."

Gailen pivoted and descended, then swam horizontally

across the ruin. It looked like a motherboard that had been fried. The ghostly outlines of old buildings, squares, and fountains were all that remained.

He continued beyond the edge of the outlines and curved into a valley.

"Huh," she murmured.

"Yes, it goes much farther than we thought." He landed in the middle of a smooth crater, bouncing very gently on the disturbed rubble. "When I told King Kadir how large the platform might be, his lieutenants grew upset. We barely have enough warriors to patrol as it is. Stay quiet here."

The blackish-red plant jutted up in a great knot.

She knelt. The vine felt oddly warm and inviting. "This is really cool."

"Cool?" He knelt beside her. "No, it is the same temperature as the rest of the ocean."

Ha-ha. "I mean I like the smoothness. Did it grow like this?"

"It does not seem to be alive here, but I also could not chip it free. That is when I realized how deep it went." He tapped it with the base of his trident.

The reverberation made a low, hollow noise, but the wood felt heavy, not hollow.

As if he could read her mind, he pointed with the tip of his trident. "Look at the bark pattern."

She traced the scalloped edges. "Scales."

"I have never seen anything like it."

"Hm." She raked through the broken rubble and unearthed halves of statues, broken cups, and urns. Very Grecian. And submerged and mystical and cool. "And we're not in danger here?"

"The danger is relative." He pointed out the distant

patrol—behind them. "I am banking on two things. The first is that the All-Council is so certain this ruin cannot be raised, they are not focused here."

"And the second?"

"You glow with the soul of a powerful queen."

Tingles spread down her back. She rubbed her neck. "A bluff, then."

"Soon it will not be." He smiled at her softly.

The tingles came again.

She flexed her ankles. Her feet remained resolutely human. Could she one day swim with the long, frilly fins of Elyssa or Lucy? Or even the functional fins of the warriors?

Gailen set aside his trident and dug a modified tool into the hard rock around the plant, puffing up dirt and debris.

She bounced on her toes and wiggled her feet. The movement inched her upward, above the cloud, and the vast ruin unfolded.

In the distance, Atlantis gleamed with the light of the Life Tree. It was like looking at a shining star, except that the whole ocean was well lit and she could see as far she wanted to in any direction. If she squinted, she could see all the way to the moon. Or so it seemed.

In the other direction, sharks chased wily fish, eels undulated like underwater rivers, and a wolffish fought with a spiny angler fish. Some different animals popped in and out of her awareness, especially big predators that passed like cars and buses. Far, far away, an elongated squid jetted across the seafloor.

All these animals shared an uneasy coexistence.

She twirled very gently in the water. It was like having the ability to fly. She could will herself higher and rise like a hot air balloon over the landscape. Or she could descend onto a broken bench that Gailen had righted and shored up one of the broken legs with a hunk of rock.

Around her, fairy lights twinkled.

This was so beautiful. Just like everywhere else.

She leaned back on her hands. A gentle current pushed her off the bench. Instead of relaxing, she had to hold on. Funny. "So this is what you do all day?"

"Yes." He straightened. "I used to patrol, but now I fight an undefeatable plant."

She flexed her too-human feet. "And King Kadir thinks you'll use your experience to raise the ruin."

"Yes." He switched tools for his trident, trying to wedge it into the space he'd cleared between the dirt and the vine. "I was so bitter about this work. Is that not funny? If I could help King Kadir, perhaps I will finally feel it is valuable."

His trident hit something with a metallic clink.

That was no rock.

She paddled over and floated close. "Okay, let me see."

He set his feet against the stem and pushed on the trident, forcing the vine back.

She waved away the murk.

A band curved around the trunk. "It's some sort of ring. The vine is growing through it. There's a pattern. Look."

He couldn't see and hold the trident at the same time, so they used his modified tools to dig out the vine, making swift progress. The ring was as wide as her clasped hands, and an ancient crust flaked off to reveal a polished blue stone. A wave pattern was etched on the top. And on the side, a diagram showed a tree growing up through a ring.

Hmm.

If she was excavating an alien technology and she came upon something like this—a diagram of a plant growing through a ring *etched onto* a ring that had a plant growing through it—she might start to think the plant was there by design.

"Are you sure this plant is a weed?" she asked.

Gailen slowly shook his head. "I am not sure of anything anymore."

A warrior shouted across the ruin. "Gailen. Queen Starr. You are needed in Atlantis."

Uh-oh.

Gailen collected his trident. She reached out her hand, and Gailen drew her against him. His thumb brushed the back of her hand.

She stopped and grabbed him.

"What is it?" he asked.

Was it her imagination? She spread his fingers. His other hand was exactly how she remembered, but this one... She stroked his thumb. His thumb bent toward his palm.

"This is the one that got hurt when you were kidnapped, isn't it? It's healing."

He made a fist. His thumb curved the correct direction. He clenched harder. His thumb trembled but wouldn't bend. His shoulders slumped. "It is not healed."

"But it is different," she insisted. "It's changed."

"Yes, well..." He tucked his trident against his elbow and pulled her into his arms. "This is still not a warrior's hand."

That bitterness and frustration made her ache.

She nestled against him as he kicked across the ruin. "It is a gardener's hand and an artist's hand."

"I do not draw. I cannot grip the tool."

"No, in your castle garden." She cupped her hands around his. It wasn't enough that she was okay with his thumbs, however they turned out. He needed to be okay with them. And there was nothing she could do but love him as he was. "What you've created is incredible."

"You really like your garden?"

"When this is all over, I'm going to lock myself in our castle and soak in the majesty. You'll never have to ask that question again."

His taut shoulders loosened. "Queen Elyssa said something similar when she saw me tending her and King Kadir's gardens. The king's garden must feed visitors, and he has so many. It is why she asked me to attend the gardens in the other castles."

"It's a talent."

"I have always thought it is not as important as defending the city, but maybe you will change my mind."

Good.

They flew to the patrol and together crossed the open land to the city.

A shadow darkened the city. As they crossed, the shadow expanded to cover the open ground and even the ruin.

Atlantis warriors patrolled with new vigor, and a low-key level of alarm buzzed in their vibrations. Everyone glanced continuously overhead.

The shadow was real. It was made up of hundreds upon hundreds of All-Council warriors. They had descended while she and Gailen had been over at the ruin and now hovered like a hand about to crush them.

TWENTY-TWO

This was the most ominous sign Gailen had seen in a long, long time.

Probably since he'd heard the eerie hiss of terrifying megalodons, which Queen Elyssa had described as "doom blimps," converging on the city.

"To the Life Tree," the warrior urged them.

Dread scratched at his nerve endings. It was good that they had left the ruin when they had, but what new horrors awaited him at the Life Tree that he should be summoned so urgently?

Lieutenant Diras gathered with a new group of dignitaries on the dais. "I cannot, unfortunately, answer any of your questions. Please be patient while I..." He saw Gailen. His shoulders slumped, and he gestured urgently toward Gailen. "The warrior who tends the Life Tree is here to welcome you to Atlantis."

The new group of visitors turned en masse to Gailen and Starr.

"Yes, Warrior Gailen will answer all questions. I must

speak with the patrols about the army. Warrior Gailen?" Lieutenant Diras swiftly exited.

Wait. Was that it? Gailen had been desperately summoned to do the greeting?

Okay...

He released Starr. She communed with the Life Tree while he greeted the new visitors.

"Welcome to Atlantis. Please inspect the Life Tree closely. Despite being such a young tree, you no doubt notice that the protective covering is broken and a large scar crosses the trunk. An All-Council raider impersonated the original warrior who tended the Life Tree, Zoan, and infiltrated the chamber where he..."

A peach warrior floating on the edge of the dais lifted his brows and made an awkward "oops" with his lips.

"Zoan," Gailen vibrated dumbly. "Second Lieutenant Ciran told us you were not coming. Why did you not tell Lieutenant Diras you used to tend the Life Tree? You could have given this welcome."

"Yes, well, I did not know I had become part of the speech." Zoan gestured toward his shining bride, Indigo. "My queen wanted to witness this historic event, so she challenged herself to transform and grow her powers in only one practice session."

"One practice session!"

Zoan beamed. "She is truly exceptional."

Queen Indigo grinned. Her white teeth flashed against her dark skin. "You are so sweet. I know you'd do the same for me."

They had a moment of communication just between the two of them.

Starr floated close. "How did you do that?"

"I wanted it." Queen Indigo spread her arms, and her soul glowed. "Here, I'll show you."

Zoan swelled with pride. "She was going to be a trainer before. It is in her blood. She will be a wonderful mother when she is ready."

Two queens working together demonstrated the vision of Atlantis better than any story Gailen could tell, and so he abbreviated his welcome to the rest of the visitors and they all watched the queens. It was so wonderful after so many dark years to see their race thrive.

"That is not the only reason we have come." Zoan lowered his vibration to reach only Gailen. "Have you seen my brother?"

"Your twin? Roa?" Gailen shook his head. "You know King Kadir would never welcome a male who nearly destroyed Atlantis."

"I know, but Roa is a king now."

That insane warrior was a king? Gailen sputtered. "Of Siyokoy?"

"Roa founded his own city and claimed a modern bride. Will King Kadir refuse another king?"

That was nothing short of incredible. "Would he dare come here?"

"The All-Council tortured him so much in the prison. He hates them even more than we do. Making a new covenant will hurt them. I think he might come."

"How do we know he will not try to finish what he started last time?"

Sadness tinted Zoan's smile. "I do not know. But I would like one last chance to say I am sorry." He straightened and clapped Gailen's bicep. "And look at you with your bride. I regret I never made you part of the welcome speech. I would have been sure to mention your thumbs."

Gailen tried to laugh, but it was weak.

"Are you well?" Zoan asked.

"Just tired," Gailen assured him and then stopped. It was okay to share his honest feelings. "It bothers me that my thumbs may never fully heal."

His old friend tipped his head. "All warriors who join Atlantis have left something important to them behind. Your loss is more visible, but your endurance gives others hope. After all, even a warrior without thumbs can become a hero of Atlantis."

He choked. "You were at the wedding?"

"I heard all about it." Zoan's eyes twinkled. "You are an inspiration, Gailen. Even though you can barely hold a trident."

"I can hold it well enough."

"Mm."

Their conversation turned to banter, and it was good to chat with a warrior who'd known him so long. The dignitaries were escorted to another gathering place, and Queen Indigo rejoined Zoan. Starr returned to Gailen.

"Did you learn anything?"

She flexed her ankles. "I'm not sure. I need more time."

"You have plenty."

She frowned.

He made a sweeping gesture at the Life Tree. "This is how I spend most of my time. Tending. Waiting. No one ever needs me in a hurry."

"You say that like it's a bad thing."

"Well, it is nothing like your work on the surface. You will see no bombs or traitors here. Zoan remembers the beginning when we few warriors slept in limited shifts, fully armed. That time is long past."

"It's best to think of my personality as a sleepy cat. I'm

done with being one adrenaline shot away from the edge of death. This is a welcome change. Although"—she rubbed her arms as she looked up at the enemy warriors lurking far overhead—"I suppose it's not exactly over."

"For us, it probably is."

"Gailen." Endi urgently waved to him. The patrol took position around the Life Tree, guarding it. He had no hint of his usual smiles. "You and Queen Starr are needed at King Kadir's castle. Quickly."

Starr went into Gailen's arms. He bounced off the dais, shifted to fins, and kicked hard.

"So what's the emergency?" Starr asked him as they crossed the open area around the Life Tree.

"I cannot guess."

"And you just said you were never needed in a hurry."

"No one needs a garden planted quickly."

The king's castle was the oldest, largest castle with the grandest gardens. A secretive group of high-ranked warriors and a few trusted kings gathered around King Kadir and a foreign warrior.

The stranger had dark red hair, iron-red tattoos, and an upturned nose. He swam pacing in the center of the group with spry kicks.

King Kadir noted their entrance. "Archivist Ulio, this is warrior Gailen. He can answer your questions about the ruin better than any of us."

Gailen jerk upright, electrified. "Archivist Ulio?"

The archivist blinked. "You have heard of me?"

"Only from General Giru."

"Ah. That warrior. He would almost be honorable if..." But the archivist waved a hand and returned to pacing. "To carry on with what I was saying, raising the ancient ruin of old Atlantis is impossible not because the mechanisms are broken, but because they are dead."

"We raised three stages," Lotar murmured. "The diagrams say there are two more."

"But those are not mechanical," Archivist Ulio insisted. "They are biological. Do you know how the city of Lusca once controlled squid? It used a mechanical system with red stones that reflected the kraken's deep vibrations onto itself. You turned a crank and moved the mechanical system to control a biological system. But I saw it myself as you"—he nodded at Lotar—"swam me over the ancient ruin. Atlantis no longer possesses the biological system."

Biological system?

The Atlantis warriors murmured.

"Are you saying..." Queen Hazel lifted her hands. "The ruin is *alive*?"

"Was," the archivist confirmed. "A beast known as the Ur controlled it."

The mutters increased.

"I don't know why I'm surprised." Queen Elyssa looped her index finger to indicate their surroundings. "The castles are alive, the city is alive, everything's alive. But it still boggles my mind that an island with an entire city built on top of it was once, what? Some kind of prehistoric whale?"

"The beast that raised ancient Atlantis was a great eel," the archivist vibrated. "Like the Life Tree, it responds to and increases the power of queens, but unlike the Life Tree, it also responds to the power of warriors. Their energies combined in a great disc known as the heart stone. When enough energy filled the stone, the Ur lifted the city above the waves. When their energies subsided, the city would sink beneath the water once more."

Incredible.

"But the warriors abandoned Atlantis so long that the Ur has died," the archivist finished. "Your idea, King Kadir, to plant seeds of your Life Tree beneath the heart stone is not a bad one, but it would take an uncountable number of queens across multiple generations to raise it. It is not the solution you seek to convert the All-Council to your side."

"I do not mind if it extends beyond my lifetime," King Kadir said. "I promised we would raise the ruin. Even a few corals' height fulfills that promise. Completing it can be the work for future generations."

"Have you found the heart stone?" the archivist asked Gailen. "It is the power center of ancient Atlantis."

"What does it look like?"

"You would know if you saw it." Archivist Ulio rolled his lips with regret. "It is hard as stone, but it is made of the crystallized blood of the Ur. Lights glimmer within it, the memory of our ancestors' souls, and when you float over it, you feel as though you are looking down at the night sky full of stars."

That sounded incredible.

And like nothing he had seen. "Much of the ruin is still covered with debris."

"Its glow was said to penetrate through stone walls and bathe the interior of buildings. No layer of mud or muck would hide its presence. Think of the Life Tree, only a hundred times stronger."

A hundred times!

The archivist rubbed his brow, defeated. "I had thought... If the heart stone survived the Great Catastrophe, there would be hope..."

"Hope of what?" Gailen asked.

The archivist descended to the garden, lost in thought.

King Kadir caught the eye of Lieutenant Diras and

nodded once. He turned away to confer with Lotar and the trusted kings.

Lieutenant Diras kicked to Gailen and vibrated quietly, "Representative Rikoy recently captured Archivist Ulio. When Lotar rescued the archivist from the camp, he discovered their plans. The All-Council army will split into two factions. The most loyal warriors will rise to the surface and murder any bride who enters the water."

His stomach dropped. "Murder!"

"And the other will fight to the death to stop us from escaping this city to protect them."

Gailen's mind reeled. That explained the hovering warriors. But murdering brides? True sacred brides? This was too horrible to even contemplate. "How could any warrior do this?"

"How could any warrior unleash a megalodon on another city? And yet that was a common battle tactic long ago. How could any warrior bring back a dormant plague? And yet your exiled healer, Balim, fought it with Queen Bella." Lieutenant Diras looked tired. "To win a war, some fighters are not constrained by honor."

Gailen had warned General Giru this was coming, but he still couldn't believe it.

"Can the army really hurt anyone?" Starr asked calmly. "The brides might not have developed their powers, like me, but they're coming with real queens."

"Queens who expect to meet us, not enemies."

"Dannika will be aware of the danger."

"I hope you are right," Lieutenant Diras said. "But all it will take is one mistake, one moment of inattention, one falter of her powers, and either she or the brides she protects are endangered. I would not accept that risk."

"We have to warn them." Starr frowned. "The cable is still in place. Some part of the original oil rig is still floating."

"King Kadir still stations warriors there. Their 'backup battery' runs the human machinery and produces air, but there is no communication from the surface."

"And I can't swim to the surface and check because of the army. Got it."

"You could after you fully develop your queen powers," Gailen said.

"After..." She flexed her too-human ankles. "I suppose if they're willing to fight to the death, they're not going to be put off by another bluff."

This time, Gailen thought Starr was right.

"In truth, I think the queens could defend the brides, hold off the All-Council army, and even descend to us." Lieutenant Diras scraped a bit of seaweed off his war-damaged, notched daggers. His weapons had seen more battle than most and yet still gleamed with honed precision. "But the All-Council armies would suffer needless deaths."

"The All-Council does not care about sacrificing their warriors, so why should we?"

"You know that when you join the All-Council army, you give up your citizenship to your home city. That is why they only take the most experienced, most honored warriors who have already met their soul mates and sired a young fry. If a warrior fails the All-Council, he is not only exiled, he also brings dishonor to his home city and son left behind."

Gailen did know that. Everyone knew that. "But how can they murder their own soul mates? It should tear an ordinary warrior apart."

"My origin city, Iara, has been at war for a hundred generations with our neighbor, Boto. There is never victory, only brief cessations of the endless violence. Some of the injured were brides and young fry."

"How!"

"Accidents. Calculations. A need to hurt others equally so that pain is 'fairly distributed' to happy warriors." His jaw flexed. "Grief will turn an ordinary male into a monster."

"But brides and young fry... That is too far."

"King Kadir convinces warriors to join him with words, never violence. Even after the first All-Council army inflicted megalodons, King Kadir forgave and welcomed the survivors." Lieutenant Diras rubbed his finger over the worn crests of Iara. "When I heard that, I came to Atlantis. King Kadir is tired of watching warriors being sent to die. And so am I."

Gailen's respect for the lieutenant grew. "Thank you."

The lieutenant's brows lifted. "For what?"

"Not causing damage when you do not have to."

His gaze flicked to Gailen's thumbs and back to his face. "The archivist was captured near where you found Starr. He was confused by the rogue currents that you navigated correctly. And when I told him that another warrior had gone that way several times, and once unarmed, he informed me that such a feat was impossible. So it seems that I owe you more of an apology for limiting you before. You should have been the leader on the patrols, not assigned to the ruin. And yet again, the knowledge you gained there from my ignorance may become our salvation."

A lump formed in Gailen's throat. He swallowed.

He was important. And his work was important.

Starr threaded her fingers through his and squeezed.

She understood what he was feeling.

The discussion of how to deal with the horrible All-Council plans grew louder.

"Lotar could sneak past a whole army," Queen Hazel vibrated loyally, her young fry sleeping in the crook of her arm. Her other arm rested on Lotar's square shoulders. "But I could go too. I know my shield would hold."

"Then you'd warn Dannika and Aya, but they'd be stuck on the surface." Queen Elyssa tapped her lips. "They're stuck on the surface with hundreds of brides and the dignitaries are stuck down here with us. We can't forge a new covenant over the telephone. Plus it's broken anyway."

"We could all surface," Queen Hazel said. "Rich people have boat parties. We could do this."

"We cannot empty the city," Lotar reminded his bride. "Someone must guard the Life Tree."

"Lucy could. She's super pregnant, and didn't she give birth during the last siege? This is like her normal birth plan."

"It was me, Lucy, and Aya," Queen Elyssa said. "I think we need at least three."

"Okay, then, she stays behind with..." Queen Hazel glanced over at Gailen and Starr, then continued. "What was Zoan's bride's name? Indigo? Plus there's Fab, Roxanne... I need to do a headcount."

"But it's not fair to make them stay behind," Queen Elyssa said. "Fab represents Aiycaya, not Atlantis. Lucy doesn't have an official city, but it seems wrong not to involve the first modern woman to marry a warrior. Lucy and Torun kicked off the underwater revolution. If not for them, Kadir would still be sitting in the All-Council prison."

Well, he would be long dead, honestly.

"Okay..." Queen Hazel pursed her lips. "We take shifts.

First shift comes up with the new covenant, second shift ratifies it, first shift comes back."

The warriors exchanged glances.

"Every time you pass the army, they will attack," Lotar told her.

"So what? We're queens. The tricky part will be trying to keep them from hurting themselves."

"Excuse me." Lieutenant Diras left them to be more involved with the plans, which wended through many more iterations, causing more exasperation and fruitless anger as the discussion wore on.

Starr suddenly squeezed Gailen's hand. "Waves."

"Hmm?"

She pointed.

The archivist had descended to a sandy corner of the garden. With a long stick, he drew a big circle surrounded by five smaller circles. One of the smaller circles had waves drawn around it.

Gailen floated down to the archivist. "We found a ring impressed with this symbol."

The archivist grunted. "Blue stone? With a drawing of an eel leaping through it?"

"Eel?" Starr vibrated.

"It is the tidal ring." The archivist pointed at one small ring, then symbols on the other four. "Stone. Electricity. Seaweed. Fish. While the heart stone was energized, the Ur eels would leap through each of the rings. You must have found it empty."

Starr stiffened in his arms. The same realization bolted through him.

"No," Gailen vibrated. "We certainly did not."

The archivist tilted his head. "You did not find it empty?"

"No. It was filled with a vine."

"Ah." He scratched away the drawing in disgust. "In a thousand years, everything but the heart stone would be covered in debris."

But it did not seem like debris. "Could these Ur eels not be the vines of a plant?"

"Impossible. In all my years in the archives, in all my studies of this ruin, the Ur have never been described as a plant. They have always been portrayed as fish. Sleeping fish, until they are awoken by the stones, but always fish."

"What about a vine with black scales?" Starr suggested. "Black with a reddish tint?"

"Black...with red?" His expression blanked and his eyes darted as though reading ancient texts in his mind, and then he focused on them. "Show me."

TWENTY-THREE

Gailen would never have interrupted war plans in the past, but now he boldly requested an escort to the ruins.

King Kadir faced the archivist gravely. "If you are captured, the head of the All-Council will not let you live."

Archivist Ulio sighed. "I forfeited my life when I left the archives. My passing, at least, will not be in vain."

King Kadir studied his warriors. "It will be suspicious if too many leave as a big group."

"I can protect them." Queen Elyssa held out her hand for her young fry, and Prince Kael took it soberly. "If the All-Council has watched us for long, they'll know how often I used to visit Gailen at the ruin."

"Very well. Raise the ancient ruin. If you cannot..." King Kadir looked heavily to the warriors assembled behind him. "We will protect the brides."

The archivist straightened. "If announcing my presence would stop a slaughter, I would give my life for that."

"You are more valuable alive." King Kadir held out his

arm, and the archivist clasped it. "I am grateful you did not catch me in the archive."

"As am I." He released King Kadir's arm. "If I die, you must convey the truth."

"You will not die." King Kadir pulled Queen Elyssa close and kissed her hard. The depth of his caring and the way her soul glowed brilliantly with their resonance echoed in Gailen's chest.

He held Starr close. She was his truth, his light, his future. And he was hers.

King Kadir released Queen Elyssa and turned to Gailen and Starr. "Protect Archivist Ulio. We must know our past to understand our future. The truth, no matter how terrible, is needed now."

Gailen gave his vow.

They exited King Kadir's castle—Gailen with Starr, Archivist Ulio, Queen Elyssa, and sober Prince Kael—and swam surreptitiously through the city.

The enemy hung over them like a building tsunami. The only question was when they would crash down and sweep Atlantis away.

"Gailen!" Warrior Endi and his patrol blocked their passage. "You are needed right away. The dignitaries have questions about the great fight that nearly destroyed the Life Tree."

Queen Elyssa vibrated firmly, "Gailen has another duty now. Who else is experienced reciting our history?"

The patrol looked at one another nervously.

"No one? Hmm. If it's that story, can you ask Zoan?"

"He does not wish to repeat it."

"Well, try your best to convince him, and listen better the next time Gailen tells you."

"But...Warrior Gailen tends the Life Tree..."

Queen Elyssa rested her hand on Endi's elbow. "Congratulations, Endi. You are in charge of the Life Tree duties for now."

The warrior whitened and clutched his trident to his chest. "I will perform them as best I can."

"That's all I ask." Queen Elyssa grinned, and their secret convoy escaped the city without another interruption.

Gailen had never really felt like he had an important job, so it was funny to see Endi look worried. Queen Elyssa hadn't laughed at Endi's fears. Lieutenant Diras had also looked extremely relieved to return the duty to Gailen.

Maybe Gailen was the only one who had underestimated his worth.

Queen Elyssa's warmth merrily deflected the looming All-Council overhead. She matched the Life Tree's soothing presence.

Starr, on the other hand, curled around him tensely like a starfish clinging onto a rock.

He would try to be that rock for her. "Perhaps Queen Elyssa can show you how to develop your queen powers on this journey."

"Maybe." She bit her lower lip. "I didn't realize the submersible was still working. I could take a look inside."

"Is the problem not at the surface?"

"Probably..."

But she thought it would be easier to study the familiar human machines than figure out how to embrace her ultimate powers as a queen.

Gailen needed to support her. "If we cannot raise the ruin, that will be our next destination."

She relaxed against him.

The archivist muttered as he swam alongside them.

"Odd submersible. Look at those tethers, so deep in the human cement..." He veered off, away from Queen Elyssa's protection, and Gailen had to call him back.

"My interest, before joining the All-Council, was in construction." He gazed up at the submersible as they passed beneath it, still noisy and bubbling, although it no longer transmitted their communications. "I did not have many opportunities in Merrow, but I learned much when I joined the archives. When I was an apprentice, the head archivist studied whatever he felt was most useful to guiding the All-Council, and his death was a great loss. His measured voice was long missed. But now, I think that..."

They entered the open water. It felt far more abandoned and ominous than their last crossing.

"It feels like we just went this way," Starr murmured.

"And yet on the surface, days have passed," Gailen replied.

"Already?"

"I was amazed when I reached Atlantis the first time," Queen Elyssa told Starr, a bright, chatty soul in the odd emptiness. "They told me months had passed! It's different when you don't have to eat and sleep every day. And now I get used to it. Time flies when you're having fun."

A few sparse patrols darted nervously, their gazes never far from the warning overhead.

They reached the colossal tower. Octopus Kong flew out of his cave.

Archivist Ulio gaped.

Queen Elyssa waved. "Coming for a walk?"

The giant harrumphed and jetted around as if to say that he just happened to be going in the same direction. He trailed them, a dangerous companion.

Queen Elyssa giggled. Prince Kael reached out a

friendly hand, which the cave guardian ignored. Even Starr smiled.

Octopus Kong was capable of rending a mer to pieces with his eight great arms. Gailen did not blame the archivist for shying away, but it was nice to have another layer of protection.

They crossed the valley, out of sight of the Life Tree, and descended into a chillier hollow.

Gailen landed at the knotted stump. Debris had buried the ring. Queen Elyssa and Prince Kael stacked rocks, and Octopus Kong pretended disinterest while Gailen and Starr unearthed it.

The archivist got down on his knees, his fins flexed to human toes, and ran his hands across the stone. "Yes, it is waves. Hm. But see this drawing? It is wrong. The tidal ring is supposed to be filled with the body of an eel."

"What if it *is* filled with the body of an eel?" Starr pressed. "Or, say, a vine that looks like a sleeping eel?"

"That would change everything we know about ancient Atlantis." Archivist Ulio touched the scaly vine with a frown. "If this is one of the five rings, that means the heart stone is..."

He pushed off, hovering to look over the valley, and then pivoted and kicked.

Queen Elyssa grabbed Prince Kael, and Starr entwined with Gailen. They hurried after him.

Archivist Ulio jabbed his angular finger into the distance. "It must be that way."

Farther away from the patrols. Farther away from Atlantis.

They crossed the barren seafloor into open territory. Queen Elyssa *would* keep them safe, but out here, beyond any hope of backup...

Over the landscape, they swam until even the threat of the hovering All-Council armies faded.

"How big is this ruin?" Starr asked.

"Larger than I imagined," Gailen vibrated. "Can you imagine how many warriors must have lived here in the past?"

The archivist glanced over his shoulder at them. "More than are alive now."

That, Gailen could believe.

Eventually, the archivist circled an abandoned crater. "This should be the center. See the strange spiral bulges on those walls? Those are the steps that humans descended into the throne room. And here was the heart stone." He landed on the dusty rock. "Hm. I see nothing."

"It's covered in dirt," Starr said.

"Yes, but it glowed through stone walls. We should see it through any layers of detritus." He scraped at the dirt. "I think."

Gailen released Starr, and together, they kicked, swept, and dug down, trying to clear it.

Bong.

Gailen's trident struck something hollow.

Everyone converged on him. He tapped it again, getting a feel for the depth. "We do not have the human earth-moving equipment. This will take some time."

"Not necessarily." Queen Elyssa appealed to the cave guardian. "Could you please brush away the rocks?"

The beast tilted his bulbous head and looked her in the eye as if to ask whether she was serious.

"Pretty please?"

Octopus Kong jetted away as though insulted, then zoomed back. They scattered in a panic. He smashed into the dirt. Rocks clattered, and murk filled the crater. They backed away until it had blown off on the current. Beneath the layers of the ocean sediment, he'd unearthed a knotted old log with a dull wood grain.

"What is this?" The archivist rested his fingertips on the submerged log. "It is some sort of preserved fossil."

"It has the same scale pattern as the vine." Gailen rapped on it with the base of his trident.

"Heartwood," Starr said.

"Oh, yeah." Queen Elyssa nodded. "That makes so much sense."

"It does?" Gailen said.

"It's what we call the center of a tree," Starr told him. "And it could turn into petrified wood."

"Or sap," Archivist Ulio mused. "As the resin of the Life Tree becomes mating gemstones, the blood of the Ur eels hardens into stone. Which means..." He squinted into the distance. "If the Ur vine is growing through the other four rings, then we could still raise this ruin. I should have looked at the tower. At its base could have been the stone ring."

"The vine has grown all through the machinery."

"Because the presence of mer 'awakened' the Ur. The city's nearness triggered its growth."

But how could they raise the whole ruin? "That growth has taken years."

"Perhaps we can increase its speed." The archivist's tone brightened with confidence. "There is still a chance. Unveil the heart stone. We must figure out how to transfer the energy collected from the rings into the heart."

The archivist shifted to human feet and pushed a boulder, rolling it away from the exposed wood.

Queen Elyssa directed the cave guardian to move a little

ways away so his efforts wouldn't interfere. Starr and Prince Kael swam after her.

Gailen remained with the archivist.

Archivist Ulio swept the exposed base where the log was embedded in more wood, seeking symbols to confirm or deny his theory. "To think that I would see the ruin in my lifetime. Your king is no ordinary warrior."

That was true. "If you had caught him when he was an apprentice, would you really have turned him in?"

"Yes, and I would never have realized my error. I, like my fellow archivists, were certain of ourselves."

"That must have been nice. I am rarely certain of anything."

"It is very easy to be certain of yourself when you give your responsibility to other warriors. In our case, we gave our research to the All-Council and paid no attention to the decisions they made with it. How irresponsible, yes? When Kadir founded Atlantis, everything changed."

"Except their treatment of 'rebels.'"

"You say that because you do not know your history." He brushed away dirt, exposing carved lines and slashes. "Did you know the ancient covenant has changed hundreds of times?"

"What?" Sick electricity vibrated through Gailen's veins. He flexed his thumbs, the weakened one and the one that still jutted in the wrong direction. "I was tortured because 'the ancient covenant is eternal and no one defies it,' and yet it has changed?"

"Oh, yes." The archivist nodded, captivated by his excavation. "It was forged hundreds of years after the Great Catastrophe. Originally, there were sanctuary cities on the mainland where the mer would meet with human priestesses, but the local warlords tried to involve the mer in their human conflicts. That was why we moved to the sacred islands. Did you know that we carried our sacred brides to those islands?"

"No." How could he? This made him reel. "Go on."

"Each island established its rituals, and the mer even facilitated exchanges and travel. Even a few generations ago, our cities were very different. There was always flexibility. It was not until the sacred islands began to empty, which started around the time Lusca rebelled, that the All-Council of the time froze the ancient covenant and stopped allowing changes to be made."

"Because of Lusca..."

"And then one generation and another were born believing that the rules could not be changed and it became the truth." He gazed up toward the distant surface. "I was deep in the archives when the All-Council summoned us. They demanded to know the military history of our most successful generals. From the way they phrased the demand, it is clear they intended to stop this reunion."

His stomach sank. "Did you tell them?"

"I suspect my colleagues did. But in addition, my colleagues protested the current attack. Finally. We, the archivists, the ones who have only ever handed over information without comment." He lowered his gaze to the wood beneath him. "And so the All-Council head condemned them all to prison. The very same prison you once stormed to free King Kadir. How amusing, correct?"

It wasn't amusing, no. In fact, Gailen felt sick.

"When I emerged from my research and heard of their fate, I left and came here." Archivist Ulio leveled his gaze on Gailen. "Once, I would have turned in your king for treason, but now I believe the treasonous ones are the All-Council. They close their eyes and ears to our history and attack the historians who keep it. And why? So that the new covenant and kings do not force them to account for their past actions. They would surely end up in their own prison."

"And so they pile dishonor upon dishonor." Gailen dug his trident deeper into the rock. "Sickening."

"The All-Council was formed to protect the tenets of our race. It was not always called the All-Council, but we have always turned to a ruling body to protect our values. Now those values are overturned. I will no longer serve one warrior or even five warriors who fail to uphold this. Even if it costs me my life."

"It is lucky you were deep in the archives when your colleagues were summoned."

"It was not luck, my young warrior. I was researching this ruin. And now..." The archivist splayed his hands across the exposed wood. "If the Ur is a vine and it is starting to grow, then we are very close to being able to energize it. In the ancient records, the mer would surround the sunken island and raise it with their energy."

"So we have to surround the whole ruin?"

"Yes. Perhaps. I do not think the entire ruin ever sank to the bottom before, but the records are clear. The sunken regions 'leapt alive like an eel' and they 'surged to the surface faster than any mer.' If only we can activate it..."

Gailen dug into the murk with renewed vigor. "I wish we had a hundred cave guardians."

"Yes." The archivist frowned across the great plain. "We must concentrate our power around the eel rings to charge the heart stone."

"How do we do that?"

"I wish I knew." The archivist swept away more muck and studied the carvings. "I wish I knew."

They had no time to waste.

Just as this ancient ruin was more massive than Gailen had realized, the history of the mer was vaster and far more varied.

Now it was threatened. If the All-Council rulers succeeded in destroying Atlantis, that history would end. And all so that just a few males could cling onto a little more power.

Unless Gailen and Starr stopped them...

TWENTY-FOUR

Elyssa frolicked with the giant octopus.

Because that's what you did when you were a mermaid queen apparently.

Octopus Kong was a grumpy mammoth beast, but surprisingly playful, flailing his tentacles in all directions. He kind of reminded her of an aloof alpaca who secretly liked to roll in the dust.

Starr's heart lightened.

This area was so beautiful and so wild. And she was out in it.

Finally.

And yet danger still shadowed her and skirted the edge of her awareness.

She flexed her feet. Her fins remained locked inside, her human toes and bones stubbornly in place.

Elyssa kicked her long, beautiful fins. "Still working on it, huh?"

"Yeah." Starr stretched. Her back popped. She sighed and shook out her shoulders. "What's the secret? What's the thing nobody tells us?"

"Sorry. All I can give you are platitudes, and I know how infuriating they are."

"Try me."

Elyssa pressed her hands to her own heart. "Think about what brings you the greatest joy and then focus on that."

Hmm. Actually, that was kind of the whole problem. "I can't."

"What do you mean?"

"I can't think about what brings me my greatest joy." She mirrored Elyssa's gesture pressing her hands against her chest. "If I feel anything too strongly, I disconnect. It's why I passed out at the surface when I tried to shift."

"Yikes. That is a problem." Elyssa twirled in the water. "But channeling your feelings is the only way I know to control your powers. Just like the way to have more energy is to eat better, exercise more, and sleep longer, which is hard to do when you have a young child and a war brewing right over your head." She grinned at Starr. "Aya's been reading me articles about how to get more energy. The last time we visited the Hague—where she's still with Soren lobbying the UN—all I've wanted to do was sleep."

"So feeling your greatest joy doesn't give you more energy?"

"Not on the surface. Well, even there, it helps."

Prince Kael darted into the dust cloud.

For the third time.

Elyssa seemed to know with that mom sense that put eyes in the back of her head. She stretched her fingers over her shoulder. The tips glowed white, and the prince floated out of the cloud surrounded by a ball of sheltering energy.

"Once I thought that I could never be the kind of person that others would look up to," Elyssa said conversationally. "I made a lot of mistakes when I first arrived. I put my foot in my mouth so many times that I've got calluses on my tongue."

She dropped her hand. The shield dissipated, releasing her son. He floated at the edge of the dust storm again, avidly watching the tentacles flail, twitching with eagerness.

"But the warriors—some warriors—kept giving me second chances. One was Gailen. He always believed in me and encouraged me to do my best. And that's why I'm so glad that he's found happiness with you."

Speaking of Gailen, he was working with the archivist. They both rested their hands on their hips and gazed over the vast crater with a frown. It was not going well for them. Gailen looked upset.

But he still had a core of kindness. His brow lightened, and he lifted a hand to wave.

Her heart rose in response.

The dangerous shadow swirled, threatening her.

No. She would not lose herself now.

Gailen let his hand fall. He didn't get mad at her for not flooding with joy. He knew her struggles.

"Despite wanting to sleep for two weeks straight, I really am having the best time of my life," Elyssa said. "Look at us, soaring through the ocean, using our feelings to make the world better, channeling the Life Tree with friends, and wielding magical powers with your mind. I wish everyone could experience this amazing life."

Elyssa threw her arms wide like she was hugging the ocean. Pure, white light danced from her fingertips. She channeled the Life Tree just like a wizard.

Beneath her fins, little lights reflected like a mirror.

Elyssa wanted all this for Starr.

And Starr wanted all this for herself.

But she couldn't have it.

She couldn't...

"You can totally have it," Elyssa said like she was reading Starr's mind.

"I never got what I wanted just by wanting it," Starr replied. "If I did, my life would have turned out a lot different. Neither you nor Bella can talk me into a new life with this froofy woo-woo."

"Well, your sister's right, and you're right too."

"We can't both be right. They're opposite views."

Elyssa smiled. "In the past, forging ahead with a peanut butter sandwich would have killed you. So you're right. But you've transformed into a mermaid. The same protective measures aren't needed anymore."

"I get that, but just *thinking* it seems pointless. There has to be something I can do."

"The mind-body connection is much stronger in the mer."

Elyssa's son darted into the dust cloud, and without breaking Starr's eye contact, she tossed her shield behind her and dragged her son out again.

"On the surface, you can't will away death. But beneath the water, you can heal a mortal wound, command energy, control your whole body with your mind. And I'm not a scientist, so I don't understand how it works, but you *are* controlling molecules with your mind."

"It just seems impossible."

"I know, but resonance is real. Scientists study it."

"Sea Opals have never cured me."

"Maybe they didn't cure you in the past, but you're not human anymore. You're a queen."

She...wasn't human anymore.

Obviously.

Was this air she was breathing? No, it wasn't.

But she still felt human. She still felt like herself.

The plastic lingered in the background, threatening her.

Crackling anger ignited in her chest.

She never got what she wanted.

Starr wanted to be wild and free.

You can have whatever you want. This is only the beginning.

Gailen said it. Now Elyssa said the same thing.

But it wasn't true.

The plastic kept her from embracing the kind of life she could have with an open heart. It had prevented her from helping Gailen when he was in danger. It had made her pass out rather than face the world head-on. Just like her allergies had always made her fall into a deadly tailspin instead of just breathing out the irritant and moving on.

But...

Her environment had completely changed. Her body had changed. Everything had changed.

And yet she still felt trapped inside. Unable to have what she truly wanted.

Was she even trying to reach for her desires?

What was the worst that could happen? She would faint? That would be annoying, but it wasn't life and death.

Elyssa suddenly stopped. Her smile froze like she was hearing something far away.

Prince Kael turned abruptly away from the dust storm and kicked as fast as his little fins could go to his mom. The mud cloud settled, and Octopus Kong rose on murky alert.

"I think we should head back." Elyssa focused on Starr with a nervous smile. "I can't tell you why, but I just feel like we need to go."

Well, in a world without cell phones, instinct was as good as anything.

Elyssa grabbed her hand and swiftly tugged her through the water to Gailen. "We have to leave now."

"We have not cleared the heart stone," Gailen replied, catching Starr.

"Yeah, we need a miracle." Elyssa looked back over the cloudy ruin. "So I guess I want a miracle. Hear me, universe?" She massaged her temples. "Miracle, miracle, miracle. Okay! Let's hurry back."

Gailen and the archivist fell in behind Elyssa. Gailen was unusually grim.

Starr hugged him. "Are you okay?"

"Yes. I just learned..." His frown deepened. "Did you know the ancient covenant changed many times?"

"No, because I didn't know it existed until five years ago."

"The All-Council is persecuting Atlantis because of the ancient covenant. My thumbs were destroyed because I planned to break the ancient covenant. King Kadir was imprisoned and nearly died because he urged us to leave the ancient covenant. And everyone told us that it could not be changed. And I believe them." He shook his head. "I do not understand how I could always honor the wrong males. I have always been misled by liars."

She patted him. He was angry with himself, but she understood. She was also too vulnerable to her own limits.

They crossed the tidal ring. Before, they'd seen patrols, but now the patrols were gone.

"Uh-oh." Elyssa pointed above into the empty ocean. "Where did they go?"

They paused over the excavation. All of them, even, it seemed, Octopus Kong, scanned the water.

The hovering All-Council warriors were nowhere to be seen.

"Did they leave?" Gailen wondered aloud. "Did they rise to attack the brides? We still have a little time before they arrive."

"Kadir must have taken this opportunity to surface." Elyssa kicked a few strokes, then paused. "I'm torn. On the one hand, we still haven't figured out how to raise the ruin. But given what's at stake, I feel like I need to be where he is."

Prince Kael burrowed into her arms.

She hugged him, seeming to need the same comfort. "I just wish I could understand their movements."

"It could be a mirror of the Oria maneuver," the archivist mused. "During the Seven Cities' War, Oria drew a rival army into a blind canyon and unleashed a megalodon."

"I know how to handle megalodons." Elyssa grinned up at Octopus Kong. "Shall we?"

"If it is not the Oria maneuver and we are ambushed, even a cave guardian would be in danger," the archivist warned. "Military history was not my specialty, but I will go with you and share what wisdom I can with King Kadir."

"We will try to activate the rings," Gailen vibrated. "Although I have been fighting the very vine that was intended to lift the city the whole time."

"That is a common mistake," the archivist vibrated, "when you do not know your history."

Elyssa's grin faded. "Starr is still developing her powers."

Gailen tightened his grip on his trident. "And?"

"I'm not going to tell you no. We need this too badly to

succeed. But you're two of my favorite people, and I worry." She pulled them into a group hug. "Please be safe."

Elyssa swam away with her son and the archivist.

The giant octopus followed them across the ruin and then wheeled away and descended to his cave. He'd had a busy day already and probably needed a nap.

Gailen dropped to the vine and cleared debris from the ring.

Starr helped him for a while, then leaned back and stretched out her legs. Being alone like this under the ocean was sort of like being alone on an alien planet.

After he fully unearthed the ring, Gailen puttered, clearing a little bit here and there, but his heart didn't seem to be in it. He kept looking out over the ocean.

It was eerily quiet.

"Do you still feel like you've been given an unimportant task?" she asked.

"No." He scraped the ground beneath the ring. "I just... I believed in the All-Council from the time I was a young fry. Every lie. Even when their loyal acolytes took my thumbs, I believed their lies. I have always been so gullible. I believe anything, even the lies I tell myself."

"I wish I could believe the lies I tell myself. I'd already have my powers." She flexed her all-too-human fingers. The film wavered at the edge of her chest. "But I like that about you."

"You like how I am stupid?" He tried to smile but faltered.

His pain broke her heart. It would always hurt to trust the wrong people.

And they were the same. She felt so out of control, and so did he. Her body betrayed her, and he felt like his kind heart betrayed him.

He turned partially away to scrape at the rock, uncovering more vine beneath the stone, doing more of what he could do regardless of his feelings. Just plain carrying on.

That was all they could do.

Wasn't it?

His muscles flexed, lithe and gorgeous. His determination was so sexy. The orange tattoos swirled over his rippling skin just like when he curved over her body and thrust his hard cock into her welcoming sex.

Attraction to Gailen welled in her, suddenly intense. Like a crush she'd never allowed herself to feel, or an obsession. She needed him, and she would never get enough of him.

Danger danced at the edge of her desire.

She could get whatever she wanted just by wanting it. It was okay to want anything.

It was okay to want him.

He looked up, surprised.

She hadn't vibrated any words, but clearly, she'd signaled some. His cock grew erect in readiness. He tilted his head, and an intrigued smile crossed his face. "Starr, you are shining."

You can have anything just by wanting it.

She pushed off the ground and floated toward him. Wicked want curled in her belly, and her core filled with need for him. "Oh, you noticed?"

"It echoes in my chest." He lowered his trident and opened his arms.

She curled a hand around his rigid cock. "Your chest isn't the only place you feel it."

His lips curved against hers as he kissed her.

Their mouths fit together perfectly.

She was allowed to have this. She was allowed to have him.

His forearms flexed, cupping her curves, slaking her thirst while feeding her throbbing hunger.

She traced the gorgeous musculature up his biceps, across his shoulders, and down his trim waist to his hard thighs. He contained such strength within him, not just of body, but also of spirit. And anyone who'd gone through what he had would get battered around and lose their hope. The fact that he continued to smile despite his past was its own strength.

She nuzzled his ear. "You're not stupid for trusting the wrong person. It's part of the kindness that makes you you. And I love that. I love you."

His irises glimmered, and he crushed her to his chest. His emotion seemed to press against her on the inside, beneath her skin, but it wasn't unwelcome.

He kissed her just as desperately and furiously as she kissed him.

Because she could. She was allowed. She was no longer human, and she was allowed to feel.

She wanted to feel.

Starr filled her hands and her arms and her skin with the sense of him. Beneath the water, enveloped in their private hollow, they found each other.

She opened her heart and her body. Entangling his legs with hers, she urged him to take her, and he buried his full cock deep into her channel. Pleasure coiled like a spring, and he turned it, increasing the tension with every rocking thrust. Gailen was her warrior, the other half of her soul, and she was his. And together, they would always be strong.

No matter what.

The orgasm shocked and delighted her as it shuddered

through her veins. Her nerves tingled like fairy dust. Energy cracked through her. She wanted to run a marathon, scale a mountain, raft down the Nile. Bring on the crocodiles. She'd outrun them if she couldn't outthink them.

They floated next to the strange vine.

Gailen buried his face in the curve of her neck and shuddered. United like this, it felt like nothing could tear them apart.

And she felt whole. Settled. Capable of more than before.

Yes, this was a new state of being. As a mer, she didn't need a filter to keep her safe from the world. She could come out of her transparent shell and just be herself.

He pulled back and kissed her gently, softly, devoting himself to her now and forever.

In the middle of the darkness, her one bright spot was him.

Well, him and the glimmering starlight reflected in the stone ring circling the plant.

Starr reached over Gailen's shoulder to touch the stone. "Hey—"

"Well, well, well." A new vibration sounded behind them, and they scrambled apart. A warrior with crazy eyes stared down. "Kadir knows how to throw a party, eh, Gailen?"

Gailen whirled her behind him and scooped up his trident in one motion. He leveled the triple blade on the new warrior. "Roa."

TWENTY-FIVE

Starr's heart pounded.

How awkward.

"Why did you come here?" Gailen demanded of the strange warrior with peach-colored tattoos. "Did you really believe King Kadir would forgive you?"

"Forgive me? Stupid warrior, I was invited." He gestured at the area where she and Gailen had just embraced. "Why are you shirking your duty burrowing in these ruins?"

"Excavating the ruins is our duty," he snarled.

Roa lifted one brow. "Sure. Now, of all times?"

"What do you mean?"

"I mean there's an army advancing on you." He pointed behind them. "About to overtake this valley."

Gailen whirled, and Starr did too.

One lone warrior swam toward them as hard as his fins could kick.

No, wait.

Behind him, a wall of enemy warriors advanced.

The warriors who had hovered over Atlantis all this time hadn't risen or dispersed.

They'd swum around to encircle Atlantis.

They weren't murdering the brides on the surface.

They'd drawn most the warriors out of Atlantis and converged upon the city to rip the Life Tree out by its roots.

Her stomach dropped.

Gailen blanched. "How did you... Did you lead them here?"

"I barely avoided being swept up in their net."

Gailen grabbed Starr and took off.

Roa laughed behind them with a harsh vibration. "You always make me feel welcome."

"We have to warn everyone on the surface," Starr told Gailen.

"You must use your queen powers to drive the army off," he vibrated urgently.

But she hadn't developed her powers yet.

"They are within you, Starr. Can you not feel your soul reaching for the Life Tree? Pressing out?"

But she... If she couldn't...

There were so many warriors. Like a cloud of locusts gathering on the horizon. A doom cloud.

Atlantis warriors kicked from the city. "Warrior Gailen! Queen Starr! Please channel the Life Tree powers and save Atlantis!"

"You are a simple warrior, and she is a queen," Roa rumbled with some strange amusement that made Gailen stiffen in her arms. "How nice."

Gailen swam abreast of the other warriors. "How many queens remain in the city?"

"Just Queen Starr."

Her heart lurched.

Gailen also did a double take on the warrior. "Just Starr? What happened?"

"When the All-Council warriors retreated, King Kadir asked for volunteers to rise and protect the brides. Everyone asked to go."

"Everyone!"

"He assumed that Queen Elyssa would remain with Queen Starr. But Lieutenant Diras has just learned that Queen Elyssa ascended, and we need three queens to effectively defend the Life Tree, so he sent Queen Lucy after Queen Elyssa."

But that was so much worse.

"You need three functional queens," Starr whispered when she really wanted to scream.

"At least we have you." The warrior beamed at her.

She was going to throw up.

"It is too bad we sent Queen Lucy, because the submersible has begun speaking. 'Hang up and dial again.' If we did not need you to protect the Life Tree, you could communicate with the surface."

That was it!

Starr squeezed Gailen. "I'll call for help."

The warrior faltered. "Is there time?"

They all looked back at the welling army surging toward their city. It was crossing the ruin now.

Gailen took her hands. One thumb brushed her knuckles. "You are a queen. Believe in your powers."

"I can do this. Please."

He veered toward the submersible. "You might become trapped."

"I'll close the door."

The warrior caught up to them. "If you do not escape in time, the city and the Life Tree will be unprotected."

They were unprotected right now. She pleaded with Gailen, "This is what I can do."

"She will defend the city her way," Gailen assured the anxious warrior. "Go. I will catch up."

The warrior turned and kicked hard for the city.

Roa floated a little ways away, idly kicking like he didn't have a care in the world. What a strange warrior.

"I do not want to part." Gailen glanced at Roa, and it was equally obvious he didn't want to leave the stranger alone during this assault.

"Go," Starr insisted. "If I feel my powers come on, I'll swim out and save the day."

"I must go to the Life Tree. We are connected no matter what. Believe, Starr. You are strong."

"Okay. I'll see you." She grabbed the submersible portal and turned to wave.

Gailen drew her into a sweet, hot kiss.

She could have the life she wanted.

But not yet.

She wouldn't allow Atlantis to get wiped out the way she'd allowed the platform to get destroyed. And since she couldn't trust herself, she had to call for help.

He released her, gazed at her one last time as though memorizing her face, and then glanced over at the army.

They were closer now.

She didn't have much time.

Gailen turned and kicked hard for the city. Roa drifted after him.

They needed reinforcements fast.

It was all up to Starr now.

GAILEN SWAM hard after the patrol.

He chanced one last glance over his shoulder.

The army welled like a deadly tsunami.

How could he leave his bride behind? Was he crazy? How could he leave his queen?

Starr entered the submersible, reached back, and pulled the heavy metal door closed. It sealed with a reassuring clank. No warrior could get inside. She would be safe.

His heart thudded. She would only be safe with Gailen! This was wrong. Parting was a mistake. She did not need to call the surface. She had the power within her. He could feel it. Why couldn't she?

If he were a smarter, worthier warrior, he would have been able to draw out her power already...

He swam hard for the city. The army boiled behind him with increasing force, and their war shouts filled the water with dangerous vibrations.

Lieutenant Diras floated with a core of warriors in a too-thin line of defense before the outermost castles of Atlantis. "Where is Queen Starr?"

"In the submersible." Gailen stopped beside him. "She is contacting the surface."

Deep lines on his forehead underscored the lieutenant's worries. He gestured with his trident at Roa kicking lazily up to meet them. "And who is that? A guest?"

"A king," Roa called.

"He betrayed Atlantis and tried to kill King Kadir," Gailen objected.

"Technicalities." Roa smiled, and his eyes opened a little too wide. "I am invited."

The lieutenant's brows lowered. "We have no queens. The patrol and I will make our last stand here. Go to the

Life Tree. If we are defeated, the fate of Atlantis rests in your hands."

Gailen's belly churned. "I understand."

"And as for this male…"

"What about me?" Roa puffed out his chest, aggrieved. "Where is my welcome?"

Lieutenant Diras's vibrations lowered. "Is he truly a king?"

Gailen gritted his teeth. "He is."

"Take him with you. Queen Elyssa and Queen Lucy must return soon. I do not like the look in his eyes."

Great.

Gailen gripped his trident and swam for the Life Tree.

Roa scrambled after him. "You forgot your guest. Are you not concerned about me being left behind?"

"I do not mind if you are crushed by the All-Council army, assuming you are not the one who led them here."

"Not this time." Roa stretched as he swam. "Look down. Any half-competent scout could breach this defense. Once, Atlantis fought as warriors. Now you are lazy and shove all defense onto the queens."

Gailen barely listened.

The castles bobbed, empty and vulnerable. A few house guardians peered out the entrances, drawn by the ominous noise. The coming army sounded like a roaring wave. Unstoppable, furious, destructive.

He reached the fragile young Life Tree.

Its pure white light calmed him.

But its tinkling holiness could not silence the growing roar.

"No security at all." Roa tsked. "You know, if it had been like this when I attacked, your Life Tree would have been ripped out of the ground. Do you hear that?" He jerked his chin at the army. "You might as well pull the outer castles down now. It will save you the trouble of failing to defend them."

Irritation crackled under Gailen's skin. It mixed unevenly with despair.

Roa was right.

These castles that he had put so much effort into growing, tending, and decorating could not be saved. He had tried so hard to make this a good, welcoming city for warriors and their brides, and all that work was in vain.

If Lieutenant Diras had been clear-sighted, he would have realized it already.

They *had* relied too much on queens and forgotten how to defend a city as warriors.

The city was empty. When the All-Council army arrived, they would flatten the meager patrol, who should have forsaken the castles and come with Gailen to make the final stand together.

He would go back and remind Lieutenant Diras, but the army was too close.

And Roa strolled far too near to the Life Tree. "Look at that scar. Hard to believe this skinny little trunk could survive such a beheading. Hard to believe it has survived with such inattentive warriors tending it."

"That scar is your fault," Gailen growled. "You did that. Why are you even here?"

Roa laughed. The delight in his face made him look unhinged.

No one would mistake him for Zoan now.

"To see old friends, of course." He grinned terribly. "Do you not remember fighting beside me to free Kadir from prison? Of course, when I was captured and you all left me behind, Kadir did not repay the favor."

"We did not know you had survived."

"And you did not bother to look either."

"When the All-Council released you, you could have betrayed them. Not us."

"I was entirely out of my head by the time the All-Council finally released me, Gailen. They promised the torture would stop if only I would kill the warrior responsible for my imprisonment. And so I came to kill the warrior responsible."

"*You* are responsible," Gailen snapped. "King Kadir did not ask you to storm the prison. And if we had known, Zoan would have done anything to free you."

"Yes, my twin seed." Roa rolled his eyes. "Do you know Zoan never wanted to leave Siyokoy? But because I wanted a more glorious future for our race, he tagged along."

"And now he has his own queen."

"Does he?" Roa looked irritated. "And after he swore to die without ever being a father in penance for failing his own blood. His promises do not last."

"It is not his fault. It is the soul mate bond."

"The twin seed bond is at least as strong."

"If it was, then you would know how bad he felt and how much regret he still has."

"And yet, that did not help me during the long *year* I was tortured." Roa's eyes opened a little too wide again and he slashed his trident in Gailen's face. "His regret did not save me one single instant of agony. I experienced it all."

Gailen floated back to a safer distance. He did not want to start a pointless altercation with this unstable male when the real fight was about to begin. "What do you want Zoan to do? He cannot reverse the ocean of time. None of us can."

"And that answer gives no satisfaction either." Roa

stared at the trunk he had sliced in half. His crazy eyes glinted. "I am sure you carry the same thoughts about the warriors who destroyed your thumbs."

Gailen's hand tightened on his trident. One thumb was almost able to curve around the long rod. "That is different."

"Oh, yes. It *is* different. Your injury was a momentary pain that led to a long disability. My torture was a vast agony from which my visible scars may have healed, but perhaps my inner scars never will."

Gailen did not want to empathize with this dangerous warrior who had stolen into Atlantis and betrayed them.

But a part of him could not help but sympathize with the broken mer.

And his sympathy was the reason he so easily made friends with warriors who would later betray him.

He hardened again. "Why *are* you here?"

"Because Kadir invited all the kings." The warrior smiled crazily and opened his arms. "And you are looking at the king of Laot. Meet my queen, Jasleen." He pointed below the dais.

A warrior—no, a female swam alone beneath the city. Her dim soul was almost invisible as she ascended the Life Tree stalk, passed the dais, and flew above the castles.

Truly, her soul was impossibly weak. She must be even less able to access her powers than Starr.

Her face was viciously scarred, and her eyes were...they were not closed. No, they were gone.

"She is injured," Gailen murmured, because it was not often he saw anyone with such deep weapon marks.

"I blinded her to keep her with me."

"What?" Gailen rotated his trident on Roa. "How could you? Your soul mate?"

The crazed king laughed. "You thought I was serious? Always so credible, Gailen. I could tell you anything."

His anger flared. "I should know better than to listen to you."

"My queen understands me." Roa tucked his trident against an elbow and opened his arms.

His queen veered away from him and soared into the empty area before the king's castle.

Roa lowered his arms. His smile fled.

"She denies you," Gailen noted, not sure whether he should feel sorry for Roa or gloat.

"No." Roa scanned the ocean. "She protects me."

"She rejects your arms."

"I do not contain her. Like me, she knows what it is to be imprisoned and tortured. We are both more comfortable handling dangers on our own."

"How can I believe you?"

"Why do I care?" Roa popped his trident from the slack position at his elbow into his hands. "Her eyes may be gone, but her sense of danger is more finely tuned than mine. Invaders have breached your city."

Gailen's heart kicked as he rotated in the water, his trident out. "The patrol has not sounded an alarm."

"Then these invaders have snuck past them." Roa studied the movement of his queen. He looked down the stalk again. "There."

A group gathered beneath the Life Tree with a long, toothed saw. They held it over the stalk.

Gailen kicked, trident out, with a war scream.

The enemy warriors looked up, startled, and then scattered.

Gailen shifted to human feet, kicked off the stem, and chased the one warrior who carried the massive saw in both hands. He was overburdened and underdefended. Gailen brought his trident down to split his chest open.

The enemy warrior dropped the saw and kicked back, avoiding Gailen's slash by the smallest margin.

The saw dropped to the coral floor and disappeared into the forest.

Gailen chased the warrior.

His enemy pulled out daggers the length of his fore-arms and crossed them, stopping Gailen's slash, then pushed Gailen's trident away. They battled, fierce. The other warriors gathered around him in a four-to-one ambush.

He broke free and kicked for the Life Tree dais. He could not fight effectively with other warriors behind him.

The enemy descended and searched for the saw, which had dropped somewhere into the thick forest.

Roa watched from the dais with a curved smile.

Gailen popped over the lip of the dais. Trident in hand, he struggled to gather his strength. "Go, Roa. Five against two is too much."

The crazed warrior eyed him. "I thought you did not care if I was crushed?"

"You have suffered enough for Atlantis. This is not your fight."

"How funny." Roa twirled his trident like a trainee showing off. "I had intended to do just that while your cries for my help echoed pointlessly again my hardened heart. But since you had to go and be noble, I no longer feel like giving you the satisfaction."

The enemy warriors gave up searching for the saw. They rose and fanned out in the center of the city.

"We will make this easy," one of them sneered. "Put down your tridents and accept your deaths. That way, you do not have to watch as we cut down your Life Tree over your dying bodies."

Roa laughed heartily, giving them pause. "I couldn't care less about this warrior's Life Tree. See that scar? I helped make that."

The warrior's sneer flattened into confusion.

"But now I am a king." Roa rotated his trident in a deft display. "I cannot have you injuring this tree before King Kadir looks into my face and recognizes me. We were both imprisoned and tortured by the All-Council. I am his equal now."

The enemy warrior shrugged. "Then you will die like him."

Gailen tensed for the coming charge.

Please let Starr have contacted the surface.

Or better yet, discovered her power.

He needed her.

This assault was only the beginning.

ailen bunched his muscles. There were too many enemies for him to take them one by one. He must blitz and hope to land blows in the confusion—

Roa's trident flashed before his eyes.

Gailen aborted his charge and flailed back, startled. "What?"

Roa laughed again. "So many warriors in this city lack defenses. This single crippled male thinks to defeat you all. How foolish."

"Two against five are no better," the enemy sneered at Roa.

"Ooh, yes, look at you, so clever, sneaking past the patrol with five skilled warriors, and not a single one thinks to guard against what might be sneaking up behind."

The enemy warriors whirled.

Roa's queen, Jasleen, floated like a ghost behind them.

They snarled in surprise and raised their tridents.

Oh, no! Gailen had to rescue—

Wham.

Roa slammed the flat of his trident into Gailen's chest, flinging him on his back onto the dais.

Queen Jasleen's faint soul flashed like a bomb. Her shield erupted outward, and the Life Tree shrieked, amplifying her damaged power.

Where most queen shields were soft and rounded like a bubble, Queen Jasleen's was hard and spiked as a pufferfish. The deadly spines pierced the space where Gailen had floated moments before. They impaled the warriors, who jolted and went slack. She darted forward, then back, as though seeking any that might have escaped. Blood dripped off the spines and landed on Gailen's face and chest.

Roa held him in place. "You must wait. Like a pufferfish, she will retreat into herself."

Lieutenant Diras and the rest of the patrol rounded the last castle with shouts. "A breach! Look! Stop the monster!"

Queen Jasleen rotated to face them.

"Stop," Roa shouted to them. "Stay back!"

They fanned out to fight her.

"Wait!" Gailen pushed off Roa's trident and rolled onto his knees. "Listen to him. She is his queen."

"A queen?" The lieutenant shook his head. "That is no queen."

"She is not like your queens." Roa rose cautiously. "She is wild, not tamed."

"She is a monster," one of the patrolling warriors cried with a quaver.

"Hold," Gailen vibrated at him sharply. "She defended the Life Tree. She deserves our gratitude, not fear."

Lieutenant Diras motioned for the patrol to pull back and lower their tridents. They obeyed. Lieutenant Diras stiffened as the blind queen advanced on him, the impaled

All-Council warriors limp and moaning. The deadly spines drew too close.

"Call her off," Gailen ordered Roa.

The warrior tossed him an amused, skeptical look, but kicked toward his queen. "Jasleen."

She whirled to face him, her spines flashing, sharp.

He slowed and eased between the bodies, vibrating calm words.

Her spines shrank. The impaled warriors slid off and dropped to the ocean floor. She popped the spines out again, twitching a few last times in warning. A spine pierced Roa's forearm.

He winced and gritted his teeth. "It is me. Are you satisfied?"

She abruptly dropped her shield and drifted as though lost.

He pulled her into his arms with such tenderness that he seemed like a different warrior. Roa proved it was possible to lose all the pieces that had once made him a warrior, and yet he could still give comfort to his soul mate. It was inspirational and deeply moving.

And just the beginning of their fight. "Lieutenant Diras, we must cede the castles. This patrol snuck in with a saw to cut down the Life Tree. I knocked it down, but any others could pick it up. We must all make our final stand here."

"I fear you are right." The lieutenant skirted the couple, and his patrol fanned protectively around the Life Tree. "What a loss."

"It is not the first time. When the All-Council army unleashed megalodons on us, they destroyed all our castles but one."

New respect reflected in the lieutenant's eyes. "I think I

am experienced in war, but you have already lived through a battle that they would write about in the archives."

"I fear we are about to live through another one."

"If we live, I will have no fears. How did you convince this stranger to defend our Life Tree?"

"I told him to go and seek safety elsewhere. He needs King Kadir alive to be recognized, so..."

"And just think, now Kadir must act grateful and thank me for saving his life." Roa grinned with that crazy gleam in his eyes again. His damaged, unpredictable queen wilted in his arms, her long black hair trailing like a ribbon, the scars crossing her face making her expression impossible to read. "This is a better outcome than I could have imagined. And it was all thanks to your insufferable nobility." He swam above the city center, laughing hysterically.

The patrol watched him.

The lieutenant eyed Gailen from the side. "And you convinced him to fight. Truly, you could make friends with a hungry bull shark."

A strange bass note filled the city.

They all squinted into the distance. The army was so vast, it was visible even above the bobbing castles.

The lieutenant's expression flattened in shock. "What is that?"

A massive shadow loomed. Its bulk stretched toward the surface. Terrible tentacles dragged over the landscape as it crept toward them.

But it did not seem to be under its own control.

Around it, masses of enemy warriors positioned red boulders. Each stone was so huge, it required a full unit to carry and another unit to maneuver. By tilting the stones one way and then the other, they drove the tentacled mass toward Atlantis.

Then it tilted upright.

Its pointed head veered for the surface like the peak of an undersea mountain. Massive squid eyes centered on the city. Its triple beak clacked.

The patrol gathered around the Life Tree.

Gailen had thought he would never see the All-Council wield an animal more destructive than the megalodons. Those legendary beasts had broken free and turned on their army, attacking both Atlantis and the All-Council equally. The All-Council had learned not to use animals that couldn't be controlled. They had gone to Lusca, mined the red stones, and captured a beast they could control.

So long as the red stones remained intact, this beast was unstoppable.

It crossed the open plane and bore down on the city. Its tentacles tossed boulders as though they were pebbles. A mass the size of a small castle flew past the Life Tree, rocking them in its current, and dropped to the seafloor below. It smashed the megalodon bones to white powder.

"That," Gailen vibrated with horror, "is the kraken."

———

STARR ALMOST HAD this communications terminal figured out.

Gailen had been so reluctant to let her go, but what choice did she have? She couldn't gain her powers just by willing them to appear, could she?

She was a special kind of broken. Broken women didn't get powers. They were for healthy, generous, friendly women with whole souls.

Starr balanced one of the two stools before the damp control panel. There were way more gauges than she knew what to do with, but the call button had blinked regularly until she'd pushed it.

Beep beep beep...beep beep beep...

On a rack beneath the controls, she'd found a soggy instruction booklet. She'd carefully peeled the pages apart and squinted in the dim red lightbulb. *When power is interrupted, you must reboot the system. To reboot, remove the power supply cable from the terminal, wait two minutes, and reconnect it.*

Ah, the holy grail of IT solutions. Turn it off and on again.

She'd found the power supply cable neatly labeled and did as instructed. How long were two minutes? She counted the seconds.

Strange thumps sounded outside the submersible.

Her heart spiked. "—fifty-nine, two minutes." She plugged in the power.

Nothing happened.

No, wait. Lights blinked on, first in one area, then another.

She rested her palms on the wet counter. This submersible was so stuffy. Her nose clogged and the air felt too heavy to breathe.

Normally, she would retreat into herself to endure physical discomforts, but she couldn't do that now. All her senses felt more acute.

Something bounced off the outside of the submersible, causing a metallic echo.

Had the army arrived? Were they trying to break in?

What if they did break in? Or what if they broke off the handle and she got stuck in here and Gailen could never get her out?

Her heart spiked higher and higher.

She tried to channel something. Anything. But she was in the air, not the water, so she couldn't channel the soothing Life Tree.

Yes, come on, she could envision it. She was nervous and alone, but this submersible was solid iron. She would be fine. And after she summoned help, real help, she could rejoin Gailen.

The call button blinked.

She pressed it.

"...Hello?" An older man's voice crackled on the line. "...one there?"

She jolted in her seat. All her nerve endings were flayed raw. "This is Starr in Atlantis."

"...arr? This is Mr. Shaw, Lucy Shaw's father. I've been trying to reach you for hours. Is Lucy there?"

"No, she's gone to the surface."

"...ood."

"No, it's not good! We need her to come back right now. It's a trap. The All-Council tricked us into sending everyone to the surface to protect the brides, and they doubled back around to invade the city. I'm here on my own, and I can't summon any powers. We need everyone to come back right now."

"...arr? This is Dannika."

Her shoulders lowered. "Hi, Dannika. You arrived, huh?"

"...did. What's this about a trap?"

"The All-Council made us believe that they were positioning warriors at the surface to attack you. But we were fooled. They're all here, and anyway, they'd never really murder their sacred brides."

"...ctually, our boats are surrounded. General Giru

warned us not to enter the water. He looks so sick at heart, I honestly believe him."

Her throat tightened. The air was so stuffy. "It wasn't a trick?"

"...haps...I once told you, Starr, that we would overcome any obstacle. But we've been stuck on these boats for hours obeying the orders of madmen. Now Atlantis is under attack? I see that I need to revisit my resolve."

But if there *were* warriors on the surface poised to murder them, they would be diving into great danger. "No, Dannika, wait!"

The submersible jolted, throwing Starr off the stool.

The power cut out. Everything went dark, even the red light overhead.

Her eyes adjusted, and she could see.

Mermaid powers let her see in the dark.

Something was terribly wrong.

And she'd possibly made it worse.

The submersible shook. Water seeped in from hidden cracks behind the machines, soaking the terminal. The power supply made a loud buzz and popped.

That wouldn't be turning on again.

The submersible tilted.

Starr slid under the now-dead terminal. More water cascaded down on her, lifting her off the ground.

And then she entered a slow free-fall, tumbling over and over in the splashing water, and landed with an abrupt stillness on the ceiling of the submersible. The water sloshed, filling up the last of the interior as the air finished escaping.

She sucked in water.

Shift.

The transition was easier than going the other way. Less

puking. She kicked to the portal exit, which was now above her, and rotated the metal submarine handle. It turned, unlatching, and she pushed the door.

It didn't open.

She wedged her toes against the side wall and pushed.

It was like pushing into a rock.

Was she buried?

Her heart rate spiked faster and faster. Her hands trembled. The submersible walls closed in on her. She tried not to scream.

This was normal. This was her isolation chamber. *Don't think about it. It doesn't matter.*

Her nerves shrieked that it did matter. It mattered a lot.

She released the door and hugged her knees to her chest. *Calm down.*

But her body rotated in the water.

Isolation, weightlessness, no sensation.

The world fell away from her. She was unmoored. Alone.

She couldn't breathe. She couldn't breathe. She couldn't breathe.

Gailen would come.

They were linked. He would hear her silent panic and come.

But he didn't come.

He'd wanted her to go with him. She could feel him now. His panic and terror only amplified hers.

We are linked.

Channel the Life Tree.

Help me, Starr.

But she couldn't.

She was trapped.

If she'd gone with him, things would be different.

The Life Tree shrieked, and she heard its pain through the iron. Starr moaned.

Gailen...

Pain pounded her.

It had been so easy for him to leave her behind. She was the kind of person who was easy to abandon.

Just like in the hospital.

Take these thoughts away. Don't think about it. It doesn't matter.

Please!

But the thoughts wouldn't go away. She couldn't even force herself to pass out and stop thinking.

These thoughts used to drive her crazy. She'd had them all the time when she'd known that no one was coming. When her birthdays, Valentine's Day, Christmas passed in the dark, and she could see the signs of other families visiting their sick children, and she got nothing because it was too much work for anyone to visit her. She'd begged for those hurt feelings to go away, and one day, the shield had appeared and granted her wish.

Now it was gone.

Starr knotted her fingers in her hair. She'd nearly made herself bald, and the nurse had chided her for ruining her looks. The tug of pain did nothing.

Thoughts swirled, attacking over and over, ripping pieces of her mind away.

She reached for the shield, but it wouldn't come.

You have to thank the shield, her therapist had said. *Thank it and say it's no longer necessary.*

But now it was necessary. She chanted her thanks and begged it to return over and over, but nothing worked. It never came back.

She had wished it away, and now it was gone forever.

TWENTY-SEVEN

The kraken tore the concrete blocks from the seafloor. The cable snapped with an audible twang, and the submersible fell. It disappeared into the debris storm engulfing the plane.

"Starr!" Gailen screamed and kicked forward.

Lieutenant Diras caught him. "You cannot help her now."

He fought the lieutenant.

"You cannot help her! She will survive this, Gailen. She is a queen."

His fighting slowed. She *was* a queen, but she hadn't found her full powers yet.

They should never have separated.

He'd convinced himself she would be safe. He needed to get to her, to save her.

"Think, Gailen. Think!" Lieutenant Diras shook his shoulders. "You cannot get to her through this storm. You must stop the kraken."

"Only a queen can stop the kraken," he vibrated urgently. Starr needed him. He must go, even though it would be suicide. "Only she can make the tone that breaks the red stones."

"Breaks the...of course." Lieutenant Diras called out to Roa. "Your queen must make the tone."

Roa, still hugging his queen, did not take his eyes off the looming kraken "What tone?"

"The tone. All the queens know it. It is low like the sound of a squid." Lieutenant Diras made the low *ommmm* that Queen Dannika had taught them after her first successful encounter with the kraken. "It soothes the animal and shatters the mirror stones. Make your queen emit it."

Roa finally tore his gaze to the lieutenant. "I do not *make* my queen do anything. She has one defensive power and it is the pufferfish shield."

"The kraken will not even prick a tentacle on her pufferfish. King Kadir will die if his Life Tree fails. Your only chance to get recognition is to do the tone. Make her understand."

Roa flattened his lips, but he turned to his bride and vibrated softly. With her, he was so patient. She struggled once, twice in his arms. He insisted, holding her with his elbows the way he'd carry a broken trident, and despite the approaching storm, he maintained an unnatural calm. She calmed too.

"I need you to say *ommmm*," he vibrated in a whisper. "Do you understand? *Ommmm*. Do it with me. *Ommmm*."

She made a couple of abortive attempts, and then finally, her chest vibrated. "*Om. Om.*"

"That is right. Longer now. *Ommmm*."

"*Omm.*"

"Yes. *Ommmm*."

She made the tone for longer and longer.

The Life Tree caught her focus and amplified her

sound, carrying the tone across the city to the dust storm. Several cracks appeared across the faces of the nearest red stones.

The kraken slowed.

It was working!

"*Ommmm.*" Roa glued his gaze to the kraken. "*Ommmm.*"

His queen, too attuned to his energies, lost control. Roa immediately focused on her, but it was already too late. Her low tone escalated to a soul-shattering shriek.

Gailen's bones ached, and the other warriors moaned and shuddered. Behind him, all the mating gemstones fell off the Life Tree. Hairline cracks appeared around the knot in the bark.

The damaged red stones shattered.

Her terrible shriek died away.

"Ah." The warriors en masse relaxed.

Beyond the city, the kraken stopped as though the All-Council army was reassessing the danger. A few tentacles went wild, seemingly under their own control again, and they smashed into the warriors.

The units carrying the red stones quickly changed formations and spread out.

The wild tentacles went limp and drifted on the current, then dug into the ground at the edge of the city. The outermost ring of castles bobbed and jostled together.

"Again," Lieutenant Diras ordered Roa.

He wrinkled his nose. "*Ommmm.*"

His queen had barely controlled the tone for an instant before escalating to a soul-crushing shriek.

It echoed inside Gailen's chest cavity and tore at his brain.

The gemstones around his feet shattered with horrifying pops, and the cracks in the trunk deepened, peeling back from the inner wood, exposing it to poisonous seawater.

Her shriek again died away, and the Atlantis warriors clutching their heads relaxed.

Gailen grabbed the adamantium knife and cut the split bark, cauterizing the Life Tree's wounds and excising the poison. He felt flayed to the muscle beneath his skin.

If Starr were here, she could make this tone. She could help Queen Jasleen.

Starr...

But all he sensed from her was pain and panic.

Another red stone shattered.

The kraken turned away from the city. A full third of it broke free, and those tentacles grabbed enemy warriors and mashed them into its one functioning beak. War cries turned to screams. It was horrifying, and the army surged away from that side of the kraken.

But that still left two-thirds of the monster focused on the city. The units controlling the red stones forced two-thirds of the kraken forward. Those tentacles wrapped around the outer castles and tore them from the ground. Pelan's castle, Iyen's castle. Endi's castle. The castle of Lieutenant Diras. Their stalks severed.

Pain lanced Gailen's chest.

The Life Tree shrieked.

"Again!" Lieutenant Diras roared.

"Your Life Tree cannot survive another cry," Roa shouted back.

"We cannot survive without it!"

The All-Council must have realized the same thing. They forced the kraken deeper into the city. It was a race now to see who could withstand the most destruction and whether the kraken would reach the Life Tree before they could break the last mirror stone.

But Roa was right that the Life Tree could not endure another uncontrolled shriek.

And Lieutenant Diras was right that they could not survive without it.

They were both right.

Gailen hugged the trunk. "Protect the Life Tree. Shore it up."

The patrol obeyed him instantly.

Lieutenant Diras hugged the bark beside him. "We are not queens."

"I know, but our blood contains its sap. We may not be strong, but we must try."

The innermost ring of castles tore away, revealing the full mud storm and the terrible clacking maws of the kraken.

Queen Jasleen puffed out her spines, forcing Roa away from her as she stabbed him through the wrist, chest, and sides, and she blindly screamed way too high.

The Life Tree shuddered. The bark fractured beneath Gailen's fingers.

He dug in and rested his forehead against the tree he had tended for years, trying to dig within him for what it needed. If he could only be strong enough. If he could only *be* enough.

The shriek needled his spine as the kraken's tentacles curled around the Life Tree and the dais shook uncontrollably.

And then another tone overlayed the shriek. "*Ommmm.*"

The last red stones cracked and disintegrated.

The dais stopped shaking.

A bright warm light glowed from beneath Gailen's fingers. The Life Tree responded to the proper tone and amplified it, cauterizing its wounds as the queen power channeled through it.

He pulled back and turned.

The All-Council warriors surged away from the city, fleeing from the stilled kraken.

A group of queens descended on the city, their bright shield glowing with soothing peacefulness across the war-torn land. One familiar face led the way with her prince in her arms.

"Queen Elyssa," Gailen murmured.

Lieutenant Diras turned and fell to his knees on the dais. "Praise the Life Tree."

The kraken's round squid eyes focused on the group of queens.

Queen Elyssa floated before it. "I'm sorry. How horrible for you to go through this. We'll find the source of that red stone and destroy it."

The kraken remained motionless.

"You're welcome to surface with us and join our reunion," Queen Elyssa continued.

"Ooh!" Queen Hazel waved. "It's going to be great. We'll have karaoke."

The kraken twitched.

"Remember when I did karaoke for you? This time, we'll have real music."

The kraken slowly backed away. Muck and debris boiled up as though she were trying to hide from Queen Hazel's notice.

"You don't remember?" Queen Hazel asked.

Queen Elyssa covered her smile. "I think she remembers, Hazel."

"Oh. You're not sticking around? The party won't be the same without you."

The kraken whirled and flounced away from the city.

"I'd call that a no." Queen Elyssa laughed, and the other queens echoed her, the relief clear in their vibrations. "I don't think karaoke is her thing."

"Aw. She doesn't know what she's missing."

Suddenly, the kraken jetted forward and attacked. A great red cloud filled the ocean. Tentacles erupted. She surged out of the cloud as though chasing things down, a whale destroying an outcropping of sea lice.

Everyone watched soberly.

"What's she attacking, Lieutenant Diras?" Queen Elyssa asked.

"The All-Council army camp." His vibration came out rough.

A mist filled the ocean, and then the kraken was gone.

Queen Hazel made a sound. "On second thought, maybe the party will be fine without an enraged cephalopod."

An off-tune warble sounded from the direction of the ruin, and Octopus Kong's form emerged from the settling silt.

"Don't worry," Queen Elyssa cried. "You're still invited!"

His great arms picked through debris and bodies, then he dug down and unearthed the submersible.

Gailen kicked off the dais. "Starr!"

Others followed—Lieutenant Diras, Queen Elyssa—as he dove to the cave guardian. They tore through the dirt to reach Starr.

Behind him, Queen Elyssa was giving Lieutenant Diras a report.

"We tried to reach the surface, but the All-Council had prepared for us. They'd bound their wrists and ankles to each other to form a living net, and had effectively trapped the slower family-filled group that had fallen behind when they were all surfacing with Kadir. I reached them but then couldn't free us. I couldn't make my shield any larger without dislocating joints or worse. The only reason we eventually got away is because Archivist Ulio remembered a successful reversing maneuver, and in concert, he and the other warriors severed some of their bindings."

"And King Kadir?" Lieutenant Diras asked.

"He must have passed through before the net formed. We never reached him or the dignitaries. I can sense that my husband is okay for the moment, but I don't think the situation is stable. I'll try again to surface as soon as we free Starr. I see I was right to leave Gailen."

"You were." Lieutenant Diras's vibrations grew rough again. "His quick thinking and decisive action saved the Life Tree many times."

Gailen unearthed the portal. The outer ring rattled and spun. Starr must be on the other side. His chest lifted. Finally, after all this horror, he would be reunited with his queen.

He forced the portal open.

Starr hugged her knees and squinted as though she didn't recognize him.

"Starr." He dove into the tiny space and wrapped her in his arms. "I have rescued you."

She didn't release her knees. Her soul dimmed. "No, you didn't."

He pulled back, shifted his fins to human toes, and rested on them. "I just did."

"You said I didn't need the shield anymore. You said you would always come. I called and I called."

"I came as fast as I could."

"Not fast enough." She hugged herself and drifted, alone, in the stale water. "Not nearly fast enough."

TWENTY-EIGHT

Starr hunched in radiating pain from her dim soul. She was even worse than when he'd met her on the boat.

But it was so unfair. He had wanted Starr with him. She had refused to come.

Gailen rested on his heels. "I am sorry you are sad."

"You said you would always come to me."

"I cannot change my past actions," he vibrated stiffly.

She rocked her head from side to side.

"It is done, Starr. I am...I am here now. If that is not enough, what else do you want me to do?"

"Go away," she whimpered. "Leave me alone."

Gailen reeled.

Starr shivered in agony, and he couldn't help her. Her agony bloomed in his chest, causing him to reflect her pain. She rejected him.

She rejected him.

Bitter unfairness overwhelmed him.

Outside, the warriors were telling Queen Elyssa of his great deeds. Starr was supposed to hear those same deeds and celebrate. He had saved the city at least twice. Him. Gailen.

She'd known the stakes. She should have fought at his side.

And how could he have come to her any faster? They had been blocked by the kraken. Starr was supposed to be reasonable.

But she did want him to go away. She pushed him, her soul wishing he were gone.

And that devastated him.

He kicked to the portal entrance and rested on the rim.

Queen Elyssa and others ranged around him on the battlefield, viscerally slamming the truth of the last battle home. Atlantis had barely survived. He had barely survived. Starr had not seen what he had. She'd been safe inside this metal submersible.

Gailen hardened inside, turning away from Starr's rejection, and focused on what was true. He had done the right thing. Not only the right thing, but the only possible thing. She would realize it and apologize to him soon.

Lieutenant Diras was finishing the report. "And all these were the actions of Queen Jasleen and King Roa, who Gailen brought to our side."

"Roa, huh?" Queen Elyssa squinted up at Gailen. "I'm sure Kadir will thank him sincerely."

"How can King Kadir forget the past?" Gailen demanded. "Roa stabbed him in the back."

"I know," Queen Elyssa said mildly. "I was there."

"Yes, he did a good thing today, but he should be glad you do not tear him to pieces."

"Tearing people to pieces isn't really my style." She tilted her head. "It may not be King Kadir's fault that the All-Council imprisoned Roa, but he takes responsibility for the warriors who are injured or killed because of his vision. Both the ones hurt following it…" She gazed sadly out on the battlefield. "And those who lose their lives because they are opposed."

"They should not have attacked Atlantis."

"I know, but Kadir's mindful. Two positions can be wrong, and at the same time, both positions can be right."

He had heard this idea many times, but at that moment, it finally drilled in.

He hadn't wanted to forgive Roa's past, but doing so had convinced Roa to join his side.

"Your answers do not satisfy," Roa had said. *"Are you not angry at the warriors who destroyed your thumbs?"*

When the Aiycaya warriors had destroyed his thumbs, they had cited honor, and when he'd later visited them after Aiycaya rebelled, they had looked away and muttered about not having any choice. That muttering had been wrong then. It was wrong now.

And he was doing the exact same thing to Starr.

Gailen descended into the destroyed submersible once more.

She hugged her knees and rested on her side like a sickening fish. Her soul had retreated deep inside. But not behind the protective layer of film. She felt everything in sharp relief now and transmitted it full force back to him in what must be an overwhelming loop.

And he'd just abandoned her to it. "Starr."

"I told you to go away," she vibrated in quiet defiance.

Hurt lanced him.

But wait. It was not only his hurt. No. They were soul mates, and they were still linked.

This acute sensation of pain and rejection he felt was not coming from within him.

It was coming from within her.

This gaping ache within him was *her* hurt.

And yet he had reacted to the sensation as though he were a child.

This uncontrollable emotion

He'd had to leave her alone, and she was hurting, still, from that necessity.

He needed to take responsibility for his actions. The good and the bad.

"I am sorry, Starr. I never wanted to leave you. You tore down the barrier to grow your queen powers and made yourself vulnerable, and I did not come."

She floated more upright. "You promised you would."

"I could not keep my promise. And because of that, you are hurting so much. Even now, I feel the fear and pain moving through you."

She released her knees and turned to him. "It was horrible. I could feel the Life Tree breaking. I was afraid you'd die and I'd never see you again. All because I couldn't get out to save you."

"That almost happened."

"Oh, Gailen." She threw her arms around him. "I was so scared."

"Me too." He held her close. Her feelings gushed into him so powerfully that his chest hitched and tears burned in his eyes. "Is this the strength of emotion your sticky barrier was holding back?"

She hiccupped. "It's terrible, isn't it? I was in here feeling sorry for myself and terrified for you, and on top of that, I started worrying that I was going to turn into a weepy emotional wreck. I still might." Her soul resonated with his and glowed brighter. "But actually, I'm feeling better. A little more like myself."

He felt better too. So much better. "I am sorry for how I greeted you."

"I'm sorry for how I greeted you!" She straightened and stretched. Her back popped. "Ugh. I know I have to feel the lows to enjoy the highs, but I hope I never feel that low ever again."

Him too.

He gently swam with her to the portal. "Prepare yourself."

"For what?" She swam out and gazed upon the devastation. "Oh. Wow."

It spread in all directions. Now that he was calm and could look at it, he shared her awe.

Half of Atlantis had been destroyed. They could see straight to the Life Tree.

Starr turned the other direction and pointed. "Look."

The ruin had been cleared of debris.

"My miracle," Queen Elyssa murmured, but her lips pulled down with regret. "I am thankful, but I wish I could have had it with less bloodshed."

"The warriors who died drove the kraken," Lieutenant Diras vibrated gravely. "They knew the risks."

"But they might have been only a few hours from reuniting with their wives. Their mothers. Brides who came to see them."

The deeper tragedy impacted them all. Queen Elyssa easily saw more sides than her own. That was why she was a great queen.

"They followed orders," the archivist vibrated heavily. His arms and legs were nicked with small wounds. "Perhaps it is already too late to stop the rest from making a terrible mistake."

"But you didn't see what I was talking about." Starr pointed again. "The tidal ring is glowing. Look."

The ring cast a light into the ocean like a blue beacon.

Gailen's chest lifted, filling with the same hope that shone in the souls of Queen Elyssa and the archivist.

Maybe it was not too late to raise the ruin, save King Kadir and the brides, and forge a new covenant.

Maybe it was not too late.

TWENTY-NINE

"You activated the stone." The archivist circled the glowing blue stone and traced the glimmering lights along a veiny path toward the heart stone. "Fascinating. How did you do it?"

Elyssa and the others who had journeyed here to examine the ruin gathered around Starr and Gailen for the answers.

So, it was a little awkward to just blurt right out. "Um... we did several things, so it's hard to say which one it was for sure..."

"You channeled the great energy of the mer," the archivist continued. "Your actions must be carefully examined. Share every detail. The smallest motion might have been the key that raised your resonance."

Right. "I told Gailen 'I love you' and fully committed myself to the mer."

"And?"

"That was mostly it."

"Mostly? We must know exactly what to do to energize the stone."

"Ah." She cleared her throat, even though she was underwater, so she didn't speak with her mouth. "Sure. But I think that was the important bit."

"Then share the rest."

"Well, uh..."

"We joined our bodies." Gailen pointed his trident at a nondescript patch of stone. "Right here."

Oh. God.

The warriors looked stunned. The women tittered.

Starr's ears burned.

The archivist's brows rose. "You did? In the midst of the excavations with the army gathered overhead, the kraken making its terrible way to Atlantis, the queens and I trapped in a net of warriors, and the enemy all around?"

"They were not around just then." Gailen appealed to Starr as if he sensed her wishing the kraken would return and swallow her. "Why are you embarrassed? We are husband and wife. The archivist must know everything to energize the heart stone."

Elyssa hid her smile. "Perhaps we will ask the brides to verbally pledge their love for their husbands and sons, just for a start."

Gailen looked unconvinced. "If you think that is enough..."

"Here, I'll test it right now." Roxanne grabbed her husband, Pelan. Their toddler scampered at their human feet. "Pelan, I just love you so much. You and Anro are my favorite men in the entire universe. I thought I'd never be a wife and mother, and now here you both are, and my life is so complete."

Pelan closed his eyes and leaned into his wife's hug.

The stone glowed.

Thank goodness.

"That is it." The archivist beamed, and amazingly, the stone glowed even brighter. "Ah, it is reacting to my emotion. And yours." He pointed at Elyssa hugging her little prince and the frowny Lieutenant Diras looking less frowny as he watched the couples snuggle their children. "It reacts to all the unifying emotions of the mer."

"And so how long until we energize it enough to raise it?" Elyssa looked up at the distant surface. "We have a lot of people waiting on a rescue."

The archivist laughed. "Just us? It would take a century. No, we must bring everyone down here to energize it."

"I was kind of hoping we could magically rise with the whole island and push the net of warriors out of the way." Elyssa rubbed her forehead. "Lieutenant Diras, we need to break through the All-Council barrier."

"You can use the patrol. They barely bloodied their tridents," he offered, and those warriors straightened.

"I want to say yes but my instincts are telling me it would be a mistake. I don't want any more violence."

Starr listened as Elyssa described the net made out of living warriors, and Lieutenant Diras recounted the strange powers of Queen Jasleen. According to her husband, she'd been hurt by human traffickers and thrown overboard. Roa had rescued her and then exacted vengeance against the criminals.

The news seemed surprising to Gailen as well, but he nudged Starr. "Your skill is solving puzzles. You have much experience opening closed areas such as archives."

And apparently, she'd been wrong to think that only a perfectly healthy woman could have powers.

Starr experimentally flexed her feet. She'd just given up her protective film, which was why everything was coming in raw and hot right now, and she felt two tissues away from a Lifetime movie. Her toes stretched...

And kept going.

Huh.

Her feet didn't feel any different, but the toes spread out beneath her, and the skin between them stretched tight. She paddled softly and boosted their speed in the water.

Neat.

Gailen flashed her a grin. "I knew you would get it swiftly."

Well, she didn't know if she'd call this swift...

"As soon as you trusted in yourself, I knew you would make your fins. And soon, your queen powers."

Her queen powers...

"I guess we can't surface." Elyssa folded her shaking hands and swallowed. "We'll stay here energizing the stones. Dannika and the other queens will protect the brides. Kadir will be fine."

Everyone listened soberly.

"You don't believe that," Starr said.

"I believe in my friends. If there was a way to get through the net without hurting anyone, I would do so in an instant. But..." She shook her head, and her shoulders slumped.

Gailen fidgeted beside Starr.

"I think there's a way though," Starr said.

"There's not. Archivist Ulio knows this attack." Elyssa nodded at the sober archivist. "I barely escaped."

Archivist Ulio clearly didn't know everything.

Starr flexed her new fins. The stone glowed, echoing her rush of power. "Show me."

Elyssa seemed surprised by her confidence, but she

turned over her authority to Lieutenant Diras, and, along with Archivist Ulio, the small group departed.

Gailen held Starr close as they rose. Their group was subdued. Elyssa carried her young son into battle, which seemed crazy, but then again there was probably nowhere safer for a kid than right next to his protective, magical mama.

"Do you know how to defeat this puzzle?" Gailen asked quietly.

"I think so based on how she described it, but I want to see it to make sure I'm not missing a piece."

"You are careful and methodical."

She nibbled his jaw.

He meshed their lips for a quick, hot kiss. "We will not energize the ruin from here."

"Sorry," she vibrated, distinctly *not*. "I thought you were seducing me."

He rumbled deep in his chest and pulled back. The iridescent threads in his eyes gleamed with promise.

Warrior snarls filled the ocean.

They ascended toward a great mesh net.

A great living mesh net.

The warriors had wound long seaweed ropes around their wrists and ankles. As their group approached, the nearest warriors quickly wound their ropes tight while the others loosened, causing the mesh to close. It was pretty ingenious, actually.

Except for one thing.

Elyssa slowed to a stop. "I can shield us, of course, but I don't want them to wrap around my bubble shield. They did that before and dislocated joints when I tried to push through." She shuddered. "I can't go through that again."

Poor Elyssa.

The queen pointed at a warrior on the other side of the growling mesh. "General Giru."

"I knew you would return." The general looked gaunt, almost ill, with purple blackberry bramble tattoos standing out in sharp contrast against his pale skin. His muscles seemed loose on his frame, as if he'd once been a much stouter man but had lost a lot of tone. "The other generals were so certain the kraken would defeat you, but I knew your escape meant the attack was over."

"It is over," Elyssa said at her most regal. "Let us pass."

"The archivist may pass." General Giru's eyes glimmered with dreadful promise at the fate awaiting defectors. "The rest cannot."

"You have to let us through."

"I do not."

Gailen floated closer to the general. "Have you thought nothing of who you serve? The All-Council head tried to hurt the brides."

"The brides are safe."

"Safe? You cannot trust the All-Council head's word."

"I do not." General Giru drifted closer to the net. "But they are safe, and you will remain on the seafloor side of this barrier until your king accepts the All-Council rule and renounces his new covenant."

"You know it is wrong," Gailen vibrated.

"I know my duty. Nothing will prevent me from executing it."

Elyssa raised her fingers. They glowed white. "Kadir will never accept the All-Council. I don't want to hurt you, but you have to let us through, or I'll have no choice."

General Giru's lips curved as though he welcomed her

attack. He didn't even bother to defend himself. It was as if he'd been in pain so long, he was waiting for someone to put him out of his misery.

"Three." Elyssa's lips trembled. "Two. One—"

"Wait," Starr called.

Elyssa dropped her hand. The light dissipated, and she turned panicked eyes on Starr. "What? Yes? You found another way?"

"I don't know what you were about to do, but why don't you just make the biggest shield possible so they can't wrap around it? Then push them all the way to the surface?"

"This is the Dekerto net," the archivist told Starr. "Very effective in this situation."

"So why don't I take one side, Elyssa takes the other, and we give it a three-two-one push and...?"

Gailen squeezed her. "Your main power is to shield?"

"I don't know, but I'm ready to give it a try." She flexed her fingers.

White lights glowed from the tips, and a big bubble grew like the sphere of a goddess.

Oh, yeah. This was going to be *awesome*.

"It will not work." General Giru sneered at them. "Do you not remember? You tried it recently and barely escaped without ending any lives."

"He is right," Archivist Ulio told her, and Elyssa nodded sadly. "This net is centrally anchored. You cannot push without ripping warriors apart."

"And we can't cut the rope? Not even with mermaid queen powers?"

"It's the platform cable," Elyssa told her.

"The *platform* cable?" Starr repeated.

"Yes."

Everyone stared at her as if they didn't get it, so she clarified. "The one that we used to communicate with the surface? That the submersible was attached to? And the giant cement blocks that the kraken tossed like they were parade candy?"

Elyssa's jaw dropped, and she vibrated her answer in her chest. "Uh, yeah. That was severed, huh? Good thing you remembered that."

"It was a memorable experience."

"I bet." A smile bloomed across her face and she wheeled toward the net again. "Okay, Starr, do you like the far side or the near side?"

"I'm flexible."

"She is," Gailen said proudly.

"I knew you would choose violence," General Giru rumbled.

"No need." Elyssa swelled. Her fingertips glowed, and she spread the shield way out, mixing with Starr's bubble and expanding exponentially. "I forgot the kraken pulled out your anchor. Going up?"

"Ding," Starr vibrated.

General Giru jolted in shock.

The bubble hit the net of warriors and kept rising. She and Elyssa kicked in unison. Gailen matched her strokes, pushing her faster and faster. The warriors braced...and nothing happened.

"Whee," Starr said.

General Giru turned and kicked to swim away.

Heh.

Starr pushed the net faster, and Elyssa amplified her power with a giggle. The net caught up to General Giru and swept him up in his own trap. Prince Kael squealed in an unusual show of delight. Even Archivist Ulio, struggling to keep up, whooped.

Ooh, they were ascending so fast, her head was starting to spin. The water thinned and lightened. Hapless fish thrashed the hapless warriors.

General Giru rolled over on the net to face them. "Wait. Stop!"

"No way," Starr vibrated.

Elyssa agreed. "I'm late for a date with my husband."

General Giru barked an order. His warriors unwrapped the seaweed and floated apart, and the net disintegrated around them.

"Aw." Elyssa kept pushing the bubble with General Giru, so Starr did too. It was fun. While the rest of his army crawled away, they lifted him toward the distant, wobbling surface.

"Let me go," he growled.

"Never in a million years," Elyssa replied.

"I will be dead soon enough. Why burden your descendants with my bones?"

"Because Nora is shielding my husband on the surface, and if you won't answer to us for your actions today, I hope you will at least answer to her."

He rolled onto his back and squinted at the approaching sky. "Why do you torture me?"

Gailen vibrated a rebuke. "She is not your torture. She is your soul mate."

"Same thing."

Hmm. Another puzzle. Although Starr had never been as good with the human ones. But with Gailen's soul entwining hers, filling her up with his emotions, she felt pretty okay with taking a stab at it.

Hazel shouted overhead. "Elyssa and Starr! You brought him. Oh, thank God. Everyone's saved."

Elyssa and Starr slowed. General Giru sat up and rose defensively as Hazel and Lotar, sandwiching their baby between them, descended. Elyssa and Starr released the shield, and the white light dissipated.

"We brought him?" Elyssa repeated.

"That's right," Hazel exclaimed.

Lotar released his family and disappeared.

Poof.

Huh.

But no one even acted surprised.

Hazel gestured at the general. "He's hidden all the brides. Nora got hurt shielding the kings, and if I try to heal her, the All-Council head will kill the brides."

Elyssa gasped. "I knew something was wrong."

General Giru blanched. The bramble tattoos stood out even more against his skin.

"Didn't you hear me?" Hazel demanded. "Your soul mate's going to die."

He swam backward, trident aimed at them. "You lie."

"It's not a lie. She was mortally injured by the head of the All-Council."

"Another lie."

"I never lie!" Hazel turned apoplectic and her hair drifted in front of her face. "Tell us where the brides are so we can save them and Elyssa can heal Nora."

"I prefer to die before betraying my duty."

Lotar faded into the open ocean directly behind General Giru as if he'd been teleported from the *Enterprise*. He hovered a dagger that didn't quite touch General Giru's throat. "Death can be arranged."

General Giru's lips flattened sourly. "Oh, it is *you*. I

thought your bride looked familiar, but all brides look the same."

"No one's killing anyone here. We're the good guys." Hazel yanked a handful of her hair out of her face. "But if you don't hurry up and talk, a lot of innocent women are going to die."

THIRTY

They were at a stalemate.

"We have to help Nora," Queen Hazel vibrated urgently. "Don't you care? Hurry up and explain."

Her soul shone with truth.

Gailen would be desperate if he heard this news about Starr. And yet General Giru did not seem affected. His soul glowed more dimly than Gailen had seen it before. But he looked seriously ill, as if he also hadn't eaten or rested since Gailen had last seen him, and he hadn't looked well then either.

"Why don't you tell me?" Queen Hazel demanded, and Queen Elyssa listened anxiously, having already exhausted her options for arguing at the net.

Archivist Ulio finally straightened. "I could turn myself over to the All-Council in exchange for the brides."

"I doubt they'd say yes," Hazel told him honestly. Her young fry reached out of her wrap to yank the older mer's red hair, and she expertly pulled Tal away. "They're like sharks circling wounded prey. As soon as Nora kicks it, the warriors are going to tear Kadir and everybody into mince-meat. And not the tasty bits in the pie. The nasty ones that get featured on Shark Week."

"I have to go to Kadir," Queen Elyssa murmured.

"You know he won't let you do anything until the brides are safe." Queen Hazel raised her vibrations. "I don't know why he's okay with Nora dying."

General Giru maintained a silent half smile of superiority on his lips. "Many lies."

It was so strange. Queen Hazel did not seem to be lying, but General Giru did not react like a warrior losing his soul mate.

Starr identified the problem. "He doesn't believe Hazel. Shouldn't he feel if Nora was about to die? I felt your fear and pain when the city was getting destroyed."

Yes, as he'd felt her terror at getting trapped in the submersible. "Perhaps Queen Nora does not call for him."

Queen Hazel jerked up. "Oh, she calls for him. She's delirious. Of course she calls for him."

"Such clever lies," General Giru said.

"He doesn't feel it," Starr mused.

"Obviously." Queen Hazel huffed. "I don't think he even has emotions."

"Emotions are not a choice," Gailen informed her.

"Yes, they are." Starr clutched Gailen's hand. "For some of us, it's a choice."

Of course!

The others argued with Starr, but Gailen floated closer, trying to peer into the general's soul. Usually, the mer could not separate from their feelings, but thanks to his experience with Starr, Gailen knew what to look for.

General Giru frowned and leaned away from him. "What are you doing?"

Lotar's silent gaze, with his dagger blade still immobilizing the general, asked the same question.

"You once told me you wished to sever your 'unnatural' connection to your soul mate." Gailen forced his vision inward to sense any barriers within the general's soul. "Starr thinks you may have accomplished it."

The others fell silent.

"Hm." There were definitely black sticky threads, not as impenetrable as Starr's, but like a frayed covering across his soul. "You may have."

The general flashed his teeth, nostrils flaring in triumph. "Then we are severed. She is free."

"Yes." Gailen met his gaze with true pity. "And you will no longer know when she is about to die."

The general's smile faded. Realization dawned in his eyes. He looked at the others, seeming to see them for the first time. "I will not...sense her?"

"You can." Starr floated to Gailen, and he entwined her comfortably in his arms. "But it takes an effort. You have to really concentrate."

The general frowned and pulled away from Lotar, who let him go and sheathed his dagger. The general tilted his head. "I feel nothing."

"You should sense that she is well," Gailen reminded him.

"But I...cannot."

"It's terrible, isn't it?" Starr swam to Gailen and snuggled in his arms. "It's easier to get it back when you're touching. Like this."

General Giru tilted his head the opposite direction, trying to catch a sound that should be as familiar as his own heartbeat and hearing nothing. "How was she injured?"

"An accident," Lotar vibrated softly. "A trident thrown at King Kadir. She swam into its path."

"Who threw it?"

"We did not see."

"I thought she was shielded?"

"She lowered the shield so I could escape."

The general glared at Queen Hazel. "Where were you?"

"Searching for the brides. Lotar was coming out to help me look."

General Giru rubbed his forehead. "Nora is free."

"Free to die," Queen Hazel said.

He glared.

"Don't look at me like that. I tried to save her. You have to tell us where to find the brides, or else Sirak is going to kill them."

General Giru pinched the bridge of his nose. His vibrations were so faint. "I tried to protect him."

"Oh, Sirak does not need your protection," Queen Hazel promised.

General Giru squinted at her in irritation. He was not talking about the All-Council head.

Mysteries within mysteries.

But Queen Nora was running out of time.

"You can see they are not lying," Gailen said. "You may be free of Queen Nora, but your protection of another dooms her. How can you fail to decide? Quickly."

His nostrils flared. "I hope you never have to make this choice."

"The brides," Lotar vibrated intently.

General Giru's shoulders slumped. "The platform wreckage. They are secured in the floating glass bowl. In the air, so they cannot use their powers. Warriors guard them."

He glanced at the others. "Perhaps too many for one queen."

Lotar nodded at Queen Hazel and Queen Elyssa. "I know where that is."

He and Queen Hazel and their young fry swiftly entwined and departed. Archivist Ulio swam after them.

General Giru kicked hard the opposite way, guided finally by his connection to his bride.

Queen Elyssa wavered. "I want to go with him, but if anything happens to the brides..."

"Go," Gailen urged her. "We will stall Sirak until you arrive."

"Thanks so much. I can't believe you figured out what was going on with him. You're wizards. Thank you!" Queen Elyssa and her prince raced after the others to rescue the brides.

Gailen and Starr flew after the general, rising through the oceans to the tumultuous sunlight zone.

———

"So how do you plan to stall the All-Council head?" Starr asked casually as Gailen rushed them through the ocean.

"How prepared do you feel to summon your queen powers?"

She flexed her fingers. They glimmered with tiny sparkles. Neat. "Pretty okay. Why?"

"We must act as soon as the others have freed the brides."

Everything depended on her and Gailen.

How funny that her depersonalization disorder had helped.

It was hard to break out of their old ways of being, but

they'd met each other and had to change and grow to grab their destiny.

And now the same collision was happening with the mer. They were about to find out which would win, the old ways that no longer served them, or the terrifying new ways that would lead to their destiny.

Gailen caught up to the general in a thick, growling crowd of enemy warriors.

Starr reached into herself and...

...a white bubble appeared around them like magic.

Cool.

"It is the same temperature as the ocean," Gailen vibrated as their enemies parted like grease veering away from a soap bubble.

She snorted. "Sure."

"Why does that amuse you?"

"I'll tell you later."

As those warriors moved back, the entire landscape opened up.

The surface was a few hundred feet overhead. Boats dotted the area, and engines rumbled as they repositioned over the last coordinates of Atlantis while the currents and winds pushed them around.

So there were still human captains. Just no brides.

She and Gailen were surrounded by All-Council warriors.

Off to her left, a faded bubble sheltered a battered, bloodied King Kadir. The other kings and dignitaries huddled behind him in the shrinking shelter had similar bruises.

The All-Council head Sirak and his fellow leaders floated way too close to the faded bubble.

General Giru pushed through the crowded warriors. "Units. Form units, here."

Sirak saw Starr's white shield. "Back!" He held his hands out to ward them away. "Do not interfere, anathema, or on my command, all the brides will die."

There was a cleared line of sight from him to the surface overhead. Warriors there waited. They must have a way to signal, like some kind of flare. Like the signal from a bomb, she had to defuse it because she wouldn't be able to stop it from going off.

"Why is the army okay with this?" Starr muttered.

"I do not know." Gailen amplified her question. "Why do all you so-called honorable warriors accept murdering your own brides?"

The heavily tattooed fierce commander who deferred to General Giru glared at them but didn't bother to answer.

"We do not," King Kadir said heavily and the other dignitaries clustered behind him, clenching weapons as their shelter continued to fade away, becoming lighter every second. "We treasure brides in Atlantis."

"You treasure anathema, all of you." Sirak focused on General Giru. "Ah, General. You have arisen?"

His movement revealed the mer floating in front of King Kadir: a pale, nearly lifeless Nora.

And she had a big old gaping hole in her chest where her heart should be.

"Oh my God," Starr murmured.

Gailen's tone echoed her grim feeling. "It is not good."

"How is she even still alive?"

Gailen moved his head back and forth. Mind over matter, the mer connection to the Life Tree, sheer cussed force of will. And Starr could tap into the same force any time she wanted. She just had to figure out how to do it without risking Dannika and the others.

General Giru's gaze sharpened on Nora. "She *is* injured."

"The rebels caused this. What of the nets? They are supposed to prevent plankton from rising." He sneered at Starr and Gailen.

"The net was compromised." General Giru's gaze did not deviate from Nora. "The kraken pulled out our anchor."

Shocked mutters echoed, and the dignitaries cried out in dismay.

King Kadir raised his bent trident. "You unleashed the kraken? On my city?"

Sirak vibrated with annoyance. "Since you still live, I surmise it spared your Life Tree. A mercy I will correct after you die."

"Who injured her?" General Giru asked King Kadir.

King Kadir flexed his jaw as if he wanted to say something else. "I do not know."

"Who?"

"Does it matter?" King Kadir gritted his teeth. "We have no healer. When you hid the brides, you took him as well. I hope that choice does not cost Queen Nora her life."

A tremor started in General Giru's chest. His muscles twitched. "I still feel nothing."

"Of course you do not." Sirak tsked with just the right hint of concern. "The death of an anathema is—"

"She is a bride," he growled.

"And the ancient covenant was created to prevent this tragedy." Sirak smoothly shifted his tone to an oration for his army. "Brides come to the mer, unite with their soul mates for a time, and return to their proper, safe home above. One needless death is sad but necessary to prevent a much greater loss of life."

"And yet..." General Giru touched the faded shield. His fingers melted through it.

His warriors pressed in behind him to pounce. King Kadir and the dignitaries stood poised to fight for their lives.

Starr called up the power glowing in her fingertips...

General Giru threw up a hand.

His army froze.

"The first one to move or touch any of them"—he indicated the trapped Atlantis group—"tastes death."

A sober silence settled over the army.

General Giru waved his fingers, and his warriors moved back, increasing the space around the surrounded group. He pulled Nora through the faded shield, tearing it away, and wrapped her in his arms.

Sirak rumbled. "Ah, General Giru..."

He held up a hand, stopping the shocked All-Council head.

Starr flexed her fingertips. Other queens had tossed shields at a distance...

The kings couldn't remain exposed. It was too big a temptation. Sirak signaled to the heavily tattooed second commander, and he floated forward, lowering his trident at King Kadir.

She could do this. She was a queen.

She could do anything.

Her fingertips warmed, and a white shield glistened into existence around the group.

The second commander checked his movement. Sirak wrinkled his nose.

Gailen subtly covered her fingers in case anyone realized that she was not only channeling a shield around them, but also a second shield around the kings.

But nobody really noticed, because the strange behavior of their general captured everyone's attention.

He stroked Nora's pale cheeks. "I feel nothing."

"Wow," Nora vibrated weakly.

General Giru's serious brows lifted. "You live."

"Of course I live. I'm just feeling pretty ill right now." Her lashes fluttered. "Gailen warned me this would happen."

Gailen stiffened, but luckily, nobody looked.

"The rebels are annoying," General Giru said.

A faint grin flashed. "Tell me about it."

He lifted his head and searched the crowd for Starr. "Heal her."

"Wait!" Sirak cried, but Starr was already doing it.

It was so easy. Her emotions welled like tears in the corners of her eyes, telling her that she was going to start sobbing at the happy parts of movies, and she directed the fullness of her feelings into Nora.

White light streamed into Nora's wound. It touched her soul, expanding and brightening. The layers sealed up from the inside out, stitching her organs and veins and everything together. Her deep stab wound just kind of went away.

Color retuned to Nora's cheeks.

She stretched and blinked awake, smiling her thanks at Starr, then looked down and became aware of herself in General Giru's arms. She softened. "Hey."

"You are a fool," the general told her softly. "Reckless and misguided. Go now with the other rebels and seek a better warrior for your mate."

"I love you."

His brows drew together. He didn't want to hear it, but he couldn't turn away.

"I love the idealistic man you once were and the tormented man you are today." Nora cupped his hollow cheek. "I love the wiser man you will grow to become when you forgive yourself for your past and begin living for your future. I just love you, man."

"I am no man."

She pressed her lips to his and vibrated, "I love you."

And they stayed that way for a long moment.

The ocean was utterly silent. Filled with a massive army, and yet nobody moved. Their kiss cast a spell over everyone. These two on opposite sides had fought destiny, and destiny had won.

"General Giru." Sirak pointed his trident. "You have betrayed your city and darkened the soul of your true sacred bride with this unfaithful human-like lust. That is what happens with too much exposure to an anathema. Your corruption disgusts me and your fellow warriors. You are hereby stripped of your position and honors."

Giru pulled Nora behind him to protect her. She grabbed his shoulders.

Sirak gestured at the second-in-command. "You are now general, Viren. Your first duty is to execute Giru for breaking the ancient covenant and changing his loyalty to this modern anathema."

Viren gripped his trident and kicked forward to face his former commander.

"Oh, uh-uh." Nora lifted one hand, and a glowing white shield wrapped around her and Giru. "No one's getting executed on my watch."

Viren focused on her hand on the general's shoulder. "Is this true? You have betrayed us?"

"I can no longer obey the orders of the All-Council." Giru's chest vibrated with roughness. "Lead our warriors well. You know your duty, but..." Giru glanced at Gailen and then focused again on his former second. "Do not let duty overrule your honor."

Viren straightened. He tucked his trident to his elbow, lifted his palm, and patted his chest in a sign of respect. General Giru repeated the motion, and the new general vibrated in a shout: "General Giru's warriors, obey me!"

The warriors barked an assent, stiffening into the same posture and patting as they did so. It echoed in a roar out to the farthest edges of the army. Despite the ones who had died from the kraken or guarded the brides or had formed the disintegrated net, there were still a lot of warriors to swear fealty to their new commander.

It was a lot calmer than the transfer of power in the Sons of Hercules, that was for sure.

"Now." Sirak gestured for General Giru to move out of Nora's shield. "Face your punishment with dignity, or we will carry your dishonor back to your origin city and exact the payment from your descendants."

General Giru gritted his teeth.

"Oh," Gailen murmured. "Of course. Why did I not think of that?"

"What?" Starr asked.

"General Giru's young fry..."

General Giru—or just Giru now—removed Nora's hand from his shoulder and kicked forward out of her bubble.

"Hey," she protested.

He held up a hand, stopping her, and then presented himself to Viren. Chest high, shoulders straight. Ready.

"Good." The All-Council nodded at the heavily tattooed warrior. "Proceed."

Viren compressed his lips. He twisted his trident.

They were out of time.

"Do something," Starr urged.

Gailen flinched. "Wait! General Giru did not break the ancient covenant."

Everyone turned to him.

His ears reddened, and he spluttered. "I mean, he did, but who cares? There have been multiple ancient covenants. It used to change all the time. The current one no longer serves the mer. The only reason it has not already been altered is because the All-Council refuses to change it."

"What is this babbling nonsense?" Sirak demanded.

"It is not nonsense. It is our history."

"You know nothing of our race's history."

"I heard it from Head Archivist Ulio, who you tried to lock up along with the other archivists because they protested against you."

A heavy silence hung over the group.

"You cannot take the word of one disgruntled male." The All-Council swam to the new general. "He betrayed us. Prove your loyalty and obey my command."

Viren faced Giru with new certainty.

Uh-oh.

Starr tensed.

But Viren did not strike.

"It is my duty to obey you," he vibrated fiercely, addressing the All-Council head, but focused on Giru. "But I cannot strike down a warrior protecting his bride."

What?

The new guy was on their side?

Sirak realized the same thing. "One death is necessary to maintain order."

"We are better than that," the new general growled.

"We? You command *my* army."

"*We* are better." Viren returned his trident to the crook of his elbow.

"You must do what is necessary!"

"We are."

The rest of the army followed his lead and tucked away their weapons. The All-Council might own the army, but he did not command them. And he'd demoted the one guy he had been able to manipulate.

"So am I." Sirak turned to Giru.

One of the dignitaries kicked out of the bubble with a shout.

It was meant to be a warning, but it just distracted everyone from the true danger. The new general looked away from Giru to the dignitary who had shouted, and so did Nora and the closest warriors.

Sirak swung his trident at Giru's unprotected back.

Gailen vibrated urgently. "Starr!"

But Starr was too slow. Nora turned back and tried to throw a shield over Giru, but she was also too late. The blades came down and sliced through Giru's—

A bright white light slammed Giru to the side, pushing him away from the main thrust of the trident so he suffered only a glancing blow.

He arched in pain from the deep but not deadly cut into his bleeding shoulder.

Nora covered them with a white bubble.

Thank goodness.

The All-Council leaders roared in surprise, and the warriors startled violently. General Viren wheeled, his trident out, defending the All-Council leaders from the shocking appearance of a new enemy.

Elyssa zoomed through the crowd and dove into King Kadir's arms. Starr's secretive shield brightened with her energy to pure radiant white.

Sirak roared. "You have broken your agreement. Your betrayal has doomed the brides!" He signaled to the warrior at the surface.

"Yeah, I don't think so." Hazel put one hand on her hip. The other cuddled her yawning baby. "Nice try."

"What is this? Who are you?"

A woman Starr had never met in person swam into the center of the action and raised both arms. Her dark hair fanned out around her. "I am Dannika." Her serene vibrations carried far and wide. "And I am here to announce the brides have arrived!"

THIRTY-ONE

Chaos reigned.

Within Starr's strong shield, Gailen even enjoyed it.

Sirak screamed at his new general to destroy the anathema, but General Viren steadfastly refused to raise his trident. Sirak tried to promote other warriors who would obey him, but the army formed up behind their new general.

While they argued, the queens took over the center, pushing the All-Council out to create a large, comfortable safe area.

Queen Nora healed her soul mate, and Queen Elyssa healed hers. She also healed the other dignitaries. The dignitary who had shouted out to try to save Giru had melted back into the group. He had sharp features, a narrow face, and dark amber tattoos. Gailen had welcomed him—a warrior named Rulin—and there was more to his story, for certain.

Although a few new souls lit the ocean, Gailen had expected a deluge. Had something gone terribly wrong?

But the warriors who joined them were in good spirits. They saw Starr's half sister, Bella, with Balim reconciling with King Kadir. If Roa was going to get an official welcome and thank-you, they couldn't possibly deny Bella and Balim. All the queens swarmed Bella to welcome her back, and the warriors began consulting with the sharp-tongued healer about minor complaints. Bella peeked through the crowds and gave a secret wave.

"I'll say hi to Bella when it calms down," Starr murmured to Gailen.

A warrior with dark-green-and-coffee-black tattoos passed with an energetic young fry. "Hello, Gailen. Queen Starr."

"Second Lieutenant Ciran." Gailen admired his and Queen Dannika's wiggly young fry. "Where are all the brides?"

"They descended." The strategic second lieutenant nodded at old friends as he rested beside Gailen. "Dannika did not want to risk a repeat with the general."

"Former general," Starr commented.

Second Lieutenant Ciran studied the male receiving treatment from Queen Nora. "I see."

"What happened to you guys?"

"Your call inspired Dannika to enter the water. She captured General Giru and forced him to tell us where he had hidden King Kadir and the other dignitaries. He acted so convincingly that even the other warriors were tricked."

"Giru denied his soul mate so much, he hid his own soul," Gailen vibrated.

"It worked. We entered the scaffolding of the wreckage, and by the time we realized our mistake, we were the ones who were captured. And yet, hearing from Queen Hazel and Lotar, it sounds as though his subterfuge was indeed meant to save our lives."

"He nearly lost his soul mate, though." Starr rubbed Gailen's forearm. "Gailen had to convince him he was on the wrong side."

"I am not surprised." The second lieutenant clasped Gailen's shoulder. "You have a talent for appealing to a warrior's better nature."

King Kadir swam up, flanked by Queen Elyssa, Prince Kael, and many queens and dignitaries. "Elyssa tells me you convinced Roa to defend Atlantis and Giru to divulge the location of the brides. Just now, you stalled long enough for the brides to be rescued. You truly are the hero of our time."

His heart swelled against his rib cage. "Thank you, my king."

King Kadir clasped his forearm. "The thanks are all mine."

His thumb jutted. This one was still broken and unable to fully close over the king's forearm, but that was okay. He had done all this as he was. This trait, or lack, no longer defined him.

King Kadir rotated to face the rest of the dignitaries, the still-squabbling All-Council, and the enemy army. "Your sad attempt to hold back the future has failed. We descend to Atlantis to rebuild, welcome our brides, and forge the new covenant."

"You're all still invited." Queen Hazel bounced her fussy young fry. "Even after all this. And even if your dad found you under a cabbage leaf or in a seaweed farm."

"Seaweed forest," General Viren growled. "For the second time."

"General." Sirak jabbed his index finger at the brides.

"Do not interact with these creatures. They have broken the ancient covenant. We are in a war to survive."

"And?" The general flicked the tip of his trident. "Like the Atlantis warrior said, it has changed hundreds of times."

"Do not believe him."

"I do not. I learned it, too. From Head Archivist Ulio."

Sirak snarled and lofted his trident in the center of the rebels where he spotted the head archivist. "You have betrayed the All-Council. Splitting the loyalty of the mer like this will lead to our destruction."

"The mer will not be destroyed by the truth," the archivist vibrated with gravelly certainty. "Only you will be."

Sirak curled his lip. "Are you so sure? Only me?"

King Kadir spread his arms. "You are all welcome to join the new covenant. Any warrior may join. We now understand the secrets of our past, and with your help, we will reactivate the ancient ruin and create a new island for warriors and brides. Come now. Leave the relic of the old order behind. Your brides are waiting."

General Viren frowned.

None of his warriors moved. They would not change sides so long as he still served the All-Council.

General Viren wavered. "Perhaps I—"

"Silence!" Sirak curled his lips back from his teeth. "You disgusting, honorless male who cannot follow simple orders to prevent worse crimes. Giru shielded me from you so that I did not realize you were so weak. And you." He jabbed his trident at Archivist Ulio. "You have encouraged all these warriors to mix with brides when you know it is impossible."

"We believe in Atlantis," Elyssa said, and the women cheered.

"Because you know nothing. Tell them, Ulio. They did not learn from their wrecked platform that humans have always and will always betray them."

Archivist Ulio fidgeted. "Things are different now."

"And yet, the past has already been repeated."

"We survived the Great Catastrophe," King Kadir vibrated. "And if the loss of the platform echoes it, we *are* different now, and we will work together to save our race."

"You are no different. There is a reason I told you that you must have a meeting place before the brides descended." Sirak sneered at the nervous archivist. "Tell them the whole truth, Ulio. They must understand why this is no victory, but our race's final collapse."

The archivist licked his lips and cleared his throat. He glanced apologetically at King Kadir.

But even his silence was damaging.

Second Lieutenant Ciran murmured to King Kadir, "We should descend. The All-Council head sows confusion and lies. The dignitaries have already endured too much."

"I still hope to bring the All-Council army to our side," King Kadir vibrated back, equally quiet. "If he retains them, he may grow his power again, and there is no telling how much harm they will cause."

"If the army is not convinced by now, no words will ever convince them."

King Kadir's gaze traveled over Queen Nora, who had been mortally wounded, General Giru, who was stretching his shoulder with a wince, and the brides who had been held hostage by a male fully willing to have them killed. A muscle flexed in his jaw, and then he nodded with regret.

Raising his arms, he vibrated, "You are welcome to join us any time. Atlantis is open to any mer who would be our allies." And then he turned and led their allies to the best current to descend.

Sirak vibrated with a deep smirk. "Look. He runs from the answer. Do not follow such a coward."

Anger crackled up Gailen's back.

King Kadir and the others seemed unaffected. They would say to ignore the taunts. They weren't true, and everyone was eager to descend. They had better things to do.

"Hey." Starr craned her neck to meet his eyes. "You okay? You seem angry."

He started to reassure her...but why? Starr wasn't asking because she needed reassurance. She was asking because she wanted to know him. His feelings, his longings, his dreams.

And he *was* angry. So what was he going to do about it?

"Do you mind if we stay here a little longer?" he asked wheeling around and weaving back through the crowd.

She grinned and flexed her glowing fingertips. "No problem. I've got all the time in the world."

"The so-called king rules over a pile of lies," Sirak ranted, having successfully recaptured his army. "He runs because he fears the truth I would reveal to him."

"I do not," Gailen vibrated at them, and the allies retreating behind him slowed and turned back to watch. "I do not fear the truth. Reveal it to me."

Sirak sneered at him. "Who are you, then? A brash young warrior? You do not even look like a first lieutenant."

"I am the hero of Atlantis." Gailen grinned.
Sirak snorted. "Hero."
But the other queens and allies returning to surround Gailen did not laugh.

He sobered. "You do not know what horrors you wish to unearth, young 'hero.'"

"If humans or mer committed a terrible crime, we cannot turn back the ocean tide, but we can atone. And we can act more wisely in our future."

His lips peeled back in a grin. "Precisely. Ulio, tell them about ancient Atlantis. The Great Catastrophe that drove us into the oceans, and why only the ancient covenant—the *unchanging* ancient covenant—can save us now."

Archivist Ulio looked at Gailen with what seemed to be an apology.

It practically made Sirak salivate. "Tell them."

Archivist Ulio licked his lips. "As you all know, once there were as many females born to our race as there were males. It is a quirk of biology that a feedback loop with a city's Life Tree creates an imbalance that, if unchecked, leads to—"

"The Great Catastrophe," Sirak reminded him. "Ulio."

"Yes." He frowned. "Atlantis was once ruled by many queens, as it is today, and also multiple kings, which is different to—"

"Ulio."

"They must understand the context." Archivist Ulio grimaced. "The most powerful queen of Atlantis ascended to claim her human husband. That was tradition at the time. But when they met, he refused her."

"Because humans cannot see souls," Sirak said.

"Well, be that as it may, the Atlantis queen lashed out, and the human king retaliated. They sparked a battle that spilled into a war. The Atlanteans lowered their city beneath the waves, and a great many humans drowned that day."

"For which they have craved revenge ever since," Sirak

said. "Through the ages, hatred has prevailed. And it was all caused by one blind king who rejected his proper mate."

But that was wrong.

No, that was all wrong. "Was it not caused by the queen? She must have been confused, wrong. How could she have been capable of attacking her own soul mate?"

Archivist Ulio shrugged. "The records are silent on that question."

"That is why the mer cannot intermix freely with humans," Sirak insisted. "Only the controlled, limited exposure dictated by the ancient covenant will safeguard our race."

"You are mistaken." Gailen looked around at his allies. Even King Kadir had returned and now listened silently. "The ancient covenant does not safeguard soul mates."

"It prevents intermixing," Sirak said. "Bloodshed is inevitable because humans cannot see souls."

"You are wrong." King Jolan of Sireno swam forward. "The mer *can* see souls, and yet my mother's soul resonated with the wrong warrior. Sireno hunted them, and both my father and the rejected warrior were killed."

"That was a failure of your warriors, not of the ancient covenant."

"It was a failure *because* the ancient covenant does not let soul mates choose."

"If you obeyed it perfectly, it would never fail you."

The sharp warrior with dark amber tattoos swam forward. "That is not true."

General Giru's chin dropped. "Rulin."

"I had not wished to endanger you with a public reunion, Giru, but I know the truth. My...real father told me after I was selected as our city's delegate."

Giru looked sick. "Do not speak."

"I must."

"But your future—"

"Is my concern." Rulin faced the All-Council army. "My mother also resonated with the wrong warrior, but instead of driving him into death or exile, Giru hid their relationship and lied so my father could survive."

Sirak gritted his teeth in fury. "And that was only the beginning of his lies."

"He had to. The ancient covenant does not allow a situation like my father's to arise."

"Because it is a betrayal of our values."

"Then our values betrayed him first." Rulin flared with righteous fury, and he gestured at Giru off to his side. "There is no more dutiful warrior, and until a short time ago, you all would have said he was the fiercest and most honorable general to ever lead this army. You would have said that. And anything he did that was not honorable was done because he was trying to protect me. A male who was not even his own young fry."

General Viren rotated to face them more fully and lifted his chin.

"I could go on." Rulin also faced Giru. "You falsely claimed me as your son, the son of a bride who rejected you, but you never denied my real father the chance to be near. He participated in all my milestones and honors. Because you followed your honor."

General Giru's eyes reddened.

Gailen felt his own nose prickle.

"I was always told I was so lucky to be doted upon and attended by two males interested in raising me. The elders joked I had two fathers. They did not realize how close it was to the truth. And I was lucky. Lucky it was you and not a less understanding warrior."

King Jolan nodded.

"My king now knows the truth. All is forgiven, and I must wear an ornament from a different ancestral line." Rulin lifted his shoulder, and all could see that the wavy bands on the epaulet did not match the one General Giru wore. "But you were and always will be my first father."

Gailen's chest lifted. Starr's energy swirled around him, and he snuggled her close, so grateful they had met in Atlantis now, and not five years earlier under different circumstances in Aiycaya.

Sirak rumbled with disgust. "You, Giru, a single warrior who has fathered no young fry, has risen to the highest rank on a lie. You should never have commanded a single warrior. Your city should be punished, and you exiled."

Giru flinched.

"And yet I will not be exiled." Rulin lifted his chest. "Our king has commanded that I create a new covenant with King Kadir that you will not stop. Warriors of the All-Council army, listen. You know Giru's honor. You see how he protects brides and young fry. That is the value we protect as warriors, and that value is treasured by the warriors in Atlantis. Come with us, now."

His impassioned plea mobilized the warriors.

General Viren kicked forward.

The All-Council army surged behind him.

Their tridents were stowed, daggers sheathed.

They came in peace.

"B-but you cannot leave." Sirak scrambled to block the new general. "We make the rules. I order you to destroy them. Hear me? As the head of the All-Council—"

"What is the point of the All-Council if not to protect our brides and young fry?" General Viren asked.

The All-Council leader gaped. "General Giru obeyed me."

"The old general must live with his choices." The new one thumped his trident flat against the All-Council head's chest, roughly pushing him aside. "I must live with mine."

"Any general who defies my orders is no commander." Sirak picked out the next warrior. "You are the general now. Remove him. You obey me."

The warrior lifted a brow.

General Viren smirked. "I do not cede my position."

"You do not cede anything. I am the head of the All-Council." His eyes flashed, and his skin grew paler. "I am the leader. I preserve the order. You cannot go against me. I am the All-Council!"

They left him far behind, descending together on the currents that would lead them back to Atlantis.

"Great job." Starr squeezed Gailen.

"I only shared what I thought."

"And that was perfect." She grinned. "You did an important thing."

They had all done important things in their own small ways.

Archivist Ulio might know the great and terrible acts of rulers of the past, queens who sank islands or kings who chose the wrong soul. But if they traced the actions of smaller warriors, they might uncover an even richer history.

King Kadir swam abreast of them as they descended through the layers. "Elyssa tells me you figured out how to raise the ruin."

"We did." Gailen squeezed Starr and acknowledged Queen Elyssa, Prince Kael, and Archivist Ulio swimming nearby. "And sending the brides ahead to Atlantis was brilliant. When the warriors reunite, their positive emotions will energize the ruin, just like Starr and I united our—"

Starr made a strangled noise. "Don't!"

"—minds and hearts."

She relaxed. "Oh."

He tilted his head at Starr. "What did you think I was going to say? As we united our bodies? You told me it would be awkward to instruct the couples to unite in front of their parents and grown young fry. It was very effective at energizing the ruin, though."

She pressed her eyes shut.

Someone tittered.

Her eyes flew open, and she jabbed her index finger across at her sister. "This is not funny, Bella."

Bella burst out laughing. "Oh, come on. It's hilarious."

Everyone roared with laughter, and the other queens clustered around as they descended.

"Don't feel bad," Queen Elyssa vibrated with giggles. "Did I ever tell you about my first time? I thought I was being sneaky in the Life Tree enclosure. Instead, it amplified everything across the entire city."

"It did," Gailen agreed. "It reassured us, though. We worried that you had rejected our king after seeing our paltry single castle and tiny Life Tree."

"Never."

"Oh, yes, King Kadir performed well. You screamed to the farthest reaches of the patrols. And so many times. We were all proud to have followed such a magnificent warrior who could bring such expressive cries from his chosen queen."

Queen Elyssa reddened. "Mm. Were you? I see."

"I tried to stop you," King Kadir vibrated nobly. "I

begged you to wait until the privacy of my castle. You would not be denied."

"You're making it worse!" She dove at him to jab his abdomen. "Oh, you!"

He twirled her through the water, kissing her, while their young prince chased after them eagerly.

The warriors from the disintegrated net fell in with the army.

And down they swam.

Starr and Gailen led the assembled mer over the devastated city, shocking those who hadn't seen the destruction. But King Kadir shared Gailen's philosophical outlook. It was not the first time Atlantis had been decimated. They would rebuild.

Octopus Kong flew out of his cave, arms waving wildly, then saw the queens and floated back like he was witnessing a great historic event.

And he was.

Lieutenant Diras had wisely led the brides to the ruin so that the joyful reunions could happen right over the energizing stones. Another act that seemed small in the course of the grand events, but if someone were to ask his story, what climactic deeds would he reveal?

Gailen and Starr greeted everyone, welcoming them one by one, and directed them to encircle the ruin until they revealed the other three rings, then cluster around them evenly. They didn't want to raise an island that was lopsided!

So many warriors and brides passed, it seemed as if they might encircle the whole ruin after all. And Starr just glowed brighter as she met all the wonderful new mer who could become her friends. Queen Nora with Giru and Rulin, Queen Elyssa's cousin Queen Aya with First Lieutenant Soren and their young fry son, Iyen—the missing Iyen!—with healing scars and a bride with what was sure to be an incredible story, and hundreds more.

And the couple that had started this whole revolution: the very pregnant Queen Lucy, holding her stomach while her husband, Torun, sought to ease her pains.

"Just put me somewhere out of the way," she requested with a groan.

"Go into the middle of the ruin," Gailen instructed.

"The middle?" She winced as her body rippled. "Of everyone?"

"I am sure the birth of a new mer will inspire many positive feelings, which will greatly charge the heart stone."

"You're the expert." She leaned on Torun's arm. "Sorry, guys. I don't know why I keep going into labor at these dramatic moments."

"On the bright side, it'll make their birth dates a breeze to remember," Starr said.

Queen Lucy chuckled and then groaned.

More familiar faces swam by. Old friends, new friends, queens, and brides of the past. And even though it took forever, seeing everyone so energized filled him with delight. This was his purpose. Everything he'd done had led to this moment. He was meant to be here, growing a new island, with Starr.

He did not see the All-Council leaders. Was the All-Council head still screaming at the surface about how he was right? If so, then he did it alone. No one listened.

As everyone jostled into place around the rim of the ruin, King Kadir swam out. He was the king, after all. Everyone paid attention, and Queen Elyssa amplified his words so that they could reach the farthest edges of the sea.

"Today, we mend a rift that has existed between our

races, between ourselves, for more than a millennium. Today, we begin the healing. Today is not the end of suffering, but the beginning of a new era, a new journey toward wholeness. You may feel grief for warriors who were lost, lives that were taken. You may not feel good tomorrow when there is still so much to be done. But so long as you continue to strive, you will reach a place of wholeness. You will feel better."

King Kadir rotated and cast his gaze at Starr and Gailen. "And you will believe."

Gailen *did* believe.

Starr linked their fingers. His healing thumb brushed her wrist.

And the other?

He would fix it.

"Right now, we channel that future," King Kadir continued, returning to the others listening raptly. "Not the energy of today. The energy of the time when we are whole. And by channeling it together, we dive into the current that will lead us to our final destiny. A destiny where our races are combined, mer and human, warrior and queen. Together. Whole."

The stones shot beacons toward the surface. Energy zipped across the buried island. King Kadir's vision had led them all here.

And today was only the beginning.

King Kadir finished his speech and rejoined Queen Elyssa. The king and queen looked to Gailen for the signal to start.

Gailen raised his linked hands with Starr. "Channel your healing into the Ur tree."

Ur tree? He was too used to saying Life Tree, but perhaps the same thing applied.

All around the ruin, souls lit up. They shone with hope, with connection, with love.

And those same lights appeared, reflected, deep within the swept-clean ruin. The whole region sparkled, brighter and brighter, like a shower of falling stars.

The ground rumbled beneath his fins.

Light intensified to a blinding level. Rock cracked and wood splintered.

And then the sea floor rose.

He shifted to human feet and rested on the trembling earth. Not earth, but living vine. It was warm and undulated beneath his toes.

They left the gleaming Atlantis Life Tree and bobbing castles far behind.

Somewhere in the middle of the ocean, a newborn young fry cried.

His own heart wept to hear it.

The ancient plant stretched, strained, exploded for the surface. How long it took, he did not know, but the water loosened, and, with a great crash, they broke into the glimmering night sky.

Surface gravity always surprised him.

He tumbled, landing on his butt with a thump, and Starr landed on top of him. She choked and coughed as she shifted, and then gasp-laughed.

He clasped her nude waist. "You are all right?"

"Yeah." The wind whipped her soaking hair. She tugged it out of her face. "I really ought to be cold, but look at that clear night."

The stars spattered the sky above, and matching glitter dusted the ocean.

And their new sacred island.

Sacred not because any ruling council said it was so, but

sacred because the love of the mer and the humans had united to create it.

"It's beautiful, and it's not a screen saver anymore. It's my life." She hugged him. "I'm so happy."

This would be the greatest living island the world had ever seen, grown by soul mates and fed by love. And the only way it could fail again was by being abandoned.

In the daylight, when the ships docked with great surprise, Gailen made sure the first promise of the new covenant was that whoever stepped foot on the island promised to hold love for it in their hearts.

"Trust me," he said. "I know about plants."

"And it's a great idea," Starr said. "Because you are brilliant."

They all signed the new covenant. King Kadir, Queen Elyssa, and all the kings, and all the queens, and all the warriors, and all the brides, and all humans, and just everyone.

EPILOGUE

Starr opened her eyes.

Cold gray light from the portal window reflected on the slatted ceiling. The splash of seawater and the sound of clanging from something unsecured broke her lonely sleep.

Her stomach growled.

She rolled over...

...into the solid form of her warm, snoozing husband, Gailen.

The sheets slid up and down his broad chest with every deep, even breath. His callused fingertips twitched. He'd been up late for weeks making sure yesterday's event went perfectly.

The grand opening of Mer Island.

Her stomach growled again.

She carefully rolled back and eased out of the super-king-sized bed. After crossing the hand-cut ocean-rock mosaic tile, she put a slice of yesterday's rosemary-infused bread into the toaster and clicked on the glass kettle. It boiled merrily while her toast popped. She spread the bread with a thick wedge of honey-walnut butter, dropped a sachet of cinnamon-apple chamomile into her favorite mug, and carried her tea and toast to the small, sheltered balcony to eat as the rising sun turned the Atlantic into glittering shards.

Shadows pulled back to reveal the playful shell-like white-and-pastel walls of the other buildings. MerMatch was nearest the docks, with a vaulted opening and peaked triple windows to symbolize two halves coming together to make a third half. Yes, three halves. The mer were insistent that two combined were greater than the sum of their parts, and the architects had done their best to reflect that vision.

Beyond it was an oceanographic institute, a center for renewable ocean-based energy, and various medical and scientific buildings for studying Sea Opals, Life Trees, and the mer. All were partnerships for mer and humans.

The architects had done especially well considering that the island had the potential to sink. The buildings were constructed with concrete pontoons and other measures so that in case future generations made poorer decisions, the disaster of the past wouldn't be so horrific.

Gailen had been so funny working with the architects.

"These are the models of the rooms for families and visitors and so forth," they had explained on their sleek yacht, using wall-sized drawings and laser pointers. "This is a two-person occupancy, one for a family group, and here's the fully loaded no-expenses-spared honeymoon suite."

Gailen had leaned forward. "Why can they not all be the honeymoon suite?"

The presenter had blinked. "All...be the honeymoon suite?"

"It is the best, right? Why can everyone who stays at this island not enjoy the best suite?"

The architects had looked at each other around the large table.

"Occupancy," one had said. "Fewer people fit in the space."

"If we need more room, we will focus our energies and grow the island."

"Some people want to live like kings."

"We should all live like King Kadir." Gailen had reached across to Starr and linked their fingers. "With our brides in our castles, growing our young fry. He wishes all may live as he does."

They'd all blinked and then the presenter had rolled up the plans. "We'll get back to you."

And so now she got to enjoy the honeymoon suite—and so did everyone else who stayed on the island.

She crunched the last bite of her toast. She still couldn't eat ordinary peanuts. The smell turned her stomach and made her sweat, even though she and Gailen were certain she no longer suffered from allergies. The honey-walnut butter was a present from Bella, who'd visited a nut-butter artisan and picked up one of each item in the whole catalog just for Starr. It was sweet and oily and coated her tongue. And she could eat it. Like a normal person! She washed it down with the tea.

Before, she hadn't had a choice in how her body reacted to allergens, but now she was a mer. The power to shift her body, to channel the healing Life Tree, shone within her.

And hopefully, the scientists studying Sea Opals would figure out a way to give that freedom to every other person who suffered, mer or human.

On the pavilion far below, chalk drawings from the great welcome ceremony were scuffed by dancing footprints. The DJ station was still there, and seabirds poked in the buckets of grasses and flowers for crumbs of cheese and crackers, grilled fish bones, seaweed flowers. The air had a twinge of dead fish rotting in the sun, which was a danger of living on a seashore, even though they were still in the middle of the ocean.

Somewhere in one of the other suites, a baby cried and a loving mother moved to shush him. A toddler crawled across the pavilion, startling the seabirds, and his father leaned shirtless and barefoot against a doorway, sipping a steaming cup of coffee. Day was breaking, and as the chief security officer in charge of setting up the networks necessary for the institutes (and Wi-Fi) to operate, she'd have to be out in it. As would Gailen, the chief gardener.

Such an innocuous title. Chief gardener, heh.

She rose and washed her dishes—gorgeous hand-turned pottery painted a cheerful blue that felt good in her hands— and left them on the drying rack.

Since the island was a plant, Gailen was basically in charge of everything. And he took the job very seriously, monitoring its health by swimming around it every day, and, since the health of the island depended on the health of the people who lived there, checking in with each and every one of them also every day. Last night, he'd thought he was throwing a huge party to celebrate everyone who had come to the island and welcome their family and friends. He'd gotten the shock of his life when his residents had begun showering him with homemade presents—a party hat made from a big conch shell and a cape made out of seaweed and so forth—and when they carried his chair around and sang him a hooray song, he'd nearly cried.

He was a real sweetheart.

Which wasn't to say there weren't still challenges.

She tidied up the toaster and added water to the potted

flowers she was now able to grow around her tables, wall sconces, and balcony.

The Sons of Hercules's leadership had never been found. Had they perished in the explosions or gone into hiding?

Since Ryerson's money and assets had been frozen, and nobody had tried to get into them, according to the rumors Dannika heard, Starr kind of guessed he was gone, taken down by the violent rhetoric he'd used to manipulate so many others to do his dark bidding. Maybe he'd been shot by his acolytes, or maybe he'd tried to yank out the wires before anyone could stop him and set the whole thing off. Wasn't it the worst irony? He would be remembered the most for something he didn't even believe in, but which was still causing fear in people that didn't know better.

His company had dissolved, and it was a pretty big disaster. There were still groups of the Sons of Hercules around, as well as a movement propogating conspiracy theories. There was backlash and suspicion against Sea Opals and how they worked. But there was also a great flowering and openness around the world of people really excited to embrace this entirely new kingdom and universe.

Tentative agreements had been formed to allow mermen into countries that had closed to them, but now that the mer had their own island for people to visit, Dannika thought the agreements would happen a lot faster as nations realized what they were missing.

But no matter what, the world was a vast place, both on land and in the oceans. There would always be dangers lurking in hidden shadows. And there would always be cities shining like beacons to gather communities and bathe them in healing light.

It was still early, so she snuck back into the bed and snuggled under Gailen's heavy arm.

Perfect.

He'd never even known she'd been gone.

His fingers curled around her shoulder, and his eyes opened.

"Ah." She knew he was still tired. "I didn't mean to wake you."

He moved to cover her mouth with his sleepy kiss. His hard cock pressed against her thigh, and his palms massaged her breasts. A matching throb of heat swelled her breasts and filled her pussy.

He tore his mouth free and pressed kisses up her jaw to her ear and teased the lobe with a light tug. "I love to wake to you."

He was always telling her in both little and big ways that she didn't have to apologize for who she was. He loved her just exactly so.

Her heart squeezed. "I love you."

"Of course you do." He trailed sizzling kisses down her chest, tugging her night shirt up and feasting on her needy nipples, then on down to her lightly swollen belly to her pounding, wet heaven. He seduced her with expert strokes until she clamped her thighs around his head and dragged him up, and then he fit his cock to her and drove into her like the waves carving out the shore. She took every delicious pounding thrust, hooking her calves around his muscular backside, until he'd wrung not one or two but three whole orgasms from her. Because he liked to do it, and he had the stamina, and why not? She could just have it. She could just want it and have it, and he wanted to give it to her too. "Watching the passion on your face brighten your soul makes me lose my mind."

She clamped onto him. "Lose it, then."

He shuddered and surged into her, filling her with yet another delicious full-body climax and pleasure like champagne foaming over with his slippery release.

It was great, really great, to wake up to him too.

Energy surged through her.

She patted his shoulder, rolled his heavy body off her with a groan, and danced to the shower. A seawater shower, because it didn't matter and because she had plans.

He got up and stumbled in after her. His yawn changed over to pleasure as she attended to washing him down, and then he grabbed a quick snack from the kitchen while they headed out to do the first part of his morning rounds. It was her favorite, and she tried to join him every day.

They greeted other early-risers—mostly warriors, including former members of the All-Council army. They returned the greetings awkwardly, and Gailen stopped to chat, really trying to get to know them.

As the Sons of Hercules still had pockets of tenacious supporters, so did the All-Council.

As soon as the island had been raised and the new covenant signed, King Kadir had sent a coalition to take over the All-Council fortress and empty their prison. They had declared a new era for the mer, and now the traditionalists were the dissenters, silent for the moment, but never gone.

Gailen resumed their walk and took her hand. His thumb curved around to touch the back of her hand, where it belonged.

And so did the other one.

His grip wasn't strong yet, and maybe it never would be, but he barely seemed bothered anymore.

They walked deeper into the island.

Once, she and Gailen had thought they could never change.

And the same thing happened with the All-Council. They were still stuck in an era where they believed that they couldn't transform. They hadn't realized that the world had already changed without them. And now they'd been faced with the proof of it, and they had to change.

One of the new coalition's first actions had been to open the archives so that the remaining representatives would go out and tell the history. Some of the historical events put mermen in a really bad light, and some of the things damaged the humans. Legitimate complaints had been forgotten over the years, and now the current generation was in danger of reopening old wounds.

But there was still a great chance to atone, move beyond, and open to new possibilities.

All the humans who fought over territory, who'd felt sorry that they hadn't lived in a time when they could explore the oceans, had to understand that actually, there was still a lot to be explored. There was an ocean beneath the ocean, where dead warriors were laid to rest, which they called the blacknight sea. It was a real place, and it was where the megalodons lived, and other creatures that awaited scientific discovery.

The surface of the earth was like the skin, and even the deepest trench was still just a pore. There was more of the world waiting to be discovered for anyone who dared to test their limits.

But pushing limits wasn't easy. Almost everyone was stuck a little bit.

Even when she had been stuck with her allergies, she had an option to be more open with her online connections, and she'd chosen not to do it. Well, not chosen, but she had allowed her illness to dictate her life and her protective shield to disconnect her even when maybe it would've been better to connect.

They reached the great pool in the center of the island. The heart stone lay beneath the gently moving waves. She left her wrap on a bench by the start of a willow tree and waded into the sultry water.

Gailen checked the willow—he was as fascinated by her land plants as he was by the ocean's—and joined her. "In a few years, when these grow up and give shade, we might introduce some fish. Did you see the portals I worked on? We should be able to clear them of muck and then let in water from the ocean."

"It will be a beautiful lagoon," were the last words she said above the surface.

He grinned at her beneath the water.

Her shift was still a matter of will. She held his gaze as she tried to serenely force the air from her lungs, clamping her mouth shut. She seemed to suffer less of the gag-drowning reflex if she let the water in from her lungs up her throat instead of the other way. That had to be the warriors' seamless-transformation secret.

He knew that she liked a little privacy to get her peace of mind back after shifting, so he kicked to the portal he'd been talking about and reached shoulder-deep into the pipe.

Brave.

She transformed her feet into fins and kicked to the lagoon floor.

And then she focused energy on her fingertips and brushed the knotted wood. It lit up with a million stars. She felt a great reverberation in her soul.

Gailen swam to her and entwined her in his arms. "It is echoing within you and within me."

It was great to swim here in the morning to wake up, but it was even better as their last swim at night. The stars beneath reflected the stars overhead. It was so beautiful living in this microcosm with Gailen. He loved her, held her, and set her free.

And she was so happy to finally be free, wrapped in his arms, swimming with Gailen.

———

THANKS SO MUCH FOR READING! If you loved this exciting conclusion to the Lords of Atlantis series, check out my new series, the Blades of Arris.

I craft extra bonuses and exclusive happily-ever-afters for my newsletter subscribers. Get yours at http://smarturl.it/StarlaNewsletter

STARLA

ABOUT THE AUTHOR

USA Today bestselling author Starla Night was born on a hot July at midnight. She hikes, scuba dives, and swims naked in the ocean. She writes about smokin' hot dragons and tattooed mermen at StarlaNight.com.

starlanight.com